ANIMALS

ANIMALS

A Tale of Terror

GEOFF RYMAN

NewCon Press
England

First edition, published in the UK June 2025
by NewCon Press
41 Wheatsheaf Road, Alconbury Weston, Cambs, PE28 4LF, UK

NCP345 (hardback)
NCP346 (softback)

10 9 8 7 6 5 4 3 2 1

ISBN: 978-1-914953-94-1 (hardback)
978-1-914953-95-8 (softback)

Cover Art and front cover design by Roland Unwin
Editing by Gillian Redfearn
Typesetting by Ian Whates
Back cover layout by Ian Whates

PART ONE
Little One

Hello

For a while in my adolescence, I wrote like a dog.

The plague had left its mark and both my parents were dead, leaving me alone at fifteen to cope with a mind that would veer off into being other species.

I could feel something cutting through my head, rumpling it, linking my brain both fore to aft and left to right. An identifiable disruption it, felt like a physical jink to my words, communication, and being? An info-genetic disorder

I hoard things like I'm burying bones. Then I find them again. Here is one page from my sixteenth year, old for a dog, the wisdom of a canine elder:

Snuffles no words
but I'd call evening primrose Ruff
and roses Rawph
and old cat piss Siff
and the deadstuff in the ground
seething black sicksweet muck Smurf,
Smurf makes me roil whine
step back be sick
But sky air ground most times delicious
great poem textbook encyclopaedia
that every breath is all field
Sunlight, ivy, shadow, flower, fungi, leaf-rot.
And human smells yes yes.
Other dogfolk
 I call us Yee
for the sound we make we meet each other
Yee, my yee
Smell our food sex excitement boredom health.
Mice voles moles weasels,
I have names for those too.

I cannot use them, they are not here.

There are no more dogs except me and yee.

In my fiftieth year I've become more human. Only at night in dreams I run and hunt. And in memory. This book is memory too – what I think happened when I was just a pup.

I could talk to cats too, if there were any, but there is only one I want to talk to. She is long dead.

I want to write this for dogs.

ONE

It had to start somewhere. And somebody would be the first to notice.

The place was our village, and the people were my father and me. Dad was the first to say, 'Something is killing animals.'

He was the first to say, 'It could be that we're the carriers. We're the ones making them sick.'

He was the first to say, 'Something is bringing them back.'

Dad was a veterinary researcher. The year before, he'd got himself a job in a London institute and had left us. Also because he'd found himself a boyfriend. By then he was coming back from London every weekend to the negotiations that were my parents' marriage. And I guess, also back to me. I was ten years old, still mystified and heartbroken. How could the Dad I knew leave us?

In those days, people had cars. You could just get in a car and drive anywhere.

You never thought about electricity. You'd just use it and whatever you wanted would turn on. And what devices. Something to grind coffee beans (coffee! Oh how I miss coffee!). Something to boil water, trim hedges, and time sprinklers. There were tiny electric chainsaws.

My Dad liked shimmying up limes or walnuts or chestnuts like a rock climber with guy ropes with a chainsaw. He'd hang in the air and bend the branches down towards him. He had also had a curved pruning saw and he'd cut the branch back in stages from the tip while sparing the roses it supported.

One of Dad's things was saving indigenous British bees. He renamed our house 'Beehive Cottage' which didn't make it any easier for the postman to find. (There were no house numbers, our post code covered four houses on two different roads, and even 'Sandy Lane' was made up, not anywhere on Google.)

Dad made beehives that were not intended for commercial farming. He made hives that looked like tree trunks and were not designed to harvest honey. He sold them to new-age country millionaires. (There were a lot of those in rural West Oxfordshire.)

He used to drive me to his hive installations all over the south of England. He would talk to the new owner who would be a pop star or lawyer or IT manager.

He'd explain that every year bees tried to find locations for new hives. He'd say things like, 'The bees have scouts. They go look for possible locations for new hives – hollow trunks or branches. When they find one they somehow share the location with the other scouts. We have no idea how they do that. When all the scouts have visited all the locations they get together on top of the old hive and parley. Somehow they decide which one to go for. And when they agree all their tails point towards it. We have no idea how they do that either.'

I think being human embarrassed him.

Dad was not much taller than I was, but he was built like a bull. In some photos, he's so big across it's like he's been pumped full of air. More than once people, sometimes strangers, would call him Michelin Man (that was a brand for pumped-up tyres on cars). His face was creased, his smile broad, his teeth gleaming in the middle of his long black beard.

It got even longer after he converted to Islam. Then he started to pray a lot, five times a day. He'd get up at 4.30 am to pray. It drove Mom crazy, but by then he was sleeping in the guest bedroom.

He found Ken and stopped living with us. I don't know how he squared being queer with Islam. My mother took it so well. 'That's just who your father is,' she told me. Well, it was not who I was. I'd lost my Dad.

He drove from London every weekend, but sometimes I wouldn't talk to him. Sometimes we still did things together. Dad had been my only male friend.

Dad found a weasel on the lawn.

He came to fetch me, trying to engage. 'Teddy, look, I've found a weasel.'

It was tiny and broken, a strip of white and ginger against the green. I'd seen it, but thought it was a piece of cardboard escaped from our recycling bin. Dad was squatting over it – he would squat without a chair even in the house, saying it was more comfortable. He hunched his whole body into a fist and pondered the weasel. 'I haven't seen one of those in a decade.' He spoke as softly as a prayer.

I'm not entirely sure that the next thing actually happened.

It was a long time ago and I know I was called 'imaginative'. That was one of the reasons for my being home-schooled even before Covid lockdown.

I *think* I remember the ground trying to pull the weasel under.

The body rocked up and down on the grass. Its face was turned towards the lawn and there was something about that motion that transfixed and appalled me, something obscene. I started to wail.

Dad stood up. 'Teddy, Teddy,' he said and kissed me. Hand on my shoulder, he started to steer me back towards the house. 'It's okay. Everything has to die. And then it rejoins the earth. That's how the soil stays alive.'

I'd heard that homily before. Yeah, things died and became compost. But I had no idea that there were things in the ground that would pull you down into it. There was something wrong. Hadn't he seen it? I got angry with him, and my fists and face clenched. Anger stopped me being upset. I jabbed at my cheeks to wipe them.

'You stay here, I'll go bury the little fella, okay?'

I didn't like being dismissed. 'I'm coming too.' We went to get the shovel from our shed. Everything in the shed was apple-pie, as if my Dad was still there to tidy up.

Then we went back out, me wrestling with the shovel. Dad leaned over the weasel and tried to pick it up. It wouldn't come free. He had to tug. Then he held the little body up and turned it over. It was like the head had grown roots, plant roots or maybe more like nerve cells. I thought they twitched. But again, that might have just been me and my imagination.

Dad held the little body up, and lost in thought, went back to the car to put the body alongside his soil-sample kit. He left the car door open. It was hot and he might have wanted to keep the car cool.

I stood alone over the patch of lawn. Welling out of it came something black, like oil bubbling out of the ground, a seething. I couldn't see what it was at first. Then I focused on fur, scraps of fibre that turned and twisted. Something like a sea anemone wriggled up out of the mess, only it was made of worms that had somehow joined up like melted wax. The surface of the earthworms was pitted, bits hanging off them, and they were the wrong colour, purple like a bruise. Then something like a tiny human hand worked its way out, a mole's hand only no longer pink. It was the wrong colour and detached from anything else.

I howled. Dad squatted next to me. As we watched an earthworm seemed to swell and gape over the mole's paw, enveloping it more like a boa constrictor than an earthworm. Worms could do that?

Dad said, 'What the devil?' It is the only time I can remember my father using that expression. Then he turned to me and said my name with concern and reached for my foot.

I was wearing shorts and sandals, and an earthworm had fixed itself to my ankle, like a leech. Dad pulled it off, and my blood trickled.

What the devil?

Dad put the earthworm in a small plastic bag. He picked up a scrap of perhaps a vole leaking yellow insides into another bag. He fingered up some soil and suddenly went 'Ouch,' and shook his fingers. He scowled. Dirt did not normally bite.

He went back to the car, then said over his shoulder, 'Teddy you didn't move the weasel did you? No of course you didn't, you've been standing there the whole time.' He gave his head a shake. He took the other samples inside with him to keep them cool.

We went into the kitchen and had a polite lunch with Mom. She asked about the Institute. I think Dad took me to Wychwood that afternoon, but I'm not sure. Then he would have driven home to Ken.

Was it the next day or the day after? I was in the front garden. There was the weasel, across the driveway by the mulberry tree. It hobbled like it was drunk or crippled, one paw drawn up and curled. It turned and stared at me with one milky eye.

Then its head snapped forward, and it opened its skull mouth with nutcracker teeth and hissed at me. Most of the left side of its face was gone, including the eye. Then with a bark, it launched itself at me, rippling and bobbling at high speed, jaws open.

I was not a brave little boy – I turned and ran. I got to the front door, but when Dad wasn't there Mom kept the front lock snibbed, and the door wouldn't open. The thing was almost on me. Six inches long, but it terrified me as if it had been a mastiff. I had the shovel with me. It was aiming for my feet, bare in sandals. I slammed the blade of the shovel down on its back as hard as I could. It was furious and turned and tried to bite the blade. One half of its face was soft, putrid. One of its teeth peeled away against the shovel. I pushed down harder, felt the blade scrape the concrete step, and I twisted it. The weasel gave away. Its lower half scampered blindly into a bush. Its top half twittered almost like a bird and began to roll over itself over and over.

I scooped it up in the shovel and used it like a sling shot to fling the half-body far out of our garden into the dog run. I stood there shivering for some time.

Then I walked around the back of the house, wiping the blade. I didn't tell anyone. Imaginative and emotional children are sometimes not believed. I wasn't sure I believed it myself.

Two

Our world was full of animals.

Mom had a friend, Dorothy across the lane. I liked visiting her. She let me read her old books, and she was old too, like a slightly crinkled blackcurrant.

She kept blonde moles in her freezer.

The first time I visited Dorothy on my own, when we'd just moved into the village, she offered me a lemon sorbet and then said, 'Would you like to see one of Oldminster's famous blonde moles?'

The moles were frosted inside Seal-Fresh plastic bags and were the colour of Labradors. When I told her that my father worked for biology think tank she offered him one for study. My father was actually very grateful, as was the lab. Oldminster Blondes turned out to be a new species.

Children now have difficulty imagining a world full of animals. Moles overturned our lawn and wrecked Mom's asparagus bed. Rabbits ring-barked our newly planted fruit trees. Voles would make me jump, flitting across paving stones in the corner of my eye. Our chimney would be full of jackdaws chuckling like a cocktail party. Our bushes would rustle with partridges or pheasants. Dad trained a male pheasant to eat grain out of his hand.

At night driving down the lanes, you'd see in silhouette a herd of deer running over the brow of a hill.

Once or twice a year Dad and I would get up at five am and drive to Wytham Wood the other side of Witney. A blanket of shadow and stillness would cover the ground. We'd creep through the twilight grey.

Foxes made love squealing like stuck pigs, or caught pheasants that would flutter up and make a rusty-trumpet sound that was cut short. The dawn chorus would start, hundreds of birds marking their territory, a waterfall of birdsong. When we got back to the car it would be covered in bird poop. Pigeons, I think. They shat massively, more like flying horses.

Nearby, in Windrush Village on the river, someone had the genius idea of opening up a Crocodile Planet tourist feature. Dad took me there, to a cluster of old buildings in which boats and cars were repaired, small parts tooled, and cheap advertising animations made. There, on the banks of a river were eighty crocodiles and alligators. They lurked behind Perspex screens in swamps made of dug Oxfordshire soil, planted reeds and heat lamps. In trays, eggs rotated like wedding rings, more predatory reptiles being hatched. You could pose, cradling a drugged, foot-long baby croc. They only charged seven ninety-nine per photo. 'Dad that's stupid,' I said. 'Who would cuddle a crocodile?' I had a vague sense that it was exploitative.

Dad got enraged. He demanded to talk to a manager. The manager came out plump as a donut and twice as tall as Dad. Dad shouted at him. 'Behind glass are they?'

'Not glass. It's unbreakable,' said the man who had a goatee to hide his fat chin.

'The Windrush floods, the floods will reach over that glass. Your predators will escape into the flood plain. They'll clear the river of swans, fish and birds. I wouldn't want to be your lawyer when people sue you for their eaten pets. Or maybe even children.'

'Cross that bridge when we come to it,' said the man, with a shrug and looking amused.

'There are no bridges in a flood,' Dad said.

The line stuck in my mind. He was right. You know things are bad when there are no bridges.

And I can still see it in my mind's eye, when the reptiles came for us.

I had a cat called Little One.

She started out as a rustling in our woodshed. The shed was as old as the house, stacked full of logs and was always full of scuttling sounds from birds or rodents.

Those rustlings turned into Little One.

At first she was called Ears. That was because her brother was called Nose. Nose had a splotch of black on the tip of his face that looked like someone had thrown ink on it. Being male, he buggered off. But Ears stayed.

Her mother had belonged to Dorothy, but she didn't like Dorothy's beagles so she darted across the road and had her litter in our shed. She was a big blue-grey Persian. Dad always said the reason Little One was so affectionate was that she was half Persian.

Her mother must have taught her to hunt when we weren't looking. Little One was a demon hunter. You'd see her suddenly arch out of the long grass in the field next door and dive down on some small animal. The rabbits, the voles even the moles became less of a nuisance.

I began to leave her milk in the shed, though both my parents had told me milk was bad for cats. I told Mom I was leaving it for hedgehogs. She told me milk was bad for hedgehogs too.

At first, I'd come back in the morning and the milk would be gone.

Then I saw a kitten waiting for me, ducking behind wood, watching me until I left. I started to stand by the door and wait. She got confident enough to sit and watch me. She would look affronted if I came in without food for her.

Then she'd be waiting for me in the middle of the shed floor. She would even let me watch her lap her milk. She would run out to meet me, and wrap her tail around my leg. I would make a mewling noise and she would echo it back to me. It was the Plaintive Meow. It was a noise we could both make, and we used it to call each other.

Dead mice started to show up on the floor of the shed.

Mom said, 'Teddy. She's leaving you little presents.'

I thought Mom was being silly.

'Cats know who feeds them. You feed them enough, they want to give you something back.'

The leaves fell; it got cold. I don't remember when I got the idea of moving Little One into the house. I knew cats liked sitting on radiators. We had a big Raeburn in the kitchen with white ceramic lids that kept in the heat. I imagined Little One curled up on those.

The previous owner of our house, Mrs Tulp, liked cats so there were cat flaps ready made.

Mom said, 'You'll have to coax her, Teddy. Step by step.'

I stopped going into the shed with her milk. I left it on the back flagstones and I would plaintive-meow her. She would answer me, but not come out. First night, the milk stayed untouched. Second or third night, milk taken, possibly by hedgehogs. But soon she was trotting out to meet me and the milk, even when wind soughed through the trees.

By then Mom had seen the cat as well. She helped at a veg stall in Witney market on Thursdays, where there was a fish stall. On Thursdays she would come back with a fish head – plaice or turbot or mackerel.

'Give her these, these are better for cats.'

Little One stalked the first fish head. She lowered herself flat on the ground and crept towards it. She went still. I blinked, and suddenly she was two inches closer. It was like stop motion animation. Finally she sprang, snatched the head off the plate, and shot into the dark.

Soon Little One would spend Thursday evening pawing the gravel of the drive waiting for Mom's car. When the Kia crackled through the gate, she would turn and run, and magically summon up fish heads by waiting at the right flagstone.

And each Thursday the right flagstone would the one a step close to the cat flap. She would hunch over the head and bare her fangs and crunch bone. I never found a single bone left behind.

Then came the night when I left the fish head on a plate just inside the cat flap.

She spun around in frustration. She looked back at me with beaming eyes. *You have got to be kidding me.*

I held the cat flap open. She stuck her head inside. I was left looking at the least interesting parts of a cat, while she crunched. So that was the routine for a while. It was as if each separate half of the cat was in another reality. Sometimes she'd panic and would battle to pull herself backwards, her feet running in place like they'd been buttered.

Mom put a heater in the back passage. The back passage was an improvisation, basically just a lean-to against the back of the house. It was thin walled and cold. But with the heater in place, it glowed with light and warmth and the smell of food.

Little One got used to eating with her head in the cat flap. And one night, bored and cold – it was winter – I just pushed the rest of her inside.

Oooh a frantic scrabbling. I ran round the front of the house and through the kitchen, into the back passage doing the Plaintive Meow. I picked her up. She didn't scratch me. I pushed her back out the cat flap. The next Thursday, fish day, I pushed her back and forth several times, and then lowered her plate. One evening, I can't remember exactly, she must have thought *What is there not to like?*

From then on, every evening, I would sit on what had been the back step of the house inside the lean-to, watching Little One lap water or crunch fish-head.

And after dinner, she'd have her Brushing. She had her own special hairbrush; a guest had forgotten it. Each bristle had a little black bobble on the end. I knew it wouldn't gouge her skin or tangle her fur. She would jump up on my lap and I'd brush, and her hide would twitch with pleasure, and she'd purr, melt, and take on the shape of my legs.

It was about then that I started calling her Little One instead of Ears. Though when formally introduced, her title was La Principessa. Mom said she was upwardly mobile. We only ever used her formal title with guests.

I had a kind of chant. 'Lit lit lit lit Little One Little One.' I only used it when we had something to share, like the Brushing or the fish.

Whenever Dad stuck his head in the back passage, Little One would shoot through the cat flap.

In the early days when Dad was still with us, he sat next to me on the step. 'She's feral,' he said. 'That means she was domesticated but she went wild. But she's come back inside. That's the best kind of cat. She can feed herself if she needs to. Like your mother says, she'll hoover up all the rats and rabbits. And she's so affectionate.' He grabbed the back of my neck, and rocked it.

Mom had a battle with Old Faithful over the cat.

Old Faithful was the cleaning lady and she fed Whiskas to Little One in secret.

Mom had a delicious, movie-star way of talking. She was always giving people or things nicknames (you've probably noticed) or finding funny ways to say things. These came with quotation marks, like they'd come from a play.

'Old Faithful. You really cannot give her proprietary cat food. You'll debauch her palate.'

Old Faithful never wore makeup and had short, snow-white hair. She was gnarled, her legs were bowed and she had vast hands with flattened fingers. Her actual name was Faith, which Mom used when being serious. Faith now gave Mom a certain look.

'You mean you want her to eat your rabbits.'

'Yes.'

'You're sure you don't want your cat to be vegan, too?'

A creeping smile on my mom's face. 'It's a moral decision. I leave it to the cat.'

'You're not marching for Mouse Rights or anything.'

Mom's eyes went wide and innocent. 'Does Whiskas do Mouse flavour?'

'Yeah. And mice cream for dessert.'

'It's full of goop. It's addictive.'

'So's my evening whisky.' Abruptly, Faith walked away. 'Work to do.'

Old Faithful was trying to seduce my cat. We'd find opened tins of Whiskas in the recycling. Faith stole my Plaintive Meow, and Little One would come running to her too, and wrap her tail around her legs. Small field species would be left crumpled next to Faith's bicycle.

Faith was a bit of a toughie, but she seemed to think we were cruel. It was always 'that poor cat'. Faith cycled from Allotments across the main road with a new wicker cat basket with a red tartan bed inside. 'Fine thing when the staff have to invest in the livestock. That poor cat has nowhere to lay her head.'

Faith was always saying 'your poor mother.' I think Faith saw Mom as a helpless city girl, abandoned in the countryside by That Man. Mom kept ducks, a pig, and greyhounds but that was nothing to Faith. Her own family had been farm labourers for generations, and she had hired herself out to do field work at twelve.

'That Man. If he ever shows up here on a Tuesday he'll learn something.'

Faith scared me. But I did say to her. 'He's a nice man. He's kind to animals.'

'Wasn't nice to you though, was he?' Her wide blue eyes didn't blink.

'He is nice to me.' I was getting upset. I could feel tears coming on, the lower half of my face swelling.

'That's why you're about to cry. For goodness sake.' She tore off a kitchen towel and passed it to me. 'Your makeup will run.'

I guess she thought I was a wimp, and I agreed with her.

I once heard Mom whispering to her, 'Teddy's a bit sensitive.'

'A bit coddled you mean. You can send him back to school now. Let him get knocked about and he'll learn to hit back.'

As Faith left that day, she bumped my shoulder. 'You'll be fine Little One.' She got back on her black vicar's bicycle which she'd bought for fifty quid.

Faith called me Little One too. I think she confused me with the cat. At least she never served me a plate of Whiskas.

All through the terrible events that were to come, through those long years, Faith lived with me and Mom.

Three

Mom was called Mom, not Mum because she was from Kokomo, Indiana.

It would have been hard to dream about being a serious Shakespearean actor in Kokomo. Somehow Mom conceived the idea of going to the Royal Academy of Dramatic Arts in London, which is how she met my Dad who at the time worked in a bookshop on Tottenham Court Road. He had no degree, and didn't want one then. He was studying virtue.

Mom was handsome if not beautiful. Because of Dad she stayed in the UK. Her English accent was never quite right, so she ended up only playing Americans. A giggly stupid American tourist got herself killed in a crime drama. Helen Mirren spent seven episodes finding out it was her sister what dunnit.

Then Mom was in a very unfunny sitcom about an irascible Scotsman played by Peter Capaldi. In one episode his American niece came to stay. (Sorry I can't bring myself to explain what TV shows were. You were supposed only to half watch them through a haze of capitalist ennui.)

'Pretty good record,' Mom would say of her career. 'Most of my year are doing panto in Hull, or are standing in the chorus at the National.'

She and Dad moved out to Oxfordshire and Beehive Cottage just before I was supposed to start school in September. The children were all from Allotments, a very different kind of village. They all already knew and hated each other – and they terrified me. Nothing I liked interested them at all and vice versa. I stuck it out until Christmas but wailed at the prospect of going back. Mom started home schooling me.

*

Mom would get up at four am every day to feed the ducks and check on her greyhounds.

In summer it was okay. The sun was up at four am, but the air was still cool. She'd scatter meal for the ducks, and I would lay in bed upstairs and listen to their little grunts and squeaks. Being vegan, we couldn't eat the eggs, but Mom sold them to The Ram's Head.

Then she would feed our Large Black Pig. Mom called her Charity Frilly-Knickers (the knickers were not made of lace). Large she was – over 300 kilograms at her finest. Charity was a vegan pig and she was particularly fond of one white duck, called Donna Duck, who slept in her pen with her. Mom once said she found the two of them fast asleep, with Donna's neck in the pig's mouth. Charity snored and was intensely odiferous. In summer her savour could fill the whole back garden.

Mom's greyhounds, the Beautiful Boys, would start yelping as soon as they heard her. It sounded like something was twisting off their legs. The sound was tormented, angst ridden. Mom always called it Dog Grief; 'They're mourning for their lost breakfast. They always think they've been abandoned.'

Mom's plan had been to raise greyhounds for racing. Then the Oxford stadium closed, and all the old men who liked the dogs passed away or went into care homes or discovered online porn (I'm not going to explain what that was).

Mom kept raising greyhounds anyway. She loved them. Dad had built them a long run all the way down the field to the river – we rented the run from the farmer – and the dog-beasts would pelt full speed up and down it all summer long. Between our garden and their run Dad built a high wooden fence. The Boys would mob it, scrabbling to get their heads over it to be scratched or to lick salt from our hands.

After lessons, while I was planting or pruning, Mom would take her Boys for long walks, up the footpaths towards Witney. I'd be weeding or watering or tearing ivy off our trees, and I would hear her voice far across the fields. She had a high dog voice. 'Here Big Boy. Here.' It sounded like the fields had become my Mom.

Then she'd get home, and we'd go back to my lessons, both of us enjoying history or English – anything so long as it wasn't maths.

Little One changed after Dad left us. I really do think she felt she had to take more care of me.

She spent even more time prowling next to me, or watching me dig the beds. She saw me filling the bird feeders, and I think for that reason, she never hunted birds. If I gave them food, they were family.

The previous owner, Mrs Tulp, had emptied her Raeburn ash at the top of the garden. It made something called the Mountain of Ash and it was surrounded by trees and ivy. I could sit there on a white plastic outdoor chair and read my books. Little One would jump onto my lap and the two of us would sit while I read.

At night, she took to bounding up the stairs ahead of me, and she'd snuggle next to me in bed. And I think that was my favourite thing. Being all warm next to Little One as her chest vibrated with a deep purring.

A yard full of animals, a pig in love with a duck, greyhounds racing up and down fields. Speedboats and restaurants serving steak and never caring about washing your hands before dinner. No hand sanitiser. No roadblocks anywhere. No dips of disinfectant to walk through. And everything full of life.

Another world.

'You do know I love you, don't you Teddy?'

The January before, both Mom and I had come down with a fever.

We assumed it was a late case of Covid. The virus had never gone away; and the danger was this might be another new strain the vaccine couldn't defend against. We were supposed to go into quarantine, but frankly, I was already living in a kind of quarantine, self-imposed.

While Mom was sick; Dad took over my home schooling by Zoom. He shrank down to a face on the screen. I was formal with him: I answered questions and did the exercises and blanked any friendly overtures. *If you want to be a Dad, be here.*

I took over all of the cleaning, cooking and online stuff. Despite Mom's ideals I started ordering food from supermarkets and I was appalled by the mountains of plastic encasing everything, even cabbages that came with a leafy packaging of their own.

That February there were floods under warm dark skies. Rain on the terrace roof didn't stop for a month. Plants lay down flat, grey and soft. Mom lay upstairs croaking. I got used to using disposable earpieces to take her temperature which for two weeks plateaued at thirty-eight and wouldn't shift. Which was weird because your body temperature is supposed to go up and down during the day, sick or well.

Then I got sick too, a terrible two-day headache. It made my brain feel like leaves being gnawed by caterpillars. Then it got fuzzy and multi-layered like those caterpillars had woven their cocoons.

On the third day I woke and all the colours were brighter. And they stayed brighter. It was my nose that felt numb – I kept sniffing things trying to smell something.

Then the sun came out and it got hot.

That July, we had four days over thirty-eight degrees, as if the air had caught Mom's fever.

We might as well have lived in the Negev. England was not designed for that heat. Everything went into a state of shock – trees, plants, animals, rivers, car bonnets, road surfaces, salt cellars, top soil. The air stuck like glue – you couldn't seem to pull it into your lungs. The meadows baked so hard you could have put chunks of earth into a dishwasher and they would have come back whole, solid as a plate. Grass went translucent, as brittle as glass.

Nothing moved. Or sang or buzzed or hooted or cooed. Animal dung and urine dried but was not washed away. Everything smelled of poo.

My potatoes baked in the ground. My runner beans which had stood so tall in May broke at the base, fell over, became skeletons. We were prohibited from watering anything, despite the floods we'd had in March. The silence grew.

Dad made his Sunday visits. I said nothing to him. He said he was sad about my fallen beans and gave my trapezius muscle a squeeze. His smile and eyes had the fixed blank look of someone who goes on being cheerful and talking to someone who does not want to listen.

On first June, we had a huge crop of apples on the best tree. Then all the apples fell in the June drop, every last one. Not even wasps ate them. We gathered them up and kept the broken ones. 'We can make applesauce,' said Mom. We did. Basins full of it.

'Where are the wasps?' Dad asked. He was inspecting the panels that separated us from our neighbours. The panels had fallen over because they were so dry. That had prized open a ground nest and all that was left of the wasps was chewed half-husks. 'Wow,' said Dad. 'Something's killing the animals.'

'No shit Sherlock,' I said quoting something. It made me feel tough and cynical like an American kid.

Mom and I watered our herb bed by hose because nobody could see us from either road or field. Dad asked us to water the grass near our wild-bee hives, even hose down the hives to keep them cool. We skipped around the garden like thieves carrying watering cans. We let all the flowers die, even Mrs Tulp's lilies that her mother had planted at the end of World War Two.

The greyhounds lay listless and panting in their pens. I kept checking their water bowls, and during the hottest part of the day, I had to refill them about once an hour.

It was a week after the weasel.

Somewhere around Thursday, 14th of July, Mom and I got up. It was three-thirty in the morning.

Dawn was already glowing on the horizon like a stove ring. I was making Mechemek Chorba, a Turkish lentil soup. Mom liked it for breakfast, with swirls of sumac spice. If you were going to cook, that was the time of day to do it, when it was a bit cooler. I was also cooking frozen beans with onions, garlic and tomatoes and bits of fennel to eat cold at noon. (The food we had! Aubergines. Cous-cous. Mangoes. Papaya. Avocados.)

Mom came back into the kitchen, wide-eyed. 'The ducks are all gone.'

'Bloody foxes.' I said.

'No, no. No feathers, no blood. Foxes leave a mess. There's nothing. They're all just gone.'

I passed her a coffee. She sipped it then made a face. 'Teddy, it's cold.'

'It's the only thing that is.' The coffee was cold because I was half asleep and the kettle hadn't boiled.

Mom sipped her cold coffee and said in a dim voice. 'We can't lose our ducks.'

I gave her a hug and went outside.

The wired pen, the baked grey lawn, the straw-filled duck-house. There was nothing. Well, yesterday's splattering of duck poo, but it had already dried into scabs. The droppings had a very odd, chemical, almost minty smell.

No satisfied grunts, no wagging of tails. No dipping of beaks into the water tub, no drinking by applauding with their beaks. Drinking ducks look like they are singing, their heads thrown back. They could preen themselves all over, arching their heads around as if they'd been doing yoga.

Our beautiful ducks.

Mom draped an arm around my shoulders. 'What could it have been?'

I stroked her forearm. 'Must be foxes.'

'Or thieves. Coming at night with a van.'

'Come on, Mom. They're not that valuable. They'd have made a noise if a fox got among them.'

'Then what?'

'Charity,' I remembered suddenly.

Charity lay on the floor of her pen, eyes open. She snorted at us but did not look up. Donna Duck was gone too.

Normally Charity would huff and puff when she saw us and kick her way to her feet. Now she just lay here.

'Oh Charity, honey, have you lost your duck?' Mom kneeled next to her. The pig blinked. Mom scratched her behind the ears. 'Where's Donna?' Mom asked.

Mom said, 'Donna' and Charity gave a thin little squeal and turned her face to the wall. I think animals even then sometimes understood what we said. They knew their names at least.

We went back in the house and I warmed up the coffee, and then realized that the soup was cold now too so warmed that up. We ate breakfast. Mom went out again. I think she hoped the ducks would come waddling back.

But she came back looking grey and said, 'I don't think Charity is well.'

By then it was seven am and Dad in London would be splashing on the eau de cologne to go to his Important Job. But I think he had told Mom to call him if there was anything strange happening to the animals. Mom had to phone early if she wanted to catch him. I heard her tell him all about the missing ducks. *Like he would care* I thought.

At the end of the call, Mom said, 'Your father asked some very strange questions.' She ran a hand across her forehead. The sweat made it gleam. 'I don't feel well,' she said, and went back upstairs.

Mom was sick all over again, for a second time. All I needed. I just stood there in the kitchen, overwhelmed, my beans sizzling. Ducks, pig, Mom, the garden – all of it had gone bad. I wanted to keep everything green and crisp and in place.

I made Mom a cup of tea and took it to her. This time she'd arranged herself on the sofa in the main room, the terrace doors wide open. Her hand moulded itself around her forehead – the same headache, the same croaky voice.

But this time, she started saying strange things. I passed her the tea, her favourite, lime and ginger.

'Misfeed,' I remember her saying. She opened her eyes, staring at me in something like outrage. 'Misfeed,' like it was urgent. 'In summary. In summary.' Or had she said *summery* like in sunlight and heat? 'Pidge. Pidge,' like she was stuck. 'Pigeon!'

Dad drove back from London that afternoon.

He was wearing a face mask. He rubbed sanitiser on his hands and gave me a rough and tumble shake of the shoulders.

'Mom's sick again,' I said.

'That's why I'm here,' he said.

'No it's not. Nobody told you she was sick.'

He looked sad, and into my eyes. 'I could hear it in her voice.' He looked disappointed. He turned away from me and walked towards the door.

'Makes a change,' I said to his back.

Mom was still on the sofa, but she'd kicked off the sheet. The roman blinds were pulled down over the windows and that made the whole room yellow. Dad put on a kind of clear plastic screen over his face that hung from a hatband.

'Him,' Mom croaked.

He stood back respectfully like he was the gardener. 'Sorry you're not well. Sorry about the ducks.'

'Still here,' she said, suddenly clear and sounding calm. She held out her hands as if at the abundance of ducks in the sitting room. I began to be afraid.

He looked up at me. I just shook my head, *No they're not.*

He sat down on the edge of the sofa and took her hand and she let him. 'Uh. Look,' he said. 'I'd like you to go to the doctor.'

She took the hand back. 'Can't fly.'

'What if Teddy gets sick too?' He was always thinking about pandemics, public health, animal health as a social function. Always. 'I'm going to give you a test,' he said.

'You're not a doctor,' I told him. That was something Mom had drummed into me in the days when I thought everything Dad said was true.

He didn't get mad. 'I am a veterinary socio-pathologist. I focus on animals, true. But we look at society as a whole and we have to know medicine, and this is a simple test.' He took out a tube with a long plastic rod and swabs and rubbed them inside Mom's throat. She couldn't talk but I think she understood what he was saying because she opened her mouth. Dad said as he sampled, 'It wasn't Covid you had the last time.' That we already knew, but Mom and I didn't know the next thing: 'We did do some tests on the samples we collected. Remember Teddy, the earthworms in the garden?' Dad looked at me. 'We've found something in them. We're not sure what it is. It could be that something new has crossed into humans again. But.' Then back to Mom. 'It could be that we are the carriers. We're the ones making them sick.'

Mom's eyes boggled and her head did a little shake, like either she didn't understand or Dad was crazy. His lips went thinner. He coughed. 'Maggie, can I take a blood sample too?'

Mom stuck out a forearm, all smooth and firm. My Mom had young arms. She understood what we said, she just couldn't find words.

Dad had the kit ready. The syringe, the clean needle, the filling up of the tube with blood pushed out of the vein in a jet, the screwing shut and labelling. The little alcohol swab pressed against the pinprick. He thanked her. He asked if there was anything around the house that needed doing.

'Turnips,' she said, as if going to sleep.

Next door in the kitchen he refilled his water bottle from the tap. Before he left us, he'd re-plastered and painted the kitchen and it all still looked fresh. There was a line of decorative tiles around the walls. I remembered when he laid those tiles – and installed the new switches in the walls. He looked at those walls with sadness. *Stay if it makes you sad,* I thought.

Then Dad told me that he was going to call me as soon he got back 'home'. So this was no longer his home. If I got sick or Mom got any worse, or if any of our animals got sick, I was to call him. He put blue plastic things on over his shoes and went to the pens, and took a sample of goop from the lawns, then trooped back to his car. He threw the gloves, foot protectors and face-screen into a bag and then into another sack which he sealed, and then started rubbing alcohol on his hands, on the soles of his shoes, and then the door handles of the car.

'Anytime you want, come to London,' he said wiping the little insignia at the back that opened the boot.

'Thanks.' *Great, I can stay with Ken.*

'We can go see a show. They have live theatre now outside in Regent Park. *The Lion King* is supposed to be pretty good. There's also a really nice rose garden next to the ponds.' His voice trailed away.

'Whatever.'

'Whatever.'

He ducked. 'Wow, Teddy.'

My eyes felt like stone and I repeated what he'd said. 'Wow, Teddy.' *Like you're surprised?* I was frightened and angry – why was he leaving if Mom was sick? If all of this made him sad? So I said, 'You better get back to your home.'

His lips went thin again. 'I'll be back here at the weekend. See ya.'

He didn't hug me or kiss me, just got back in the car, but that might have been a health measure. The little electric Golf drove away, as silent as he was, as hunched as Mom's back.

Only then did Little One come trotting out from the ivy on the Mountain of Ash. She'd never liked Dad, always hid when he came. I took the watering can back to the herb bed, and she trotted alongside me.

That evening, Mom's fever went back to thirty-seven. More to the point, she started to make sense. 'I'm sorry Teddy. I hope I didn't scare you. I kept trying to find words, but it was like my brain was rewired and they kept finding the wrong ones.'

Everything my family did was to help save that old world. We were right there at the beginning of its end.

Four

Charity stopped eating.

All that day and into the next, I pushed plates of leftovers at her and she didn't respond, our huge pig and family friend. She even stopped sighing.

I pushed plates of food at Mom too – something gentle like vegan macaroni warmed on the Raeburn. She would only nibble a bit at the end of her fork. But at least she was eating – and drinking at least three big bottles of water a day. We went back to algebra and history.

My head buzzed all the time. I knew I had the sickness again too. It felt numb inside. And my stomach was weird – weak and burning like I'd drunk too much coffee. I didn't tell her that.

'Your father will be back at the weekend.'

'Thanks for the warning.'

'Don't be like that, honey?' A damp, ice-cold hand on mine.

Old Faithful clanked down our drive on a Friday – not her usual day. She glided down the gravel, swinging a leg over the bar and standing on one bicycle pedal while it was still coasting. Faith didn't like anything to slow her down.

'Your Mom's poorly,' she said, as if I hadn't known. 'Thought I'd look in to make sure you weren't smashing the place up.' She gave my head a stroke as she passed.

My kitchen was tidy. 'You been keeping the place up,' Faith said. 'Your mum been eating?'

I just shook my head no.

'Let's take her a plate. Nothing warm. You got any of that paste?' She meant the mushroom pate.

Little One had been pawing the kitchen rug all the time Faith was there. When Faith moved to the fridge, Little One ran in front of her. This was Little One planning ahead. If you went to the fridge first, the human would follow and give you food.

Faith held up a warning finger. 'Your job is to hunt.' She said that for show. I knew she had a tin of Whiskas in her rucksack.

'Maybe we should feed her something. Else,' I said.

Faith spun. She knew what I meant. She always moved so quickly, everything she did looked unintended, like it surprised her. 'Well that's a turn up.'

'If animals are getting sick then maybe eating other animals isn't such a good idea. So. Mmmmm-maybe Whiskas?'

'That's the most words you've ever said to me in one go. As it happens.' Faith scooped up the rucksack and pulled out not one, but four tins. But they were dog food. She laid them out on the counter, and said as if in passing 'My old dog died this morning.'

'What, Leeroy?' He was a huge slow fubbsy Labrador.

'Wall. He was sixteen. Had good innings.'

'Oh.' I couldn't think of anything to say. Faith started pulling celery out of the fridge. I said, 'What do you do when a dog dies?'

'You bury him in the garden. In his favourite spot. Does your mum eat crackers?'

I nodded yes. For some reason I began to feel a mounting distress. 'Did you have to bury him yourself?'

'Who else?'

'What, all alone?'

She paused. 'Leeroy had good innings. He was a dog. Dear old thing. I'll get another. Come on.' She slapped my butt to get me moving. We gave Mom her food. Mom sat up, looking worried. 'Faith, you shouldn't be here. You'll get ill too. Teddy, get my purse.'

'I'm not here to be paid,' said Faith, offended.

Together Faith and I went out to see if we could get Charity to eat. 'Water's more important,' she said.

She pushed the water basin under Charity's nose.

I was having a distraught morning. 'Please, Charity, please. You've got to drink something.'

'It's the heat. Go get the hose.'

'There's a ban.'

'The hose. Now.'

So, it was okay to break the ban. I ran. Little One followed, getting underfoot, hoping still for a fish head. As soon as she saw me reaching for the wall tap, she scarpered. The only thing in the garden she hated worse than rabbits was that hose with its jet of water.

We watered Charity with the hose to cool her down. It ran in rivulets off her back and soaked her straw. Wet bedding would help keep her cool as well. She didn't shift, or snort or look up to say thank you. She kept her face buried against the wall. The water gathered in beads on her coarse black hair. For a moment her back looked like Dad's beard.

Faith hooked a finger under her nose. 'She's not right, is she? Keep watering her and we'll see tomorrow.'

She clanked off on her bicycle. I was fed up carrying the watering can, so I took the hose and drowned my vegetables just in case they would somehow revive. Potting and planting out had been so much work that spring. I thought I was weeping for my vegetables and hating myself for being a cry-baby. I stood and didn't move, water splashing into the ground over brown and brittle, fallen stems.

Maybe if Faith had watered old Leeroy, he'd have raised his head.

From under the bushes, Little One glared at me and the jet of water. *Traitor.*

I made up for it by spooning out great meaty gobs of dog food for her. The smell made me feel sick.

Faith came back on Saturday which was totally unheard of. She felt my forehead.

'How long have you had a fever too?' She cooked me bratwurst while Mom slept on the terrace. 'Stopping a child eating meat, it's not right.' The sausages made me feel sick, but I ate them anyway to please her. While I was eating she nipped out, I think to have a word with Mom. On her way back, she picked up the cat and stroked it. 'It's okay Little One, it's okay,' she said her eyes hooded. Then she looked up at me, and dropped the cat neatly on all fours.

'Let's check on Charity,' she said. She kept a hand on my shoulder the whole time. Charity didn't move, not even to flick her ears. Faith said, 'I'm sorry, Little One, but I think you should know. She's in a decline.'

I really didn't like talking any more.

'She's pining,' pronounced Faith. 'For her duck.'

'Donna?'

'She's lost her duck. We all need company, Little One. I better get going or I'll be here to give That Man a full portion.'

That Saturday Dad came late.

They still didn't know what Mom had. But the Well Being Institute had formally told the renamed (again) public health body about a potential new pathogen. The Social Health Agency apparently had hit the roof, demanded the WBI's samples and went full swing into drawing up a public health protection plan. This time they would not be caught napping. Swing into action.

Dad came into the kitchen covered in blue and the clear face-mask. He turned on the radio, always set to Radio Four, and it was already in the news. A new pathogen present in both animals and people.

Epicentre in West Oxfordshire.

I took Dad in to see Charity. I had some of Faith's dog food in a basin and water but she didn't move. I shook her. Dad said sharply, 'Stay clear of her, Teddy.' He pulled his gloves tighter and rolled her over.

Charity always had a smug smile, as if her life was particularly satisfying. Now her mouth had turned down and showed yellow jutting teeth, like a nasty old man chomping a cigar. I'd never seen eyes like that. They were flat and grey and dry. I knew without being told, knew all the way down into my bones – Charity was gone.

'We should go,' Dad said. 'Come on, Teddy.' He didn't touch me with his blue-gloved hands but walked towards me, herding me.

I remembered what Faith had said about her dog. 'We should bury her.'

'Possibly,' said Dad.

'Possibly what? What else could we do?' I was shouting.

'She died of a disease,' he said.

'And of a broken heart.'

'Okay, okay,' said Dad.

I turned and stormed off, wailing, 'Mom. Mom. Charity's dead.'

By the time I got round the shrubs Mom was easing herself down the steps from the terrace, holding onto the rails with both hands. She'd thrown on one of Dad's old white shirts and her khaki slacks that tied up at the shin and her Moroccan string sandals. Her skin was grey and there were bags under her eyes.

'Teddy, I'm so sorry,' she said. She enveloped me in a hug. I could feel her sway, as if there was a high wind. 'You wanna have an ice cream?'

The hot air was like a boxing glove in your face – I yearned for an ice cream, even one with no milk and no sugar. I nodded.

'Can I ask you to go get it? One for Dad as well.' She eased herself down onto a terrace chair. She knew I had to be told to get one for Dad.

He stood away from us, outside the family circle, still in his masks and gloves. As I left I heard Dad ask Mom, 'Do you have an old sheet? We need a sheet.'

When I came back with the trolley Dad was sitting on the terrace on a third foldout chair. He and Mom sat in silence, hands neatly folded, like they were strangers waiting for a bus. Mom tried to make happy noises when the ice cream came out. I shoved a bowl and spoon towards Dad but didn't say anything.

'I'm going to have to take some samples,' Dad said.

That was too much. *Mr I-went-to-uni-late-and-now-I'm-a scientist.* 'Oh my word,' I said, which was about the strongest epithet I used back then, and took my ice cream down the steps. Over my shoulder I said, 'Sell her for bacon why don't you?'

Mom's voice trailed after me, sounding weary. 'Don't be unkind, Teddy. There's enough unkindness.'

Dad followed me down the steps, and squatted like he always did, to look into my face, only from a distance.

'I'm sorry, Teddy. But we don't know what this is and we have to find out. To save other animals. And possibly other people, older people maybe. All I will do is take swabs from her eyes and throat, and blood and fluid samples. Okay?'

I stomped back up the steps. They were made of wooden decking material and always bent under any weight. I drove my feet down, hoping to break them. 'That's not what you do. A decent person finds a spot in the garden that they always loved and buries them there. *That's what you do.*'

I shovelled in my ice cream in hurry, determined not enjoy it. But I did put the cold bowl against my forehead.

Mom stood up, I think to climb the stairs and fetch a sheet. 'Don't!' I said and ran up the stairs, and pulled a sheet from the linen cupboard and thundered back down. 'Here's your sheet.'

We all went to see Charity. Mom had a hand on my shoulder for balance.

Charity was already stiff. Dad could not roll her by himself onto the sheet. Mom told me to go fetch either Bounce next door or Mr Keppel across the lane. Off I went.

I found Mr Keppel in his garden and had to explain. 'Our pig has died and we need someone to come and help bury her.' My ears seemed to be ringing with the unreality of it. I felt like I was faking it a little bit, with the sting of tears around my eyes and the shaking voice. I felt a bit of a fraud like I was performing. But then how was I able to go teary if I didn't feel it? Mr Keppel looked solemn, nodded yes, glanced at his watch and followed me back across the lane.

Together he, Mom and Dad rolled Charity onto the sheet. Her legs stayed stiff and folded up like chicken wings along her belly. Her face looked like she was about to swear.

Dad took swabs from her ears and nose. He used a long needle to jab into her stomach. There was a hiss and he filled a tube with grey water.

Little One peeked in. She kept pawing the grass, sitting in alert position. Men made her nervous. I think she liked women better than men.

Then Dad took some kind of blade to cut a strip of skin and I wailed.

'Leave it, Michael,' said Mom. Dad started to say something, Mom cut him off. 'She's a pet.'

'In the garden,' I shouted.

Dad nodded and folded up the blade. 'Where in the garden do you think, Teddy?'

'I don't know!'

'How about the Forest Glade? Shall we bury her there?' The Forest Glade was a strip of big trees along our fence where we'd planted wild garlic and bluebells. Charity had liked to root around the plants.

Somehow Faith was there, walking round the corner of the house. 'Brought an extra shovel,' she said. Maybe Mom had rung her; or maybe Faith just knew that Charity was going and we'd need help. I remember thinking that she must have cycled down the hill from Allotments with that shovel on the handlebars.

We dragged Charity on her sheet round the toolshed to the Glade. The rest of the day was spent digging, Faith and Dad mostly. Mr Keppel had a portly stomach and short thin arms, and kept mopping his forehead in the heat. Mom kept struggling out with bottles of water from the fridge. 'Don't get dehydrated.'

I made her stop. 'Mom, you should rest, I'll get the water.' But I didn't.

I was ashamed of crying, so I tried to help dig. But it was too much for me. Our ground was clay on top, baked hard and then stones held by roots. Dad was in blue plastic, which he did not take off. The plastic clung to his clothes with damp. He took an axe and chopped roots, pried stones up with the shovel, and broke the handle of our old gardening fork. Faith had big arms with wizened skin and huge fingers like sausages. Her upper body pumped up and down digging the whole time. Dad had to balance big flat stones on his knees to hoist them up. Soon he had built what looked like a cairn.

'Those are good,' he said. 'We can pile those on top.'

'Why?' asked Mom.

He was panting. 'Stop anything digging her up.'

Mom and stood there, both us swaying in the heat. 'I'm taking Teddy inside,' she said.

Dad nodded. 'We'll call when we're ready.'

I wanted to help, but shamefully I also yearned to sit down in shade. I slumped onto the sofa and wished that we had TV.

'You can look at the tablet,' said Mom. That was a dispensation.

'Maths?' I asked.

'Something fun,' she said.

We found a series of South Korean anime about two friendly larvae. They made me laugh. Little One was allowed up onto my lap. I stroked her and Mom stroked me.

About an hour later Dad shouted, 'Teddy, we're ready.'

The rhyme struck me as funny. I had just been watching two slug-things acting like Laurel and Hardy, and I giggled. That made the cat jump. She didn't like it when people laughed.

The hole was rectangular and deeper than Dad's waist. Charity weighed about twice my Dad's weight, but they had managed to drag her up the lawn and into the trees. Mr Keppel and Faith were also now wearing blue gloves. It took all of us, Dad, Mr Keppel, Mom and Faith to overturn her into the grave, still wrapped in her sheet. She made a gurgling sound when she hit the ground and something sighed, like she was still alive.

Mr Keppel chuckled. 'If that's what she weighs after starving to death, that was one prize pig.' Then he saw me. 'Sorry, Teddy.'

Dad staggered as he shovelled soil back in, and then lugged the stones to drop on top of her.

Mr Keppel stood back, his shirt and face looking like someone had thrown water over him. 'My God you really mean it don't you?'

'We don't want the foxes digging,' said Dad. 'We need to keep other animals away.'

So they couldn't catch the disease.

But I preferred my version. Charity had died of a broken heart.

One thing I've learned in my long life: two things can be true at once. There is no dialectic.

Dad stayed to cook, since Mom was still unwell.

He showered and put his clothes through the laundry and put fresh ones on, and rubbed alcohol on his shoe soles and washed his hands. He jittered like a speeded-up film. He chopped up mint, drained chick peas, made a tomato and paprika sauce, let it cool and smashed up ice cubes and cut lemons to make a chilled salad.

'Both of you. Eat.' He stood over Mom, who ate not just nibbles but spoonfuls. That made him calmer. He kissed me on the forehead and told me I'd done well. My brain buzzed and I couldn't find any words. He got out his wet clothes and said he'd dry them when he got home. Again, that word 'home'. Home was not here with us. I wanted Ken buried, but in a garbage dump. Dad walked up the drive towards the van, and just before he got in, turned and waved to me, knowing I wouldn't wave back.

The heat woke me up, in the dark.

There was a smudge of dawn outside my window, but everything looked grey and sooty like we'd been covered in hot ash. I was just drifting back to sleep when I heard a snuffling noise. I must have been dreaming. I dreamt I heard a squealing, piggy sounds, and a clatter of stones and of trotters on loose rock.

I woke up. Of course it was silent. But Little One wasn't snuggled against me. She was sitting on the windowsill, bolt upright, her back towards me. Her fur was raised and caught moonlight in a halo. She was staring out of the open window, her tail flicking back and forth. She kept sneezing.

I got up. 'Oooch, Little One. Hay fever?' I stroked her head.

It was two-thirty am, so I swept the kitchen, and made tea, and took out Dad's salad and poured off the ice water. That would be breakfast. Mom came downstairs. 'I feel fine, Teddy, I'm fine,' and she went out to see the greyhounds. I went to water my plants, and dump the compost bucket which was stinking under the sink. I heard rustling in the elder trees by the compost and I got scared (of course). The dogs yelped for love and food. I heard Mr Chukwononso's van in the drive delivering our newspapers. I got the newspaper and baked it to kill any viruses and then we ate breakfast. I washed up. Mom went back upstairs to sleep. I took out my book *Dinotopia* to read on the Mountain of Ash. Little One did not come with me.

And there, in the front garden, like my dream had come true – the heavy rocks were scattered, the loose soil spread all over the Glade. Charity was not in her grave.

Maybe Dad had been right: Something dug her up?

You Staying Long?

Years later the Big Bake blasted everything and I went back to Oxford to live in a walled settlement.

I was there for about ten years. Everything in those days was Nationalized. The gates opened at six am to let in the lorries delivering food and water. The estate had its own shop, hairdressers, post office and clinic so most of us could stay put. Save on energy. I was put to work digging in the huge allotments out back. We were experimenting with prickly pears.

The nights were silent. No animals left.

The birds were still free though. By then babies were terrified of them and ran screaming. These new kids couldn't differentiate between animals and birds. Anything alive and not human was an object of terror.

Including me sometimes.

People like me were monsters. Even when my being able to talk to dogs and cats and ducks meant I could explain the sudden sounds that sometimes welled up from beneath the earth. Well, especially when I did that. I once barked a mound of soil back down into the ground.

There were posters in bus stops urging tolerance. One of the posters was a photograph of me. I was literally a poster boy for the compromised. HUMAN the poster said. SO GO SAY HI. It meant: poster boy's safe, let him live.

The ad campaign got me beaten up. Some compounds drove people like me away. I'd sit in our aluminium doorway and listen to the birds: blackbirds singing, pigeons making that rootling sound.

I stayed in the estate because I had friends. By then I was in my twenties, and I had tons of friends. Well, you had to have friends, things had become so terrifying we all had to work together. We'd all seen our parents die and food was rationed. The vaccine only really worked on people. Immunity for animals was only about fifty per cent, so there were no herds, no meat except chicken or insect mash.

We'd cook, we'd clean, we'd fix the cars, we'd grease windmills and recycle water. I'd been doing practical stuff since I was six. I could rewire light fittings, fix pipes, and even service a car. Let alone cook, bandage wounds, darn socks, and fix clocks. I realized that the kids were asking for my advice, help. In the middle of the night the younger ones would even come to me for comfort, their faces streaked with tears.

To my surprise, I'd become well liked, even a bit of a leader. For a time.

I would tell the younger kids about animals, especially the babies. I tried to get them to understand what animals were.

Animals weren't like all those nostalgia videos where the creatures are motion-controlled by actors so they have human eyes, human hearts. I try to get people now to imagine that animals couldn't talk, not at all, not a bit, despite what happened later. They were the victims, not humans. We ploughed their habitats, poisoned their litters, ran over them with cars, trapped them or hunted them. People had killed so many animals that they ran when they saw us, hid when the smelled us.

'Good,' say the young people, and I don't know where to begin.

I tell them animals were beautiful. I tell them about Charity, Little One, the Beautiful Boys. They look at me like they don't believe me.

Sometimes I howl for the past, as if at the moon.

Five

All that summer, heat roared like a lion.

In the shade, it was forty-one degrees. Our garden was so full of the stench of death that it smelled like fire. The very air slumped, exhausted.

I noticed Little One's food dish was untouched. I was as nervous as a trip wire. 'Mom. Little One's not eating.'

Mom was in her bathroom, washing. 'What?' She flung open the door, still wrapping her bath robe. 'It's probably just the heat.'

'I don't think she's touched her water.'

She took hold of my arm. 'Let's go see how she is.'

Mom was feeling a bit better, one of her good days. She didn't wait to put on shoes properly, just slipped her feet into them, cracking the backs. I will always remember that. She knew how much Little One meant to me.

We couldn't find her. The first place we checked was the Mountain – it was always cool and shaded and it had a chair. Then we thought she might be in her first home, the woodshed, so I peered inside that, making the Plaintive Meow. I called her, 'Lit lit lit lit Little One, Little One.' My voice was soft because if I'd really shouted and she didn't come, it would make it real.

She liked to sun herself on the old garden table, but she wasn't there.

I went back up the Mountain of Ash. I sat on the white plastic Weatherproof Throne. I didn't have a book to read. I just stayed there, not wanting to move or cry aloud. She was a private cat, she liked to be alone sometimes. I was being silly. I'd see her soon. It was just the heat. I tried not to meow or call. She would come, I'd see her any minute.

But she didn't come.

I knew I was making my wimpy face, my mouth bunched up against itself. Then I heard Mom call me, and she sounded worried, so I came out.

I sighed theatrically, lightly like nothing was wrong. 'I can't find her, Mom.'

'Oh. She's probably out in the long grass hunting. Shall we do your math?'

I said okay, to make things normal. She tried to explain how make percentages out of fractions, turning things upside down or something, but we were both distracted. I kept looking out the big terrace windows, at the big old yew, and the lily circle. I kept trying to see her coming back.

Finally Mom put her hand on top of mine. 'Let's go try and find her again.'

This time we looked together, both of us calling. Finally we heard a tiny sound, a squeak more like a hedgehog than a cat. I shouted and she came crawling out from under the winter jasmine, on her belly.

'I'll get her blanket. You get the vet cage,' said Mom.

Little One was always so tame when we took her to the vet's. It was like she trusted us to do no harm. She never hissed or clawed or fought. She would just slip into the cage. She might yeowl a bit when the car turned or bounced.

This time she crawled onto her blanket in the cage. I put my hand on her back, but I didn't have to push her in. Mom came back out with her brush and bowl, then dived breathlessly into the front seat.

'She'll be fine. I'm sure we caught it in time.' But her hands shook and she stalled the car. She took a deep breath, then edged out of the gate into Sandy Lane and very slowly gained speed. I kept my hand on Little One's back. Her breathing was fast and shallow.

'How's your husband?' the vet asked.

Michael Spaulding had a reputation locally, not always a good one. He had been in the press with a think-piece saying we should imagine animals as being a kind of person. He'd written articles attacking current veterinary practice.

'Good, he's fine, good. We've come with Teddy, my son. This is his cat. He's so fond of her.'

The waiting room was full of people, standing room only. Maybe fifty people and only five chairs.

'It is doing the rounds,' said the vet. 'Of course in this heat, some of them are having kidney problems.'

'Don't put her to sleep,' Mom said.

The vet's face fell. 'No, no. We'll rehydrate her. Intravenously. If we think there's anything else, we'll also give her an antibiotic. You did well to bring her in so quickly.'

Mom look relieved, her smile fluttering.

'We'll do everything we can,' he said. 'But.' He shrugged.

'There are a lot of sick animals.'

The vet scowled. 'As you can see. Something's doing the rounds.' The vet bent over to look her in the eye. 'She'll be okay. What's her name?'

I tried, but I couldn't say it. Mom kept rubbing my shoulder like it was a magic lamp. So Mom told him, and he said the name again.

'Leave her with us and we'll give you a call.'

I looked into Little One's face and told her we had to leave, and not to be scared. We'd be back for her. Her eyes looked into mine and I knew she'd understood.

'She'll be home tomorrow,' the vet promised.

We drove home slowly.

When she wasn't changing gears, Mom had her hand on mine. Back home, there was no sound in the house; it was as if all sound had turned into heat. The French doors, the terrace door, all the windows were open, but nothing moved. Mom and I tried to focus on fractions and percentages.

I still can't do percentages.

Beetroot salad with pine nuts for lunch. The salad was hot by the time we got it to table.

'I think I'll put up shutters,' said Mom. 'You know, like Italian or French houses? Shutters block the sun.'

The field and the sky were grey with haze. They seemed to merge, as if the Earth curved upwards.

The phone rang. Mom jumped up and said, 'Yes, hello. Yes?' A wary, 'Yes, I see.' Pause. 'Yes. Thank you, Doctor.'

Mom stood like she was in church, though she was in shorts and a halter neck.

'I'm sorry, honey, but Little One has gone.'

'I thought so,' I said.

'Do you want to go get her?' She was peering anxiously into my face. I couldn't move. 'If you don't want to...'

'I want to.' I still couldn't move.

Mom dangled the car keys. 'Do you want to stay here?'

I stood up.

The funny thing was that I felt like we were going to see her alive. I almost felt happy. I was going to see her again.

There were even more cars in the parking lot – this time there were no spaces at all, at the clinic or along the street. We had to park in the building next to M&S. So it was a ten-minute walk. I took the vet cage with me, like she was coming back alive. The heat from the pavements came through the soles of my sandals.

The vet's assistant looked stricken when she saw me. She came out wide-eyed carrying something wrapped in a blanket, another blanket, not her blanket. I still expected Little One to stick her head out from under it, to give her head a shake, her ears a twitch. The woman passed the bundle to me and I could feel that what was inside was already stiff.

Mom snatched up the vet cage from the floor.

I was amazed at the grief I felt. She was just a cat, a wonder of a cat, but she was gone and that was that, all used up. Dust and bones.

Stupid, I did a little mew to call her. I bit down on both my lips and stopped myself.

'Oh Teddy,' said Mom.

I walked out carrying the bundle at arm's length like she was trash.

The vet ran out after us. 'Mrs Spaulding. Sorry. But. You should probably burn the body?'

'How much do we owe you?' said my mother coldly.

'No, no, please, we'll send you a bill. But really. It might be better to leave the body with us.'

'My husband is an expert.' Mom started to walk.

'Yes exactly, I'm sure he'd say...'

'This is extremely upsetting.'

'... that perhaps its best to dispose...'

Mom almost shouted. 'So thanks and have a nice day.'

Outside the car, my Mom said. 'Give Little One to me, Honey. Okay. Let's make sure she's comfortable, so we can take her home.'

I'm not stupid Mom. I'm not a baby.

'Just. Just there we go.' Mom put the bundle in the cage. 'Do you want to sit in the back seat next to her?'

'She's not there.' It had been good to hold the body. It told me at a very deep level that whatever Little One had been was no longer with me.

'No honey, she's not.' She leaned in and put the cage on the floor to stop it sliding around and I got into the front seat.

Home. Mom ran into the house with the vet cage and hid it somewhere. Then she went straight to the phone and rang Faith.

'Hi, this is Maggie. I've got some bad news I'm afraid about Little One... Yes. Yes. He's taking it very well. Yes of course. Thank you, Faith. Thank you so much.'

Looking to me: *Faith is on her way.*

Then another call.

'Michael, this is me. I'm afraid Little One died. Yes, we think so.'

She looked up and asked me. 'Teddy. You want to talk to your father?'

No, I did not.

'He's shaking his head. He's pretty upset.' Mom looked up at me again. 'Are you sure, honey? Talk to Daddy?'

I kept swinging my head from side to side, no, no no.

'I think we'd better leave it, Michael. Can you get here?'

By the time Faith sailed down the driveway. I already had the shovel out. I knew where Little One was going to rest. In the Mountain of Ash, where we always sat reading. We still could read there together.

'That's the right place,' said Faith. 'You're no use with that shovel though. Give it here.'

I didn't let go.

'You don't let the chief mourner dig.'

I let a seventy-five year old woman finish the work. I had thought of the Mountain partly because the ash was light and easy to shift. In short order, Faith had dug an elbow-deep trench.

What were we going to do with her bowl and brush – give them to another cat? I lay them next to her. I felt like an ancient Egyptian, burying her with grave goods to help her on her long lonely trip, so that she would know that we thought of her. I just wanted her to have them.

'There you go Little One. There you go. Lit lit lit lit Little One.' I stopped.

'It's hot. You go inside,' said Faith. I knelt and started scooping the coal ash back with my hands. It left my hands as black as ink. The dark lodged under my fingernails and stayed for days. I patted down the ash. The sun was so strong through all those leaves that my skin felt wrinkled like the surface of an old pot of cream.

I went in and sat down on the sofa and just stared. Mom sat next to me and snapped on the radio, and got out her darning.

Thin-voiced Witney Radio and its five-minute News.

First the heat, the hottest blah blah since records began.

Then two disappearances in West Oxfordshire. One from Witney, the usual eighteen-year-old girl, a goth last seen in Rapture Records in the Walk. In a separate incident, a middle-aged man from Allotments has been reported missing. His abandoned vehicle was found in a passing place, the door still open.

Then: the Witney Animal clinic reports a five-hundred-fold increase in illness of pets, with many animals succumbing to a flu-like illness. This follows reports from the Well Being Institute of a potential new virus in the West Oxfordshire area.

Mom switched to Radio 3. It was the Jazz show. (Jazz was an improvised music, very complex, created mostly by black Americans. You had to be a musician to understand it.) I sat. I didn't want to eat. Mom stood up and came back with more of the same salad we had for lunch. She'd added some kimchee, so I plucked that out to eat first, all crisp and cold. There had to be small joys. Mom leaned over me and asked if maybe it was time for bed. She was always telling me that it was time for bed. Did she think I didn't know when I was tired?

She knelt in front of me, eyes wide.

It's all right. I get it. I have to lose everything.

I had no father, no friends. I had my Mom.

'Honey,' Mom said. 'I know you loved that little animal. I'm sure she loved you. She came when you called, she got into the cage just like that? She knew you were only going to help her.'

She pressed her cheek against mine. It was as slimy and sticky as a slug.

'I'm okay, Mom,' I said in a voice that was far too loud. 'Everything dies. I know that, Okay? She wasn't old yet, but it was the heat or maybe yeah she died of this new thing. Which is nobody's fault. So. Mom. How about you let me grow up a little bit? Huh? Who knows, maybe I might even be able to face school. And get out of this house.'

I'd left the hose on. Great way to be an adult. I stomped down the terrace steps to the wall tap. No little cat to be scared of the water now. The shrubbery and trees at the back of the garden were a solid silhouette, untended and wild.

I had my back to them, reaching across the tomatoes to turn off the tap, when I heard a rustling. I stood up. 'Hello Boys?' I said. I thought it was one of our greyhounds, got out of his pen.

I heard a rasping sound, like air coming out of the leaky bellows we kept by the fireplace, wheezing air through a rip in the leather.

The thing both wheezed and gurgled, with a dragging sound as it came closer. I didn't like it. I scampered back up the steps, and closed the terrace door behind me and locked it for good measure.

Mom was back on the sofa. 'You heard it too?' she said. 'Best to keep the door closed; we wouldn't some sick animal to come in by mistake.'

No, we wouldn't.

The next day, as soon as it was light, I went back out to check. The rocks over Little One's grave were still in place.

I went back to the shrubbery at the bottom of the garden. I'd flooded the lower garden by leaving the hose on. I was dreading seeing in the mud either cat prints or the imprint of pig hooves.

Something rustled in the deep shade of the holly, the yew, the elder.

I felt a tickle in my brain. I was trying to smell it. I didn't have the basic equipment, though I did have some human sense of smell.

You know sometimes when the volume is turned down very low, you can still hear? You can focus and concentrate. You know how when you look at something far away, something you couldn't photograph even with a telephoto lens, but your eyes can somehow focus and pull it in closer?

It was like that. There was a scent, under the smell of wet lawn and pigeon do-do on holly leaves. I knew it was the smell of death, and I knew it was the smell of duck.

And as if made of that stench, wafting on it, out came one of our ducks.

I recognised her. It was the big white one, Golden. Her feathers had come out in patches; elsewhere they were sticky with what looked like tar, and her lower beak had dropped off. She saw me and managed to hiss, and then, her neck extended, she charged at me.

I didn't want to make it real, so I walked slowly up the terrace steps and closed the doors behind me. When I looked back there was nothing there.

'What was that sound, honey?'

'Nothing,' I said.

What was I supposed to say? Mom, our ducks didn't go away, they're waddling around the shrubbery with bits dropping off them. I am such a wimpy crybaby that the duck actually scared me, and I got goosebumps because I'd understood the quacking. It was a food signal. I was the food?

I'm so 'imaginative' that I actually believe a sick duck is attacking because it wants to eat me. And I'm trying to grow up.

I had a pretty good idea, right then, of what was coming and I said nothing because I didn't want to look stupid. I was made of fear.

Goodbye

Why am I writing this?

Well partly because I can't stop. I try to stop for a meal, or stop for a day, maybe a week, but then I remember something else and have to get it down before it goes, like fireflies, like bluebells. Look at the appendices to see more memories of animals or of Mom and Dad.

During my lifetime, I have seen at least five whole worlds of culture come and go. It feels so good to use this language again, like stretching aching muscles, the language my parents used, the language of my first world.

Even then, the way I talked was old-fashioned, the English of my grandparent's books, of my parents' even-toned discussions. There was no television in the house; my use of the internet was gate-kept.

We were unconventional for the time My dad was studying for a qualification in Islamic Studies. He would read aloud in Arabic. My Mom was a retired journeyman actor from the early days of the century. She could recite long stretches of plays, Shakespeare or Bernard Shaw, by heart. And she could say anything she liked, just like that, using any word she wanted.

These days I have to put every word through the checker first. It always pings with alarm: *dog, pathogen, organic, vegan, Islam, heat, boyfriend, father, mother*. Even *he* and *she*. All of these words set off sensitivity alarms. Even now I could go to prison if I mention the dark days of sterilisation. (Oops I just did.) Sterilisation is why I don't have kids, you may have noticed. Well, the main reason (another reason is I just don't fancy human beings). My children would have barked. So they made sure I can't have any.

So I rewrite this. It's easier to cut, lie a little bit, avoid the controversies, and then post the cleaned up version. (Oh, and wipe the history so there's no record of what got pinged.)

I don't need trouble. And there will be trouble if anybody reads this version. They'll know Edx Spaulding is still dog, still cat, still howling at night. I tell everyone that the treatment worked. People would be revolted to know that a cat had once slept in my bed or that we'd lived with pigs and dogs.

We were alive. It was a good world.

Dogs would never destroy a planet; bees had wireless and built cities; pigs could love other species than their own; cats knew how to love without possession, knew that food was love, all food. Cats knew not to hunt birds if you fed them; food meant birds were family.

I want you to know what you have lost. Then I'll go back to my olives and the mountain of ash and only whisper my stories in the language of dogs.

Goodbye.

PART TWO
Oldminster

Six

Dad called again to say he was sorry about Little One, and I still wouldn't talk to him.

Mom said, 'Please Teddy. Please?' She held out her phone and her eyes had that no-nonsense look. There would be hell if I disobeyed. I knew my Mom.

So I took the phone, and launched myself at him. 'It's okay, Dad, you don't have to come. It was only a cat, and you did your weekend visit so why come back? I get it. We are fine here by ourselves.'

I knew how he would sound – stricken. 'Teddy. Teddy I'm sorry. But please understand. I've been with our lab the whole time, we're trying to work out what this thing is.'

(Meaning: *I haven't been with Ken.*)

'But I'm thinking of you all the time, Teddy. I'm so sorry about Little One. I really am.'

'Don't strain anything.'

'The chances are *good* that I will be staying with you and Mom for a long time.'

I just held the phone back out towards Mom. I looked away but she stepped in front of me to give me a glare. Her eyes softened when she took the phone. 'Mike? Well. You know. He's lost his best friend.' Then she almost chuckled, except that her eyes watered at the same time. 'I don't mean the *cat*. I meant *you*.'

I went out into the garden to do my chores, but I just stood there. The garden was a sunny tangle and I didn't know where to begin or what to do. I just stood there.

Mom took me by the shoulders and eased me towards the terrace. 'Come on Sweetie, let's do English. You've got your SAT skills, vocabulary to do. We could do the flash cards?'

The day was like any other. I thought the days would go on and on the same, doing the National Curriculum. Ten year olds are supposed to be top of the school and prepping for the Next Big Step. Only I was the top of nothing, I was nowhere. Yes, I could use vocabulary powerfully and I was an Independent Reader. I'd missed school full stop so that just made the next step even more of a climb.

I probably pruned the tomatoes that day so they would fruit. They at least seemed okay with the heat. All our other crops were toast. I probably sat on the Mountain of Ash and stared into space. I don't remember listening the radio, but I think, I *know*, that the Well Being Institute was mentioned.

The next day was a Tuesday, so Faith would have shown up again. I don't remember her. I imagine she was a bit hearty and brusque. 'Get out there into that fresh air. All this sitting. You'll get square eyes.'

I do remember one radio broadcast and I think it must have been on that day. The WBI had made public what data it had, all its photographs of the pathogen. The WBI had called it a virus. The Chinese government declared that the pathogen was too large to be described as a virus. They were testing to see if antibiotics were effective. They had learned the lessons of Covid. As we all had, only too well. Fast action was key; the Chinese had already banned all travel to and from England, while exempting Scotland and Ireland. All imports of animal products from across the UK were to stop. Not that they were using it for politics.

The shadows got long; the air grey and hot, twilit and still. It was so hot that it was like a bull had its snout up against your nose and was sucking out the air. I had the never-ending headache; the disconnected buzz.

And I felt a yearning in my heart for love and attention and care that I'd never had before. I would do anything – get down on the ground, roll over, show my stomach – just to get some praise. *Good boy, good boy.*

That's what dogs are. Part of their genetic code is missing, so dogs are love-seeking mutants. Now I was mutant too.

I had a pretty good idea what had happened to me, I just didn't want to face it. If anybody had asked, I could have told them *the thingy is copying parts of animals into us*. I'd caught this from the greyhounds. Which means I could have warned Mom: the Boys are already sick. And maybe I had something from the cat and the ducks as well.

I didn't know anybody my own age, just Faith and Mom. There were no kids in the village, which is how I liked it. It was Oldminster, full of oldies.

I sat there and I knew – *this old life is going to end.* I knew I was going to have to grow up and I was young enough to like the idea of everything being overturned, most especially me.

Whatever happened, I was going to go back to school. However much I hated it; even if I was bullied and the kids were as alien as Martians.

I hadn't been able to handle school at six. It was like I had a phobia of other children. They sounded harsh and mean, even their laughter sounded like they were breaking something. Now it would be different. I'd join sports teams and if I wasn't good enough for any team then I'd stop with the bloody beans and bees and I'd practice football day and night until I was good enough to at least be invisible, normal. Being normal makes you invisible.

I remember, I got quite determined. I got very cheerful. That was it. I was going to be less of a baby. I was getting out of Beehive Cottage, and going to West Allotments Junior. I stormed back into the house and crammed a lentil roll into my mouth and turned off Stephen Sondheim's *Company.* I promised myself I would listen to cool stuff. Not that I knew any cool stuff. Ed Sheeran? Was Ed Sheeran cool?

It was all for nowt. The next day we were back in lockdown.

Dad's boss had been at some government meeting.

He rang Dad right afterwards and told him West Oxfordshire was going to be locked down, so to get moving now. It may be that he wanted Dad to be in the epicentre and report.

Mom nodded on her phone glancing all the time at me. 'Uh-huh. Uh-huh.' Sure sign I was being talked about. 'Yes,' meaning probably *yes he's listening.* Then. 'So what do you need us to get?'

She flicked her hand at me: *I need a pen and paper.* Our dining table was full of school stuff, so I passed both to her..

'So nothing fresh is what you're saying. Power failures? Okay. So nothing frozen either. Tins?' Her lip curled. We never ate from tins. 'Rope,' she said this ruefully like it was the punchline to a joke. 'Oh come on Mike, they had a run on toilet paper the last time. Bird food. Right. Batteries. We only have two fuel tins Mike. Yeah sure. I have no idea where to find a generator.' More uh-huhs. Then. 'Come on Teddy, we're going shopping.'

I dreaded shopping. I always got horribly self-conscious. Here I was nearly leaving primary school and still going everywhere with my mom. I saw other kids in Witney. Some of them had skateboards and wore black leggings. They walked about the mall like they owned it. I felt like a dog on a leash.

Well.

Waitrose was half empty. Mom bought dried beans, rice flour, tofu, all kinds of tinned vegetables. She muttered 'Sod it,' under her breath and also bought bags of frozen peas and broccoli and vegan ice cream and vegan apple tarts and bags and bags of nuts that we couldn't afford. Even jam. She never bought jam. And flour and yeast. Sauces, for curry, for pasta. She'd never bought sauces. Fire lighters for some reason. Clothes pegs. Cleaners, screws, light bulbs, big packs of batteries and, yes, toilet paper.

The bill came to over three hundred quid. And that's without any booze at all. Our family never drank.

'Stocking up?' asked the till lady, being pleasant.

'Yes,' said Mom. She hesitated. 'We're going back into lockdown.'

'Honestly, I wish the people at the top would make up their minds.'

'This is something new,' said Mom.

'Really?'

Mom nodded, yes

The till lady said, 'It's about the animals isn't it? One of our neighbours got attacked by their guinea pig.' And I thought. *We all already know, really.*

We went to Boots and bought tons of first aid, but of course no antibiotics. Mom tried to buy most of their hand sanitiser, but they had the three-item rule back. Also travel items. Insect repellent. Water purifiers and water purification tablets. A mosquito net. Mouthwash. Three bottles of surgical spirit.

There was a queue outside the butcher shop on the corner. We had no need of butchers. The very faint smell of meat was enough to turn my stomach.

So why was I salivating?

Without saying anything, Mom took a tissue out of her purse and wiped my chin. She murmured, 'Teddy. You're drooling.'

New adult-me let her have it. 'It's the sickness.' I checked to make sure no kids had seen my mother wiping my face.

We went to the country store and bought seeds and nuts in big tubs to feed the birds. But then weird stuff too. *Leather harness, chains and muzzles?*

For the Boys. In case they get sick.

Driving back having filled two canisters with petrol, Mom finally told me. 'Your father is going to come back to stay with us for lockdown.'

I found myself waiting outside the gate scuffing my feet, staring up Sandy Lane, trying to make my dad appear.

I just stood, thinking nothing. I kept thinking Little One was still there next to me. She would have waited with me. I kept expecting to feel her winding around my ankle. I think I even gave the Plaintive Meow without realising it.

Mom came out with water, told me to come inside. I said, 'Yes, in a minute,' but I didn't come back inside. It got to late afternoon and Mom gave me a little push. 'Do I have to get angry with you? He'll come when he comes.' The sun was starting to set, and my lip curled inward and my heart clenched into a fist. He wasn't coming. Of course, he wasn't coming.

Mom gave me a coconut milk ice cream. I didn't eat it. She said I could use the tablet, sat next to me, jumped straight into the South Korean larvae. But I didn't laugh.

It was nearly dark when we heard a crackle of gravel under the silent electric car, and the automatic outside light switched on. Mom jumped up, light glistening on her face. She flung the door open. 'What took you so god-damned long?'

Dad was carrying a TV set. A huge dome of rucksack swelled over his head.

'Hello Teddy,' he said.

'He's been a waiting outside for you all day. What's that thing? Why did you bring that?' Her hand flickered in disgust at the TV screen.

'We may be here for quite some time,' was all Dad said. He looked worn and tired. He'd given up on wearing all that blue stuff – it was almost a shock to see his face. Whether Mom realized it or not she was blocking him in the hallway. Dad turned sideways past her and staggered into the sitting room where he lowered the TV. I stared at it. It was as big and black as death. Dad hugged me. 'I'm sorry about Little One.'

'You're hurting my neck.'

Mom was standing her ground. 'Why a television? We didn't need a television in the last lockdown.'

He patted it. 'It's how the nation talks to itself.' He had some kind of aerial.

'Thought they had social media for that.'

'That's how little cliques talk to each other. Teddy? Can you come with me and help carry things?' He rubbed my hair. He thought I was a couple of years younger than I was. I nodded yes.

More tools, some we already had. Nails, fresh-cut two-by-fours, drill bits, wiring, extra plugs, charger batteries and tons of replacement light bulbs. Barbed wire – ouch. Locks. Boxes of face masks, gloves and face screens. More surgical spirit. Mom found a small white box of bee smokes, and turned them over in her hand. 'But we don't farm honey,' she murmured.

And, crammed somehow into Dad's little Golf, were two generators. One petrol, one diesel. Four empty fuel canisters. And Dad's Dr Frankenstein box as Mom called it. Phials and tests and syringes.

And then under it all, a shotgun and boxes of ammunition.

'What the hell is this?' Mom asked.

'We might need it,' was all Dad said. Mom glanced at it and grunted. 'I suppose we might be attacked by Tom's tumbler pigeons.' She had a way with deadpan theatrics.

When we'd unloaded, Dad threw himself onto the sofa. Sighed. Mom shouted from upstairs, making a bed, 'There's a plate in the top oven.' He groaned back onto his feet to go get it.

I heard his phone ring in the kitchen, and I imagined him hunched over it, keeping his voice low. 'I got here okay, no problems. They're both fine. Yes. Yes. I've only just got in. I will ask, okay? I will ask.' Then murmured low, what might have been, 'I love you.'

Dad perched on the edge of the sofa and ate with just a fork. It was the standard beany nosh, but he thanked Mom, said it was delicious.

Then he sighed and put both his hands on his knees. 'Um. Look. If this is like lockdown last time it could go on for months, so Ken has asked me to ask you: would it be okay if Ken stayed with us?' His eyes latched onto Mom's, away from mine.

Mom sat up straight, her face neutral. 'If it was just me, I might say yes.' She sounded like she'd thought about it already and rehearsed her reply. 'You and Ken could stay in the third bedroom. And if Teddy liked Ken, I would say yes. But, Michael. I'm saying this so Teddy doesn't have to? The answer is no. Teddy is not well, and I think he needs both our attention.'

And Teddy hates Ken.

Dad gave me a glancing, wincing smile and nodded. Nothing more was said. Dad stood up and set up what looked a bit like a Valentine's heart on the windowsill and plugged it into the TV. We knew we were too country for Virgin cable, and Mom refused to have anything to do with Sky since it was Murdoch, so it was Freeview or nothing. Very nearly nothing.

To my wonder and amazement, up came BBC 1. Just like that. Dad could do anything.

The ten o clock news – more trouble in Parliament, and then, yes, West Oxfordshire was in lockdown. Some minister said they were taking the necessary steps speedily and following scientific advice.

And suddenly on TV, there was Dad's boss, Ivan Szenas. It said his name white on red, and Well Being Institute.

'Yes, I think the government has acted quickly and on good advice. This pathogen affects both people and animals and we should do everything we can to get on top of it. As we've heard, the Chinese have already stopped flights from England and banned UK meat imports.'

The announcer asked, 'The Chinese are saying you've got it wrong, that this is bacteria not a virus.'

'We're not calling this a virus. It's something new, very large, so I can see why Tsinghua University might call it a bacterium. The hope was that antibiotics would be effective against it. They're not.'

The interviewer sounds dazed. 'Antibiotics don't work?'

'We're still testing it, but the first results suggest no.'

'But the government said it has adequate stocks of antibiotics.'

'Indeed it does, but this is not a bacterium. The Chinese have jumped the gun in this instance. Which is why we should all wait until we know more.'

Dad was shaking his head.

'Want to go for a walk, Teddy?' he asked.

'While we still can,' said Mom.

'Walks outside are allowed even in lockdown.'

So we went for a walk along Sandy Lane in the dark, with just a flashlight. We got to the hill where the church had its parking lot, looking down on the line of old cottages. It was a full moon, a hot night, no clouds. You could see the sagging roofs, the doors right on the roadway, the thatched rooftops – a postcard village full of rich people's second homes. Not to mention a government minister. The lights were on in our fourteenth-century inn, The Ram's Head.

The north side of the street perched on a steep slope, a bank with shrubbery. The village had one streetlight at the bottom of the hill. One of the few houses with a big garden looked out over the hill, which was where a famous ballerina lived with her less famous manager-husband.

Somewhere a dog was barking. There was something not right in the sound. It was ragged, like it had a sore throat, and somehow I knew it was not signalling correctly. The bark seemed to me to be a *Where?* A lost yipping, like a pup might make for its mother. But it was backwards, confused, almost *Where am I?*

We started to walk back. The bushes rustled. The dog howled again, and it sounded much closer. My head started to buzz.

My mother touched my arm. 'Teddy, why are you making those noises?'

Dad stopped too and took my arm. 'You okay, Son?'

My head buzzed and I kept trying to see in the dark more clearly.

'Here,' said Mom, and turned on her phone flashlight.

There on the bank, on its haunches sat a cat. For less than I second my brain said *Little One* and I felt joy and a smile jump onto my face. But it wasn't her. In the glare of the flashlight, this cat's face was all white but misshapen. It was as if there was something in my eyes, blearing my vision.

Then the cat jumped and landed on my head.

Its claws began to gouge into my scalp. I screamed, or thought I did. I could feel skin peel back, and my hair caught in its claws being painfully pulled.

Mom shouted and grabbed it. It hissed. I felt the hiss coming from somewhere down from its chest and the smell was putrid, the metallic smell of death, but also like a wound, infected.

Dad pushed it forward from behind, so the claws had less grip. The cat came away from my head and I was making as much noise as I could.

Later Mom told me I wasn't screaming. I was yeowling like a cat.

I had an impression that it was holding onto my mom's arm. 'Get it off, get it off,' she said. I think Dad seized it and flung as far as he could up the bank. 'Ow!' my mom wailed.

The door of the ballerina's house was flung open. A tall, athletic man came out with white hair, white beard. 'Is something wrong?'

Mom picked up her phone. The flashlight was still on. She shone it on me.

'My God,' the man said. I could see a trail of blood down my shirt. I couldn't breathe. Mom had a large slash down her arm.

The man said, 'Do you need some first aid? I've got some in the house.'

Dad said, 'We're near, we'll go home.'

'We got attacked by a cat.'

The man stared. I still couldn't breathe. I was hiccoughing. I somehow couldn't find any words or any signal to make words.

'I'm Mike Spaulding from down the lane. I'm a researcher at the Well Being Institute. We've been getting some odd reports, and we think, because of this pathogen, that some of the animals are attacking people.'

'What, pets?'

'And livestock yeah. Be careful is what I'm saying.'

Mom and Dad ran with me, trees arching overhead. My trainers kept tripping me up, catching on potholes. The street signs stared back at us, reflecting light:

NO PASSING PLACES FOR 1.5 MILES

We heard a rustling in the shrubbery that kept pace with us. Mom said later that I started to growl. We turned down our drive.

The automatic light was already on. That meant something had moved past our front door. I thought I saw something shoot under the hedge of forsythia and flowering currant that masked our door.

Mom's hand was shaking as she tried to find the right key. There were too many keys for the house, she always got the wrong ones. The fingers of her right hand were dripping with blood.

Finally the door shivered open; she pulled me inside, and slammed it shut. She pulled me into the laundry room where we kept bandages and creams.

'Your head!'

I could see in the cabinet mirror there were great long gashes, like the cat had been frantically digging into my skin to peel back the scalp. Blood was dripping from my nose.

'Jesus.' She got me to lean forward and started to dowse my head with cold water. Blood swirled down the sink.

'We need to get you to a doctor.'

Dad walked in and said, 'I called Feeb.'

I waved in the direction of her hand. I still couldn't find words. There were tooth marks in her arm; it was a very bad bite.

The automatic light flicked on by itself again. Mom jumped. Then we heard the settling of a car in our drive. Mom went to the door.

I stayed rooted to the spot.

'He's in here,' said Mom.

A tall red-headed woman strode in, wearing an old-fashioned white face mask. I recognised her but I couldn't think of the word for what she did. I knew she lived across from the ballerina.

Immediately the woman began to examine me. 'Yes. That is quite nasty. From a cat you say?'

I knew which cat it was, too.

'It'll need stitching.'

It had been Nose. Little One's brother, who'd also been born in our shed.

'He needs to go to the hospital,' Mom said, 'Well, that little clinic, you know?'

Feeb had big blue bag with her, a sports bag maybe, and she pulled out what looked like a stapler gun. Nothing quite made sense.

'They won't be open. The nearest A&E is in Oxford.'

Nurse, she was a nurse. More than that, a Ward Sister. I was finding words again.

'Just stop the bleeding,' Dad said.

She washed the wounds and they stung. More blood washed in thin trails down the sink.

The automatic lights kept flicking themselves on. Something was moving outside. Mom's eyes would leap up and catch Dad's

Phoebe. That was the Ward Sister's name. Dad always called her 'Feeb' – I think because she was a hearty product of the middle class. I could feel her laying flaps of skin back in order. 'This has got tucked under some other skin. I'm so sorry Teddy,' Feeb said. I could feel loose scalp twist back into place. I started to shake.

'Needs a chair,' said Dad and with the speed of a flick knife, a chair was there. I sat down. My wimp face had fallen into a million pieces, my lips were shuddering and there I was blubbing again.

'Poor little fella. Poor little fella,' my Mom kept saying, which made it worse and made me cry more.

The nurse said, 'I'm going to be straight with you Teddy. This will hurt.'

It did. She stapled the slices shut and I screamed. I screamed and kept wailing and I buried my head against my Mom.

It was all too much for me. Not just the attack, but all our animals dying. And it was Nose. Little One's brother, from four years before.

Nose – and most of his face had been missing.

I did sleep in the end.

I was afraid of dreams, though I was too ashamed to say so. Mom must have heard me moving about. She came in and asked if I wanted to sleep next to her. I followed her down the corridor. Dad was in the middle bedroom. In the middle of the night, the sky rumbled and it was like a cat purring.

Mom and I had settled on her bed. There was a flash of light.

Mom said, 'Let's count.' We waited for the rumble to reach us. The lightning was far away. Another flash, and when we counted to the thunder, we both said, 'Getting closer.'

'I wish it would rain, I said

'Me too.'

We counted as the sky seemed to come closer. Then there was a flash and boom right overhead. We both jumped and laughed. Mom said, 'Let's go see.'

We trundled down stairs in bathrobes. Dad was on the terrace I guess to pray – there was a matt on the floor. He was talking on the phone. 'Give it another twenty-four hours. Thanks.' Then he turned around. 'How are you, Teddy?'

I told him I was fine in a small voice. He reached for me, but I stayed where I was. 'Good,' he said.

The terrace's view of the sky was blocked by the big chestnut and Mrs Tulp's old yew. The holly tree was always in silhouette – we called it the Goldfinch Skyscraper because sometimes it seemed there were as many birds as leaves.

All of us went to the east-facing French doors. We saw the sky dance and laugh. It threw up confetti and lit torches, jigged around a bonfire in the sky, Guy Fawkes overhead. Then a beautiful bolt. It looked the sky itself had cracked. You could see blinding daylight through the break.

'Do you think it will pass over?' Mom asked. She meant without raining.

Oldminster is the seventh driest place in England. It lies between the Cotswolds and the Chilterns in what's called a rain shadow.

'Too late for my beans,' I said.

Both my parents laughed and for a moment stood side by side.

For once the sky didn't hate us. A drumming began on the glass terrace roof starting slowly but becoming almost as loud as the thunder.

I jumped up and down and clapped my hands. It felt like all the bad things had passed. The terrible smells would be washed away and I could splash through puddles. I started to run outside, but Dad grabbed me. 'Stay inside.' He looked up at my Mom with heavy eyes. 'We've been getting reports.'

The rain sounded like an audience applauding. I went to the only north facing window. The automatic light was on. The driveway was already full of puddles, like right under the Good Apple Tree, where the car always turned.

The raindrops were fat and gloopy like saliva. I felt my smile fade.

There, in shadow, two yellow eyes caught the light.

I stood not moving, not really thinking anything at all.

Mom touched me gently, like she was afraid of startling me. 'Honey. Why are you making those noises?'

'What noises?'

'You're growling again.'

Seven

I woke up late in a grey light, with a trickling sound in the gutters.

Downstairs there was a new noise: the television blaring. Half asleep I could hear what it was saying. New disease, West Oxfordshire in lockdown, residents told not to travel except on essential business.

I trooped downstairs in my sleep T-shirt and yesterday's chinos. Mom sent me back upstairs to wash.

I saw myself in the mirror and I burst into tears. Underneath all my posh manners and shyness, I was a vain little fellow. I looked like Frankenstein's monster, a row of stitches right across the top my forehead and my hair in weird twists where the blood had not quite washed out. I remember thinking: *I won't be beautiful any more.*

I was also angry: *bloody cat, why did it have to pick on me?*

I could smell green through the open window, like the shrubbery and fields had breathed a sigh of relief. Water reflected on the rear walkway, still pimpling with rain. The air was sweet again. And the sound of the rain was like someone stroking your cheek.

I ran downstairs, and the TV noise was louder.

'Your Dad's going to be on the radio,' Mom said. She'd made a bean salad for breakfast, but was still pouring water through the coffee filter. 'Your Dad wants to know what they're saying.'

Dad was squatting on the sitting room floor, knees up around his ears. He looked like an old Indian shaman, eating the salad with his fingers. 'They've got it all wrong, Teddy.'

Mom came in with her bowl and the coffee. 'So why watch it then?'

'Because they get everything wrong. You need to know what people are thinking.' Dad never watched TV when he lived with us. Mom and I glanced at each other. *That's Ken talking.*

'You say the same thing about social media.'

Dad chuckled. 'We live in a world in which mainstream media are more reliable. Or maybe just less crazy.'

The Beeb's political correspondent was detailing how the government was embarrassing party members. Then came a lot of sport, and then an interview with a pop star who had travelled to Manchester. This was the first time I'd seen TV news, but even at ten, I thought it was thin soup. This fed the nation?

'They still haven't got it.' Dad sighed and stood up, blooming like a speeded-up flower on a nature show. 'Sorry. Got to have the radio and TV off for the call.'

Ivan had given Dad's name to the Beeb as one of the WBI's experts, the man who'd seen the first cases and was now locked down in the epicentre. BBC Radio Oxford was going to interview him.

'You and I have an essay to go over,' said Mom, hand lightly pushing my back. She left Dad in the kitchen where the main phone plug and the broadband were. I can't remember what we were studying, but I could hear Dad talking. I remember thinking mostly about how I'd made up my mind to go back to school, join the world, and now I couldn't because of lockdown.

Dad came back out, chuckling and shaking his head. 'Well, that went well.' Which meant it hadn't.

We gave it a half hour and then listened on the Sounds App. You could listen to all the BBC's radio shows for free; it was like an aural encyclopaedia. I downloaded the file, and for many years afterwards would play the recording, until I had an OS upgrade and it was gone for ever. I know it, if not exactly by heart.

The interviewer gets it wrong from the start.

The reporter introduces Dad as a biologist. He corrects her – he's a veterinary socio-pathologist and she plainly doesn't think that's relevant. He explains his profession at length.

The interviewer tries to help out. 'So it's about the interaction between people and animals.'

'And animals with each other. Unless you think animals don't live in societies themselves.'

She wants the personal angle, the dread of lockdown in another pandemic. He wants her to understand that the policy is wrong. 'We're reacting to the last pandemic. It's what humans do – try to correct the last mistake instead of looking at what's happening this time.

'What's different is that today animals are dying, not people. In fact, from what I've seen, the mortality rate among infected animals is close to one hundred percent. We should be taking steps rather more like we did against hoof-and-mouth disease. Only more extreme.'

'What would those steps be?'

'Excluding people entirely where herds have been infected. We are the carriers. Making sure people wash completely before they leave or enter an area. It's not clear that disinfectant works, but at least wash hands thoroughly and hose down their feet, wash it away before travel. Driving cars through disinfectant. And I hate to say this, but culling infected herds. You remember hoof-and-mouth, those piles of burning livestock. That's our future.'

'The Chinese have already banned meat exports from the UK.'

'Quite right,' says my father, endearing himself to meat and dairy producers across Oxfordshire. 'But we may have to cull wildlife as well. By now I reckon, a cull in a wide corridor along the A40 and M40 between Gloucestershire and London.'

'Cull wildlife?'

'And cattle. Now.'

The reporter sound stunned. 'The Chinese are saying that this is not a virus but a bacteria.'

'A bacter*ium*.'

Great Dad, let's keep our grammar perfect in a crisis. The announcer laughs at him. 'Very well.'

'It's not a small point. This is not a virus and it's not bacteria, it's something else, something, we don't know about. It's too big to be a virus, but antibiotics don't touch it.'

What Dad fears and suspects pushes its way out in a gabble of information. He lists all the species he's seen infected, with not a single case of an animal recovering.

'The good news is that people don't die. The bad news is just get very sick and stay very sick. My wife and son have been ill with this pathogen for months. Their fever won't go away. I think that means that a fever doesn't kill this pathogen.'

'A kind of worst-case scenario then.'

'I'm giving you a best case. If what we suspect about this pathogen is true, then believe me, it's a lot worse than what I've told you.'

'Worse?' The reporter is beginning to sound like she's been collared by a drunk in a pub.

'It's large, highly structured and carries within it three pouches of genetic material not its own. We think it transfers genes between hosts.'

'Can you give me an example?'

'My son barks like a dog and meows like a cat.'

The announcer chortles. 'Perhaps he's just having fun.'

'Especially when he screams in terror. Or can't talk for a day or two.'

He was saying this about me on the radio. I looked like Frankenstein and I barked. How could I possibly go to school now?

The reporter says, 'And I'm afraid that's all we've got time for…'

'You'll have to make a lot more time, believe me.'

'Thank you Dr Michael Spaulding of the Well Being Institute in lockdown in West Oxfordshire.'

By the end of the interview, Dad was hiding his eyes and smiling in shame.

Mom was red-faced. 'Did you have to bring Teddy into it?'

He shifted, like he was under a burden. 'Face it, the whole interview was a mess.' He laughed at himself. 'That will teach Ivan to put me on radio.' He looked up at me. 'Sorry Teddy.'

My Dad's been on the radio calling me dog-boy or something.

Mom's voice was still curdled in anger. 'And least she cut you off.'

'She gave me extra time. It was a great interview from her point of view. Crazy freak-of-the-week.' Then he sighed. 'I got scared.'

I ran out of the room, determined never to talk to him again.

Mom went after me, hugged me. 'He's not good with the media. He said things he shouldn't. Like he said, he was scared. This thing is very scary, Teddy.'

It was still raining, and suddenly I hated the rain as well. It trapped me in the house with all of this.

Dad's boss called him. He came back into the sitting room. 'Ivan says I really put the cat among the pigeons. He sounded pleased, like I'm a useful idiot.'

Mom was concise. 'He set you up.'

The rain kept drumming. Mom went out to check the greyhounds and I went out with her in raincoats and wellies. Each greyhound had their own pen, so they wouldn't attack each other. Alone in his, Big Boy lay, panting, glassy eyed and silent. Mom stroked his head and said in a tiny voice. 'He's burning up.'

So that's why I'd slept so late. The dogs weren't barking. In each of the pens, the dogs lay quiet, but at least they were able to raise their heads. They stood up, shook their tails, whined to be let out.

Mom walked back, rubbing sanitiser all over her hands. 'Big Boy is ill. He has a fever. He was quiet this morning.'

Without a word, Dad stood up, left, came back with his green box of tricks. He walked down from the terrace into the rain as he was, barefoot.

Mom sat down on the terracotta-coloured sofa, looking like someone had kicked her in the stomach. I sat in front of her on the Persian carpet, and she pushed a hand into my hair. 'I can't lose the dogs as well, I just can't.'

Dad came back in looking solemn.

'Have they got it too, Dad?'

His head-shaking was tiny but continuous, like he was helpless. 'I have no way to get a test sample out of here. So I don't know. I'll have to keep these into the fridge until I can get them somewhere.'

'Post it,' said Mom.

'Send a new infectious pathogen through the post.' Dad said like it was the punchline to a joke.

Outside, the rain finally trickled to a halt.

Dad needed to talk to people, I think to undo some of the damage done on the radio.

'Just the few people in the village we know,' he said. 'Just make sure they are okay and see what we can do together.'

Our potholed lane was flooded. The puddles already stretched from one bank to the other. The potholes were so deep you couldn't ride a bicycle. In one of them, the water slapped around the top of my wellies and cooled my feet – they felt wet but weren't.

The Averys next door had put a row of bricks across their driveway to keep out floods. Dad stepped over the bricks. 'I'm going to make sure Tom and Bounce are okay,' he said. He scrunched onto their driveway and rapped their door-knocker that looked like Tutankamun.

Bounce answered. Her husband always called her Bounce so we did too. Like us they raised ducks, also hens, but they came at things from the other end. Tom was a retired butcher. 'But I gave up the knife. Whisky for me from now on.' Both of them were rolly polly in faded blue jeans. Dad loved having them round for drinks. 'Breath of fresh air,' he called them. 'From the days before us weekenders crowded everybody out.'

Bounce was pleased to see us. 'Hello! How are you, good to see you. Have you lost any more of your ducks? Tom tells me you lost some of your ducks.'

'All of them.'

'Oh my God, I'm so sorry. Some of ours are poorly too.'

Dad said, 'I might look in on them later, if I may, Bounce.'

Mom told her about my cat. Bounce said, 'Oh, Teddy, you must feel awful. And what's happened to your head?'

'Teddy was attacked by another cat.'

'Gave him a right going over. What's a cat want to do that for?'

Dad sighed. 'It's possible that some of the sick animals attack people.'

'You know. My friend Heather by the shop? She got attacked by her neighbour's dog. It was sick too. I better be careful about my hens attacking me then.' She chuckled. We didn't. Mom mentioned that at least we had the Smartway at the top of the hill.

Bounce shook her head. 'You been up there? It's closed. Andrew's buggered off to Witney. I reckon he couldn't face another lockdown.'

Mom went very still. 'How are we supposed to get food?'

'We'll just have to go into Witney. If they'll let us. Maybe the government will drop food parcels. Though with this lot, they'll probably forget they locked us down and just leave us here!' Bounce laughed. She always did. Her real name was Mary, Mary Avery. I looked her up. She was born in 1952. There's no gravestone for her or record of her death.

Mom wanted to check on her friend Dorothy.

Dorothy was the one who kept moles in her freezer. Dad called her Dotty Dotty. Mom rather loved her.

Dorothy lived in a house that her husband had re-named *The Manse*. It was a perfectly ordinary 1930s big house, all sharp edges and straight lines. Dad, with his sense of humour called it The Pants, which made Mom wince. 'The Manse' looked good on a business card. The real big house in the village was the farm behind us.

'She hates the name too,' Mom would always say.

I think Dorothy had once been beautiful. Now she was round with dyed black hair and perfect red lipstick. She had a scrumptious way of talking like she had a mouth full of Haribos, and was sad-eyed with a smile that seemed to say *I'm being so brave*. She loved talking to me, I think because she loved and missed children, but she always called me Eddy, or Bobby. Once, once only, most bewilderingly she called me Ethel. She always called Faith by our pig's name, Charity. She never understood why Faith responded to her hellos with an oink.

Something middle class in Dotty chimed with theatre, though she hardly ever went out. There was something lilting and upside down in how she spoke, which warmed Mom's heart.

She once said something like, 'It's so embarrassing what Stan did to our house name. I wish we'd called it *Cold Comfort Farm*. That would have been good for a giggle. Or possibly *The Old Dark House*.'

Dorothy's husband had been a brute. He'd hit her a couple of times, then did her the favour of leaving her for a hairdresser. One of his reasons: 'I hate this bloody house.' He was the one who'd insisted they move there, but Dorothy was the one left stuck in it. Her only child, a student at Keele, had been killed in a car accident. Even I could see that the shock was never far from Dorothy's face.

The Manse and its drive were walled in by leylandii, her husband's choice to block out the fields and the sheds. Dad railed against those trees, an import that grew 45 feet high and blocked all the light. From behind that hedge came the yelping of more dogs, a beagle pack. Dorothy had been the leader of the local hunt. The law changed, but she kept the beagles. The hunt still met, swarming over farms and crashing though hedges. They supposedly no longer killed animals, except for the odd domestic pet.

Mom had gone with Dorothy on the hunt once out of courtesy and curiosity. She came back amused and bemused. 'It's just an excuse to drink warm sherry and eat cake. Some of them went to all the trouble of dressing up. They looked like something out of Jilly Cooper, at least the ones on horses.'

The horses followed the dogs as the hounds chased hare. Those on foot got tangled in brambles, and never quite caught up to the hounds or the horses.

'I don't think I met anybody who cared a darn about the hunt. They were all fertiliser salesmen hoping to make contacts. Poor Dotty. The dogs did catch a hare and she turned her head and said, "Oh I hate this!" and when I asked her why she did it she said "To be part of the world".'

Dotty greeted us at her doorway. 'Hello! Hello!' I can still see her: stone-washed crimson shirt, with the fluffiest pink cashmere sweater over her shoulders. Beautiful tailored grey slacks and neat flat black shoes. (The time people spent on grooming and dressing and shopping for clothes. Their hair was multi-coloured, streaked and trimmed. They wore a new shirt only twice.)

'I heard hound music and I thought it was a fellow dog lover.' Dorothy always called barking 'music'. She beamed at Mom with cigarette-yellow teeth and she said with special warmth. 'Maggie. No kissing! No handshakes. They've locked us down again, the brutes. Are your dogs well?'

'Oh Dorothy. One of them's ill. Mike says it's the dreaded lurgy. Sorry to cast a blight.'

'Mine too. Isn't it awful? And we've lost our lifeline, the store. Mr Chukwunonso has left us.'

Thirty years ago, Mr Andrew Chukwunonso had been West Oxfordshire's only African, a Igbo gentleman who'd bought the local store. Dorothy's ex-husband was called Stan Stanwell and he'd called Mr Chukwunonso 'The Nig-Nog.' For him the Allotments were 'Dodge City' and Mr Chukwononso's store 'The Last Chance Saloon'. The Oldminsters called Stan 'delightfully working class'. With glassy grins. Dad called them The Old Mincers.

Dad stepped forward. 'Dorothy, do you mind if I have a look at your dogs? Just to check them out?' He strode off on his own, taking out his face mask and gloves.

'Come in and have some fruitcake. I've made it and now I need someone help me eat it.'

So we sat in her parlour full of old watercolours done by family, dried flowers in vases, polished dark furniture, and blue hardcover books with faded gold lettering. (We lived in museums.)

As for the fruitcake, you could have built Whitehall out of it or thrown it like a brick. It was solid fruit peel soaked in so much brandy it was a fire hazard. I couldn't eat it; to me it tasted like medicine. Nowadays it would feed a settlement.

I was determined to make conversation – this was the new, outgoing me. 'Do you still have moles in your freezer, Mrs Stanwell?'

'Oh yes. I found a new one the other day. Running around in circles biting its own leg. Well, I popped it in the freezer. Add to my collection. It was the most extraordinary thing. I took it out a few days later, just to check, make sure the frost wasn't damaging its coat – and it bit me and ran away. Zip, right out the back door.'

Mom gave me a heavy eye. We'd once checked Dorothy's fortnightly recycling bin. It had been full of about thirty sherry and brandy bottles. Dorothy's grasp on reality was as sodden as the cake.

I ruined the moment by starting to growl. I couldn't stop it. There was a smell from the open back door.

Dad came back in, looking grim and making the smell stronger, putting sanitiser over his hands and even his lower face – his shoes were off. 'Your dogs are very sick, Dorothy.'

Her face seemed to wither. 'I know.'

'I've put the stable door on the latch so they can't get out. Check in on them, but don't get too close to them or you might spread the lurgy. If any of them die, call me, and I'll come and deal with them for you.'

She saw us to the door, and this time, she gave Mom a hug. 'Everything passes,' she smiled and said in light almost merry voice, 'C'est la vie.' Mom saw it too – a little tear trickling down Dorothy's cheek.

We stopped to thank Phoebe, the Nurse.

She had a tiny cottage perched on the steep slope that ran along the north side. It had a stone-paved ledge for a garden with a trough of lavender. Mom and Dad thanked her for last night, and she looked at my stitches 'Well there's no sign of infection, so by my reckoning we got there in time.' In exchange, Dad looked at her cat Puffkin. He was a big old Tom, a plumped-up cushion of a cat. He was healthy if overfed.

'So what do we do about this new thing?' Phoebe asked.

'Stay in lockdown. Lockdown Puffkin too.'

'Oh he won't leave the sofa. I heard you on the radio this morning. I thought the announcer's questions were *stupid*. Do you have a name for this thing?'

Dad grimaced. 'My boss wants to call it a Marsupium, Plural Marsupia. He says it's something new.'

Phoebe nodded. 'Because of the pouches.'

'And the size. Too much like a kangaroo for me.'

'Well, it makes the point. We don't know what the hell this is or how to deal with it.'

'They should have put you on the radio not me.'

The Toy Boy hailed us as we passed.

He was sixty at least, tall and rangy with snow-white hair. He'd been a dancer and then a promoter. The ballerina was as sparse as a dried flower arrangement. Mom was edgy around her, smiling. The ballerina was famous, well, not like the Kardasians but pretty good for Covent Garden. (The Kardasians were famous for having big buttocks and breasts and spending huge sums on hair and makeup while being filmed. Covent Garden was a place where visiting investors were taken to show them something old and European like opera and ballet.)

'Sorry about last night,' said the Toy Boy. 'I hope we didn't sound unsympathetic.'

'No, no, not all!'

He looked at me. 'Whatever it was gave you a right going-over.'

The ballerina had a delicate, translucent face, quite old in daylight with very fine lines. 'Harcourt!' I have to suppose that was Toy-Boy's name. She looked at me. 'Teddy may not want people drawing attention to it.'

Small things win your loyalty.

Dad asked about their animals. The ballerina said, 'We don't have any, it's my allergies I'm afraid.'

'You may be one of the lucky ones,' said Dad.

*

We popped in to see the Dobbs.

Both of them were in their nineties. Mrs Dobbs had been born in that very house in 1930. She came to the door, looking bright and happy to have guests.

'Mustard. Tustard. Ah, yes! Calendar.' Her back hunched she strode into her kitchen. 'Munchkins! Munchkins!' she called out to us as she went.

Mr Dobbs and his walking stick were rooted to his chair, his cheeks a smear of weeping. 'She been like that two days. No sense.'

Mom sat on a chair next to him, Dad knelt at his feet. Mom felt his forehead. She looked at Dad and nodded.

'Do you have any animals?' Dad asked.

'No, no. Can't take care of them.'

'Have you been able to get to a doctor?'

'No. And the kids out in Netherfield, they're not allowed to come to us and drive.'

'It's the wrong lockdown,' Dad said, grimly. He looked at Mom and then said. 'Mr Dobbs, I'll be back this afternoon to drive you into Witney, to the clinic there. Would that be alright, Mr Dobbs, take you both in for a check-up?'

Mrs Dobbs came in with a porcelain cake tray, all faded pansy frills with muffins. 'Penis,' she said and tottered out for the tea.

'Excuse her, she don't know, she don't know.'

Mrs Amelia Dobbs was one of the few recorded human deaths directly attributed to Marsupia-1.

The village even had an archaeologist.

Well, a retired professor who translated ancient texts and was often on digs. Even then, the village was full of types whose whole way of life had gone. Universities were focussed on teaching animation and Gantt charts not ancient languages.

Dad liked to take me on visits to see the Prof. The old gent was frail now, with blotches all over his face that Dad said were from too much sun. The Prof would read us his translations of funeral texts, showing me what each of the hieroglyphics meant.

He came shuffling out to greet us. 'Hello Michael! Hello boy!' he shouted. He had to shuffle but his hands kept jumping up and down to look sprightly. 'Come in. Too early for a beer even for me. Tea? No?'

He hobbled ahead of us into a sunswept south-facing room with huge bay windows. The sills were lined with pots of bright red geraniums. 'I thought you would be interested in this.' He shuffled forward and took out a photo album. He still had photo albums. 'Now this was my last trip to the dig. Just a visitor by then of course, younger people now as site translators. But this was fascinating.'

He showed us what looked a bit like a maze, a series of walled compartments of all equal height. 'They'd found a huge cat cemetery. Now some of the cats were ginger, which is very significant because you wouldn't get a colour like that in nature. Too easy to spot either as predator or prey. So it's likely the Egyptians bred them for their colour. The cat goddess Bastet is the daughter of Ra the sun. So it's possible the colour of the cats was something to do with that. They had to look like the sun, Bastet's father. Thus the fiery colour.'

His grin was goofy and lopsided, but it lit him up. 'The Egyptian director couldn't think why there were so many cats buried all together. And mummified. One theory was that they were all offerings to Bastet. Or they might have been some sort of spirit army to protect the temple. That many cats, it must have been a breeding programme on an industrial scale. Possibly they were bred as sacrifices.'

He'd been used to lecturing.

'Though it is possible they all died at once, in a sort of epidemic.'

He showed us a sculpture of Bastet – a cat that looked somehow human. Or maybe a human that looked like a cat. A hybrid. With gold rings through her nose and ears.

He stared at us grinning, expecting us to say something. He had teeth like a horse. He waited and when Dad and I glanced at each other, he said. 'Well it's obvious. That many cats bred together like a chicken farm, you'd run the risk of disease. I thought it would be right up your street, Michael.' He showed us another photograph of a little ginger-furred paw emerging from wrappings. The claws were out. 'There were thousands of these cat mummies. As a precaution we had to walk above the graves on planks. Well, I'm a bit unsteady on my pins – and I fell off. Typical me. Well, I got back home, and I fell sick. High fever. Couldn't speak for days.'

His grin was fixed. 'I'm Ground Zero.'

Dad grimaced. 'I think you might mean Patient Zero.'

He looked pleased. 'Yes of course. The dig was run by Egyptians. The Director was Faysel Mohammed Siri, University of Memphis. You might want to get in touch, see if they've had any cases. That's the University of Memphis *Tennessee*, not Egypt.' He looked even more pleased.

Dad asked if he could take the Prof's temperature and a blood sample. 'Of course! It's why I asked you in.' His grin – I could see the skull underneath. 'Fit as a fiddle as you can see.' He had a fever of forty degrees Celsius.

As we walked across the street, Dad said something very strange. 'Just so long as those mummified cats didn't start walking.'

It was the Minister of Transport Dad really wanted to talk to.

He lived right across from the Prof. The house belonged to his wife's family, opposite the one post box and next to our fourteenth century inn. The Ram's Head was made of sagging black half timbers. It had once been a pub but was now a conference centre that offered fine dining. 'Fine Dining' was a phrase Mom quoted with scorn.

The sky had broken up into white cloud. Sunlight and shadows chased each other across the playing field. A little green hutch had been inserted next to the Minister's house. An armed security officer stood inside it, wearing a green rain poncho and a blue face mask.

Dad introduced himself as a researcher on animal epidemics for the Well Being Institute and a village resident. Could the Minister spare the time to see him, if that were possible? He then asked the man if he'd been asked to take any extra precautions during the lockdown and congratulated the man for sticking to his post.

The man's eyes above the mask were narrow and hard. Not interested in being probed. He keyed in a number. 'A Mr Spaulding from the village, Sir.'

'Dr Spaulding,' Dad corrected him. We were frisked and then ushered in. The man kept his hand on something on his belt.

The Minister was a scholarly looking gent – deceptively so because he would turn on you if you said anything foolish. He had done it to me once, at the top of our drive. I thought I'd impress him by saying something about the leadership election in his own party. I was out of my depth, and he made it quite clear that I was a fool. I was also nine years old.

'Good timing on your part. I heard you on the radio this morning. Well done for trying to get people to see how crucial this whole thing is, but I think it all got a bit too complicated. Not clear messaging.'

'I'm not a spokesman,' said Dad.

'But I agree with you, Mike. And we're very lucky to have someone like you here in the village to give us accurate information. We've got this thing wrong, and I'm not sure the village can afford to hang around waiting for us lot in Westminster to get it right.' The Minister's eyes strayed over my stitches and flickered for a moment. But it didn't interrupt his flow. 'So I'm minded to set up a village meeting, maybe in the church.'

'Uh. No,' said Dad. The Minister flickered again. 'Social distancing,' said Dad. 'We infect each other and then we infect the animals.'

'Zoom meeting, Zoom meeting. Though, hang on, can we get thirty people onto a free Zoom?'

'The WBI has a subscription, we'd be happy to host it. It works very well with large numbers of people and there's no time limit. I'm sure Ivan Szenas – he's our Director – I'm sure he will be happy to underwrite it. Show up as well, if that would be helpful.'

'No no no, too official, keep it local, deal with the issues here.' The Minister looked mild, but being with him was exhausting. He punched home his words. But you heard every syllable. 'So how do we tell people?'

'There's that Round Witney Facebook group. It's also on WhatsApp.'

'Just local is it? Not many people from outside?'

Dad had not sat down. Mom stood too, and it looked like they were supplicants. In a way they were. 'All due respect, but there have already been people missing from the town. This lockdown won't stay limited to just the three villages around here. It's going to spread.'

'No harm in more people hearing the issues.'

I suppose that was all agreed and then the Minister started to bustle us out, very friendly with stabby body language. He wanted us gone, he was also a bit shaky. We'd taken off our rain gear because it was getting so sticky, and the sunlight was blazing. As we left he called. 'Don't forget your umbrellas.' We had no umbrellas. His face was glistening with sweat.

Outside Dad rang Faith.

'Faith, Maggie and I were just wondering. I know you can cope with things by yourself, but this lockdown is going to get very bad, especially with the store closing. We were wondering if you'd like to come and stay with us for the duration. Join forces. Safety in numbers kind of thing. Yes. Yes. Ha ha. I promise you, Maggie and Teddy and I will do everything you tell us to do. Well thanks for the warning. If you want to bring a few things with, I could come and collect you. Really? All right. Fine. Great. See you.'

He looked at Mom askance. 'I can't tell if she's coming or not. She doesn't want us to collect her.'

'She hates cars.'

'She said all she needs is a change of smalls.'

'If she didn't tell you off, she's coming.'

We walked home.

Mom went straight out to look at her dogs. She started hosing Big Boy, who still lay panting on his side. 'Some of them must get better,' said Mom. Even with the Spanish Flu, people got better.'

I took the other four dogs out to play. They bounced up and down and play-snarled. I knew what the noises meant. *Boss sick. Not me. This good! Play!*

I snarled back. *Play. Fun. Ball.*

And they answered. *Ball ball ball!*

I opened the gate out into the field run. Sunlight sparkled on the grass, which had gone green. It had turned into a sarcastically beautiful day. The rain seemed to have scrubbed everything clean: *You're all dying so we'll make the weather perfect just to mock you.* It was actually a bit cooler and the sun was brilliant and the sky was lockdown blue.

The dogs pounded up and down the run panting. *Me me me, I'm fastest.*

They were made of joy. It didn't seem odd to me at all that I understood what they were saying. They ran and ran all afternoon, as if they could never tire.

When I came back, jumping over the wooden gate, I saw Dad driving back in. He'd taken the Dobbs to Witney and apparently the Prof as well. The Prof had staggered out of his house, saying he didn't feel well. Dad stayed with the three of them in the clinic, and a doctor soon saw them. Dad had taken all of his samples with him and he managed to convince the clinic that they could send the samples by Medi-safe to the WBI in London.

When Dad saw me in the field, he waved and smiled, and half jogged down the driveway to intercept me and steer me into the house.

There was something he didn't want me to see, on the Mountain of Ash.

Little One's grave had been dug up.

Dad got a text message.

I saw Dad standing, reading his phone, hand over his mouth. 'The Minister's ill,' he said. He showed me the screen. It was from the Minister's wife.

> *Hi this is Liz. Owen ill. Can type*
> *but can't speak. Stroke? Can you take*
> *Zoom meeting tonight?*

Later there was a sound of chopping wood in the sky. I ran out and saw a helicopter coming from the direction of Brize Norton airbase. I saw it descend into the fields behind the north side of the road. That was a Ministerial Airlift to get him out.

Back home, Dad was sitting cross-legged on the sitting room floor, laptop on his legs. On the screen was a ghostly grey image of bones. It was the University of Memphis website, an x-ray of one of those mummified cats. The back was arched, the back legs curled, the front claws out.

'It's like it was moving when it was bound, almost like the linen was there to hold it still. See, Teddy? The claws are out, the back arched. But if you weren't preserving them, why scoop out their internal organs? And how does a cat with its organs removed, tear its bindings?'

He turned around at looked at me, but I think the answer was already there in our eyes.

I don't remember much about the village Zoom.

I only saw the start of it. The Oldminsters didn't know enough not talk over each other, so the speaker screen kept jumping from face to face. Dad knew about pinning screens, but he had such a scrabble to keep up. One of the older men really didn't like Dad. He was some millionaire who seemed to think Dad was a socialist and that the WBI were after his taxes.

'*Think tank*. It's a lobby. Some of us work for a living.'

'We used to work,' he was corrected by someone else. 'Comfortable retirement now.'

Dad: 'It's a research-based policy-making body on social health issues.'

'Well, that went well the last time, didn't it?' The man kept chuckling. His name was Mr Day. Mom's had nicknamed him Muggy.

Dad kept trying to explain that this was not Covid. It was very different from Covid. If we were going to go into Witney to shop for food, it would be a good idea for as few people as possible to go. One person could drive with a shopping list for four others. Dad could get us disposable foot protectors to wear when we went into town.

'Yes, yes, let's get everybody else under control.'

Dad began to get angry. 'This is about stopping the marsupia from spreading.' He was beginning to sound brow-beaten and distracted. He kept glancing at me.

I heard Mrs. Stanislaw, the manager at The Ram's Head say that they had a lot of food in their freezers that they would be willing to sell at cost to the people in the village. She invited villagers to come in groups of six to look at the provisions and to have a light lunch courtesy of The Ram's Head.

Mom edged me away. She whispered. 'Teddy, could you try not to make those noises? Can you control them?' Her eyes were swimming.

'What noises?'

She went very still.

I could hear noises, sure, noises from outside in the creaking night. They buzzed, scanned, blipped, clattered, sang. From across the road came another sound, like someone was filing their nails inside my ear. It came from all the hedges across Sandy Lane. It was the no-food signal, like you were in water but had found no succulent reeds.

'The ducks are hungry,' I said. I heard myself say it, like I had another brain, so I knew how it would sound to my mother. It was a crazy thing to say. But it was true. The ducks hadn't eaten. Something stopped me from asking *What ducks, where?*

'Teddy. I need to hear whar peopoe are saying. Can you go upstairs?' She passed me the tablet which looked so small after Dad's tank of a laptop. 'Maybe read for a bit? It's just about time for bed anyway.'

I went upstairs, dismissed as an embarrassment.

As I got to the landing, I began to hear the Plaintive Meow.

I snapped on my bedroom light. It had been hot, the window was open, just above the roof of the back extension.

And in the bed, meowing, covered by a sheet, was the shape of a cat stretching its front paws. I thought of the cats in the x-rays.

I screamed. I ran to the top of the stairs and I wailed. 'Mom! Mom! Mommy!' And I screamed again.

Mom thundered up the stairs eyebrows scowling her mouth open. 'Teddy what is it?'

'It's Little One! It's Little One. She's in my bed where she always was.'

She knelt, hugged me. 'Teddy, Teddy.' She looked into my face. 'Teddy. Little One has gone.'

I grabbed her hand, and hauled her into the room, and I pulled back the sheet. And of course, there was nothing in the bed.

I heard Dad's feet. 'What is it?'

Mom said. 'There was something in the room.'

'Did it attack you, Teddy?'

'It was Little One. It was Little One!'

Dad almost imperceptibly nodded, and then eased me down onto the bed and sat next to me, and took my hand. 'Did you actually see her, Teddy?'

I snatched the hand away. 'I didn't have to! It was *her*! She was where she always was.' I was angry at myself for being a baby, bawling again.

Dad said in a choked-up voice. 'Well sometimes, Teddy, it's easy to make a mistake.'

'It was her! She mewed.'

'Maybe it was the other cat.' He looked at Mom. 'I did say to keep all the windows closed.'

'Ssh now Teddy, ssh.' Mom kissed the top of my head. 'There may have been a cat, but it's gone now. So I want you to calm down, okay?'

Dad grunted and went back to his meeting. Mom tucked me in. Then she too went back downstairs.

No other cat would make the Plaintive Meow. It had been her.

They didn't understand why I was crying. I wasn't crying because I missed Little One. I wasn't crying because I thought it was the cat who'd attacked me.

I was crying because a dead cat was walking. Little One was back from the dead. The animals were dying and coming back.

I locked the window. Then I thought maybe it was still in the house, so I looked under the beds and in my closet, and then I closed the bedroom door and pushed the two spare chairs against it. Then I thought: what if I've locked myself in with it? So I opened the door again.

I lay on the bed and listened to the night and I heard the Plaintive Meow outside. But it had a new rasping sound to it. And then Little One asked me for food.

All that night, all of the animals were asking for food.

Hunt.

Hunger.

Bad smell Bad food.

Bad.

Eight

Mom, Dad and I were three of the six people who took the noon slot at The Ram's Head.

The ballerina, the RAF Officer, the senior cleric who lived at the old vicarage and us.

Mom always waxed satirical about The Ram's Head. Rows of labourer's boots were lined up across the fireplace as if to dry, without a speck of mud on them. The fireplace was filled with a flower arrangement in a vase. The farm implements on the wall had hand-lettered notes. *This spring-loaded instrument was used to fire pills down horse's throats.* The bar made from an old church door with its sign: *No bar service. You will be served at your table.*

Mom growled, 'What an *opportune* little sign. Otherwise you might think you were in a pub.'

Mrs Stanislaw came out from the back. 'Welcome, welcome, hello, lovely to see you all.' The smile was trained on each of us in turn. 'I thought it might be interesting for you to see our kitchens and where the food is stored. So. Please come on through.'

The kitchen looked like a 1950s film set for the inside of a rocket ship, gleaming metal and lots of dials. There was a wall of freezers, again all metal, looking more like a morgue in a Scandinavian thriller. (I saw old films on YouTube partly because in older movies everyone pretended to be nicer and more sensible.)

In front of a chopping table, a lanky man stood at attention in a cupcake cap.

'This is Anton, our chef for today.'

I recognised him. When Anton shopped in the Allotments Smartway, the staff called him Billy.

Mrs Stanislaw: 'I thought you might all like to sample our produce. As you know we grow most of our own vegetables. Anton has prepared a warm salad of our lettuces, chives, and summer squash with… his own truffle oil dressing.'

The food, we had; the food *they* had – they'd certainly not stopped watering.

A murmur of anticipation from all of us. The bowl did look handsome – some purple leaves, some green, with orange slabs. The senior cleric pressed forward with a plate. Others lined up behind him.

Mom and Dad were staring in horror. I followed their eyes and saw opposite one of the freezers, on a metal draining board, a skinned carcass of a deer carcass.

'Oh Dr Spaulding.' Mrs Stanislaw jumped forward. 'Just to reassure you. That is local game. It WAS shot in season, last October, eight months ago before there was any problem.'

'Interesting experiment,' was all that Dad would say.

'Well, we are famous for our venison marinade tartare.' She turned to the other guests 'I set it out to thaw last night, so I'm hoping – those of you who aren't vegetarians –' A dazzling grin directed at my parents '– that some of you would like to take home a cut for your larders. Free of charge of course. A shame to let it go to waste.'

I found myself backed against one of the freezer doors. Mom was rubbing my shoulders. I was growling again.

I remembered Tom, our next-door neighbour. Someone had run over a muntjac deer and we'd given it to him. For some reason I'd watched Tom skin it. He slit it open and jewels spilled out, rubies and emeralds. He made cuts in the hide and then coaxed off the hide like a kid glove.

This time I understood what I was barking.

Dog
Eat
Deer

Dog
Hunt
Hunt.
Hunt.

No one was standing near the draining board, but the skinned carcass fell off as if by itself. As if it had heard me.

Dad was staring into my eyes, stricken. 'Teddy. Teddy stop.'

All I could do was point behind him.

The other guests started to shout.

The thing on the floor was thrashing, kicking with all four legs.

Dad turned.

Without a head, without any feet, the carcass managed to rise up onto its knees. It was muscle memory. Literally. Nowadays of course we know that its entire body had been converted into a nervous system. It didn't really need a head. Dad got out his phone and began to video it. I remember the thing's long neck, and its cut throat. The gullet opened and closed like a goldfish's mouth.

Watch the video and you can hear me begin to yeowl. I made a noise I'd never made before but I knew exactly what I was signalling.

Bad smell
Don't eat
Bad food

It swayed in place.

From somewhere in the village, a dog that was still alive took up the signal.

Bad food
Bad food

Then, the carcass stood up on two legs like a man and began to run.

The bloody stumps slipped out from under it, like Bambi on ice. It slid into the fire exit door. Perhaps it was an accident that it managed to stumble against the release bar.

A fire alarm bell rings. The image jerks and follows the deer. Dad is running after it. In the video you can see the thing, bipedal and spinning in confused circles. It can't see and it's possible that the new nervous system remembered running as a man, not as a deer.

You can see a car park and a lawn and a kiddies' play area with a coloured slide. The thing careens into a dry stone wall and rolls along it, leaving a trail of black seepage.

Then suddenly it drops down onto all fours, gathers itself like deer, and leaps over the wall.

The image jerks again, then the phone is held up over the wall. You can see the thing in the video, bounding across a field of broken stalks of wheat.

I was still in the kitchen, my head buzzing. Everyone was still silent, staring, in shock.

Mom's face was full of suppressed fury. 'What an unusual recipe.' She drawled like Tallulah Bankhead. 'All that from a marinade. No wonder it's famous.'

Dad wanted to get that video uploaded to his boss.

We left at once. Bugger the truffle-oil dressing. I wasn't terribly sure what had happened. I began to get very frightened and to sob.

'What was that? What *was* that?' I meant the deer, but I also meant what had come out of me.

Dad was focussed on his phone. He keyed something in. He left a voice message. 'Ivan this is Mike. I've just sent you a video. You have to look at it. The deer in it was shot in October and had been frozen since then. Text me when you get it.'

'So what does it mean?' Mom asked.

'I don't like to think,' he said.

'Well, it just can't come back to life. Was it like a chicken, when you cut off its head?'

Dad said nothing

We passed Dorothy's driveway and the carved-stone sign *The Manse*. It looked like a tombstone.

'I just want to see if Dorothy's okay,' said Mom. Dad nodded but murmured, 'We all stay together, yeah?' For some reason I noticed that, suddenly, he was developing a pot belly and some of his hair was grey.

It was silent, all along that driveway. No birds, no wasps, no insects. 'Her dogs aren't barking,' said Mom. The stench hung like a fog – death, dog-death. Even Mom could smell it. 'Oh!' she said and covered her mouth and nose.

In her front garden, Dorothy's azalea and acanthus were wilting or crisp in patches. Her front door hung open. Well, it was hot; perhaps it had been left open for the air. Mom rapped the door knocker, then rang the bell. 'Dorothy? It's Maggie. Dorothy? Are you okay?'

We waited. Mom said. 'I'll go in, just to make sure.'

Dad shook his head. 'None of us should be alone.'

In the hall, a small table had been overturned, envelopes fanned out across the rug. Sunlight on the light mauve fitted carpet, nothing else out of place. Then, into the shaded back parlour that was linked to the kitchen where the back door was still open.

Then I smelled the new smell.

Chemical and minty. The stench seemed to jerk my head back and stretch the ligaments in my neck, and I began one long unwavering howl. Even I could hear it. I knew what it was. A warning. I seemed to feel hair stand up. I began to bounce up and down in place. *Move move move.*

A teacup was on the parlour floor, not broken but with an exclamation of tea dashed across the carpet. The back door was open. Lying on the lawn, pink against sun-dappled green, was Dorothy's cashmere, abandoned.

Dad grabbed my arm and Mom's, and started to pull us.

'Dotty...' Mom began.

'Whatever Teddy's doing is a warning. We need to get out of here.'

Mom pulled away. My head was buzzing; words became meaningless sounds. I saw Mom trundle upstairs and heard her call. Dad bayed, shouting words. I went frantic and danced on my back legs and howled: *Pack broken! Pack broken!*

Hunting. You want to encircle and drive prey into a trap. There was only front door and back and no other escape. *One way out only, go, go now!*

Dad pulled me up the staircase. On the landing, no Mom. She came out of a small room, shaking her head, saying something lost as if my ears were clogged, though I could hear her heart and smell the sour sting of fear. Dad grabbed her wrist and bundled us down the stairs, our feet thumping on the carpet. I could hear yelping from the back yard, like someone was shouting backwards, scrambled, as if trying to be another kind of noise. 'Rrrrrtheyrrrthey'.

Mom was still shouting, but now she was running too, and the stench was all around us and inside me making my throat and sinuses itch. I started making a screedle of sounds. I think I was howling in both dog and English, scrambled. Mom was a jogger, Dad a rugby player. Dad scooped me up and ran with me, and all together we sprinted down the leylandii drive, all in shadow with green scents, death stench and a weird rasping chorus of howls, as if those lightless trees had joined in the hunt. The yelping was behind us. The yelping kept pace alongside us, just on the other side of those trees.

We didn't stop running until we were down our drive, into our house, and Mom had turned and locked the front door.

Dad immediately rang Ivan.

Mom panting, almost sobbing, kept trying Dorothy's number over and over on her mobile. 'She's not answering. She's not answering.'

Dad shouted at Ivan on the landline. 'Do the heat trials!' I think he rang Ken too, because his voice went low and quiet and desperate. Then he ran upstairs because he had to pray, and Mom was left alone, whispering over and over to the phone, 'Answer Dorothy, please answer.'

Dad came down from his prayers, looking calm and solemn. He took Mom by both shoulders. 'I'm sorry, Maggie. I'm so sorry. We have to cull our dogs.'

Her eyes closed, her lips pressed together, she nodded yes.

But he kept on explaining. 'It's like the herds that got foot and mouth. Even if some of them survived, they might still be carriers.'

She nodded again, but more sternly and gave him an angry push.

'Teddy, let's you and me do this. Leave your Mom here? Okay?'

'Kill the dogs?' I asked.

We kept a glass jar full of bratwurst, for guests. It was the only meat in the house. Mom liked to serve it with proper Polish sauerkraut. The stupid jar wouldn't open. I found a pair of secateurs in the tool drawer and stabbed the tin lid over and over. That broke the vacuum. The sausages, warmed, were soft and smooth like bodies.

'Thanks, Teddy,' said Dad. I ignored him. We trooped out to the pens, leaving Mom still phoning Dorothy.

Four of the dogs were outside their cells in the pen.

Two came bounding towards us, wanting to be stroked, to have their heads scratched, or to taste all the wonderful traces of sausages on our hands. Petra, one of our two dams, bumped me with her head. I gave her a sausage, which she gulped down in two huge chomps. Of course she came nosing back for back for more. The other dam Jenny whined and bumped me with her head. I gave her a sausage too and she gave a nip of pleasure. Her teats were swollen, and I wondered if she was pregnant.

Dad murmured. 'We don't want to panic them, so we'll do it in the run, okay. I call, and you bring another one out, one at a time. Poor old Big Boy can't move, so we'll do him last in his pen. I'll call when I'm ready, okay?'

I gave all four of them sausages, to snarls of pleasure. They didn't believe me when they were all gone, so I got out the green ball. They spun around in place. *Ball Fun Ball.* I threw the ball and they rolled over each other, growling for real. *Mine. My Ball.*

Dad called my name.

I led Petra out. She nittered at being singled out, and wriggled with happiness to be let out of the pen into the run. The run was long and narrow going from the Sandy Lane hedge all the way to the river. Petra started bounding along it. Normally she would have pelted the whole distance, but she bounced to a halt and whined for the ball to be thrown.

Ball I yelped and threw it towards Dad. It was a feeble throw, not worth chasing. Tongue hanging out, Petra lolloped over to Dad, jumped up, paws on his chest, trying to lick his mouth, but he had the face screen on and next to him was his Frankenstein box.

'Teddy. If you could just hold her still. Hold her neck. Be very careful to avoid the needle. '

Petra wheedled and strained. *Fun! Field! Run!*

'I want to throw her the ball. Just one more time.'

He looked sad, and said yes, and I threw the ball and she brought it back to me. I hugged her neck. That confused her. She threw her head up and down and stepped back.

'Hold her calm Teddy. Avoid the needle.'

I was starting to shiver and cry a little bit, and I think she sensed that. My whole face crumpled and I started to bawl like a little kid.

'It's okay, Teddy.' He knelt down, whispered to her, she came to lick his face again, and then a quick jab. She made a little squeak and fell over, and was still.

I wailed. Dad hugged me. 'She wouldn't have felt anything, Teddy.'

'I know, I know.'

'Can you go and bring the next one when I call? I'll make sure they won't be frightened. Okay?'

I had to do that three more times. I petted them, hugged them, let them lick my hands. I told them there would be a ball to play with. Jenny the other dam came bounding out. She'd seen Dad and was delighted.

Pack Pack, she said. They loved it when we were all together.

She made a nittering sound, and somehow I knew it meant that she knew she had puppies coming and was proud and wanted Dad as pack leader to know. 'Good girl, good girl,' said Dad. I chickened out and stood back and Dad did it quickly – boom. I was still holding the ball. I'd said we'd play a game with the ball and I'd forgotten and I'd broken my promise to her.

I didn't know what Dad did with the bodies, but he was lifting them over the main garden fence, out of the way. Schizo was fine; he pelted up and down the run, jumped up for the ball and I threw it too far and raced all the way down, past the first of the ruins. He brought it back.

Jameson, though, knew something was wrong.

When I led him out, he stopped, kind of hopped skittishly backwards. He was a smart fellow so maybe he wondered where the other three had gone. Or maybe he smelled something, death, in the air. Dad called him, and I heard what was so unfair – without Dad quite knowing it his voice echoed a pack safety call. Jameson came to him, full of trust. To me his squeak sounded louder, as if Jameson had time to feel betrayed.

Dad stood up, gathering his box, then looked up and froze. I turned and there was Big Boy, who had been flat and still all morning, standing in the field, wavering slightly as if the ground was moving under him.

Pack, he said. They were all out on their run and he wanted to join them.

Ball he said in a kind of wobbly whine.

I did a terrible throw. I blew it. The lime green ball dropped down about three yards away. He walked towards me slowly, shivering. I could see Dad stand and walk closer towards us with the box.

'No no no not that one, another one, one more.' I begged Dad and picked up the ball, and threw it pretty far. Big Boy tried to run in a kind of lollop. A cloud passed and the sun seemed to blaze out I wanted him to keep running away and never come back.

He dropped the green ball at my feet. I hugged his neck and buried my head so I wouldn't have to see and called him by his name. He trod impatiently, wanting more fun. My face was buried in his coat, which was far too warm, and seemed to have a thrill to it like a plucked string. He made no sound at all, but collapsed like a heap of sticks.

And that was it, job done.

I mark that moment as the last of my old world.

PART THREE

Our Parents,
Our Children

Nine

Just the other side of our old big gate, Mom stood over the bodies of the dogs.

'You must feel awful,' Bounce said, hand on Mom's shoulder. 'Can I get you some tea or something?'

'No, I'm okay, Bounce, but cheers.'

Bounce was wearing gardening gloves and a face mask. She and Tom had come to help pile up wood for the fire. The cadavers were to be burned.

Dad got off the phone and addressed us all. 'So long as we keep the fire to the dog run, the farm manager says it'll be okay.'

'There'll be more of these fires, I reckon,' said Tom.

'I think you're right. Sadly.'

'Come on,' said Faith, 'Let's get cracking.' She went into the shed and came back with a huge log on her shoulders. 'Did more'n this when I was the only girl up at the Hastings.'

'Don't you want gloves, love?' Bounce asked.

'Grew me own,' said Faith.

Mr Keppel was there to help as well. Phoebe came in via the footpath gate and stopped. 'I've got plenty of firelighters if you need them,' she offered. Dad said, 'If you can spare them.' Phoebe and turned around and went back out the metal gate to get them. I don't remember her coming back. I don't remember seeing or hearing anything about her ever again.

Dad had made a teepee of garden clearance – gnarled old quince twigs and the like. 'It's got to be a very big fire, bigger than you think. It will have to burn for a long time.' He interspersed a whole recycling-week's worth of newspapers to help it burn. The pile was already up to his knees when the first substantial logs were laid across them.

Mr Keppel winced. 'The forecast says it's going to rain again.' Indeed, that fleecy horizon had advanced and was now a wall of grey.

I really admired Mom. She and Bounce started carrying the bodies through the gate, and though she looked grim, even angry, Mom didn't cry. Bounce said something and Mom just said, 'It has to be done.'

During Covid, that field and the ruins along the river got as crowded as Blackpool – river, shade, and the lawn full of sunbathers and people barbecuing on the thirteenth century stone walkways. Their cars had created parking places where there had been none before and they'd worn a new path from the gate to the ruins through the long grass. Visiting had become a habit.

A crowd of grockles gathered the other side of the run's barbed wire to gawp. When Mom and Bounce swung the first of the greyhounds on the pyre, there were comments.

'What's that in aid of?' a man asked with three pale children, towels around their shoulders.

'They've died of this new disease and we have to get rid of them.'

'Ow!' said the man, and began to pull his kids. 'Come on kids, keep away.' A woman in sunglass and sunhat, said angrily. 'Do you have to do that around other people?'

'With due respect Madam, this is away from people.'

'It's a public footpath.'

Dad straightened his back and smiled. 'Actually it isn't. The footpath goes from here to the next village.' He pointed to the trail across the fields that ran east. 'The right of way doesn't go down to the ruins at all. This field is private property, we have permissin for this fire, and this is a run we rent.'

The woman muttered something. 'What's your name?' she asked.

'What's yours?'

'Cass Pothstern. I'm not the one burning animals in public.'

'You are the one coming into a village in lockdown, though. Don't blame me if you get sick. I'm Dr Michael Spaulding.' She wrote it down. She took out her phone, camera-eye pointed at us. Faith laid the last of our dogs on the pyre.

They all knelt with matches in a ring. The wood from the shed was dry but the kinding had been soaked in the rain and it smoked. A lot. Billows of grey, which meant at least we didn't have to see the bodies.

A few more people drifted over to the barbed wire perhaps from the village. We didn't know them. Some stuck their heads over the kissing gate or the old stone walls on Sandy Lane. Maybe they were afraid of infection. The fire began to dance, flashes of orange inside all that smoke.

Faith was angry. 'People think we're not educated cause we're rural,' she said.

Dad stood next to her. 'Maybe they don't think that now.'

She glared him down. 'The schools here were good. You had to work. We learned everything. I remember in sixth they taught us Charles Darwin. And I said to myself, Mr Darwin you got it right. We come from the animals. They're our parents. And now, they are our children.'

For about twenty minutes the fire roared while the rainclouds advanced.

There was a sound of shifting, logs falling as the smaller branches and kindling were consumed. One blazing log rolled off the fire all together. Some of us stood back. The fire wasn't smoking as much now.

Something inside the pyre moved. Another log rolled off.

Dad said in a little singsong voice. 'Juuuuuust as a precaution. I think we all should stand further back.'

The sun went in. Suddenly it was grey overhead as if all that smoke had gone to heaven.

'Teddy,' my mother said holding out a hand and waving her fingers back towards herself. 'Come on, do as Dad says.'

A little string plucked in my head, and I did what she asked.

'Bounce, Tom, Faith. Come on.'

Tom smiled, still watching the fire. 'Good thing we had all that rain, no danger of setting the field alight.'

Another log rolled. Something was shifting inside the fire. There was a crackling sound, and what looked like a flaring-up of flame stood. A gust cleared the smoke.

Standing on top of the fire, black and streaming with smoke, was Big Boy. You should see his dark shape amid the white and grey. There were little flickers of orange along his fur.

Someone screamed on the other side of the run.

'Somebody with a phone video this. Tom, get back,' said Dad. I pulled out my mobile. I fumbled the code, then fumbled the app. 'Teddy,' Mom hissed and pulled me back, gathering up Bounce by the elbow. Faith was already at the gate and she said one word, 'Hellmouth.'

I jogged backwards getting a jumbly video.

The torch of a dog shivered and shambled and growled. Tom was backing away when Big Boy leapt and seized him by the throat.

Dad hit the dog with a branch. The woman in the sunhat was bellowing 'Oh My God! Oh my God!' Mom and Faith held Bounce back. Tom was on the ground, and the Halloween shape, orange and black, had fangs like candles. Dad kept pushing the dog back with a smoking stick. Tom sat up holding his throat, blood pouring over his hand. Mr Keppel scuttled forward with rake, and tried one-handed to pull Tom to his feet while holding off the dog. Tom tried to stand, but his legs gave away. He sat staring, immoveable.

From out of the fire, another dog stood up. It was making the grief sound.

And it started to rain. Dad joined Mr Keppel and they both pulled Tom away by his shoulders, dragging him like a dead weight. Dad was shouting. 'Close the gate behind us. Close the gate!'

The rain sizzled and hissed as it hit the flames. Yelps and howls from the fire. Another dog kicked free and nosed burning logs out of its way. The whole fire spewed out white smoke like steam as the rain started to drum down.

Mom pulled me and Faith inside the garden, Faith saying over and over to Bounce, 'Leave them to it love, keep inside love.' Tom was not moving.

All five dogs tottered towards us in a phalanx, limping, paws blackened, fur gone, claws welded shut, rainwater steaming from their backs, seeming to see with their burnt-out eyes.

'Get into the house,' Dad roared.

Big Boy blinked, and the ash cleared from his eyes. I saw into them. Grey as the sky. I couldn't move. He stepped forward and a bone in his shoulder seemed to click back into place.

Mom pulled me back. Dad and Mr Keppel kept dragging Tom. Bounce broke free from Faith and ran towards her husband. The dogs had shivered their way close to them. Dad dropped Tom, grabbed Mr

Keppel and ran pulling him. Just inside the gate Dad caught Bounce with his other arm and held her while Faith swung the gate closed behind all of us. All except for Tom. A smouldering dog, tar-coloured leapt and snapped at us over the top bar.

The dogs' heads were ranged over the top of the gate, unable to jump over it as always, chomping and whining as they always used to when they wanted their heads scratched.

They were baying the hunting call. They were hungry.

Bounce was shouting, 'We can't leave Tom!'

Mr Keppel, Mom, Faith and me were all somehow in the front hall. Dad slammed the door. Hands shaking, he fought his laptop out of its bag. Rain hammered on the roof like it wanted to be let in. 'Teddy, did you get any of that?' I was numb. 'Pass me your phone. PASS ME YOUR PHONE!' I wasn't used to Dad shouting at me.

Bounce was still struggling. 'I've got to get back to Tom.'

'The dogs are still out there.'

'We can't just leave him!' Bounce was raging.

Mom was looking into her eyes. 'We don't know what this is. We have no idea.'

'They're your bloody dogs.'

Mr Keppel tried to calm her. 'It's, it's just this new disease.'

'You didn't put em down properly!' Bounce was shouting. 'TOM IS STILL OUT THERE!'

Old Faith had a brandy bottle in her hand. 'You should have this. Those dogs were dead, missus. I carried them. You can't kill them twice. They're already dead.'

'Well, they look dead don't they?' Bounce was gnawing the tips of her fingers.

Dad was rattling away at his keyboard. My phone was USBed into it.

Mom broke next. 'What are you doing on that bloody computer?'

'Getting Teddy's video to Ivan.'

The rain made a sound like the sea on our roof. It was as dark as twilight outside. Mr Keppel was looking through the hall window. It faced east, out towards the gate and dog run. His face when he turned had gone slack and jowly as if it were melting. His eyes were unblinking, ringed with bags.

Dad stood up went to cupboard under the stairs, and pulled out the shotgun. Mom's eyes widened; he stood a bit taller and thrust out his chin. She gave an almost imperceptible nod. He loaded two cartridges, and passed Mr Keppel a box of ammo. Mr Keppel's eyebrows hitched.

Dad snapped the shotgun back. 'I'm going to back the car up while there's some light. I'll need you Faith and you Francis. We go get Tom if we can – no, sorry Bounce, it's best you stay here.'

'Not on your life,' she growled and stood up. I looked down at the red tiles, in case Dad saw what I intended to do.

'Right,' said Dad and ran out the front door, holding a gun and key fob. The car chuckled to itself and the folding mirrors spread in welcome. Dad revved the car back, boot-first, nearer our front door.

We ran, all of us. Faith being the tallest hunched into the front seat next to Dad. Bounce, Mr Keppel and then me crowded into the back. Dad was shouting at Mom, 'Close the door!' and maybe didn't see me.

He was looking over his shoulder as he swung the car around, backing up toward the gate. Bounce held up her phone as a torch – everything was being swallowed by darkness.

We stopped, slam, as Dad pushed the brake button.

Behind the gate, the dogs were crowded around Tom.

Something gurgled up in me, like fat in a chip pan, and I heard something else in me growl something like: *Ours.*

Meaning, *Tom is ours.*

Big Boy spun and bounded snarling towards me, barking over and over: *Ours ours ours.*

He slammed into the gate and tried to climb it, bared his fangs and chewed the air. Something slammed my head like a fist – a gun blast, close to my ear. I staggered and looked up. A lot of Big Boy's head was missing. I covered my ears; a second blast slammed through the air and into that head. More of it was swept away, only the lower jaw left, still trying to bite.

'Light,' coughed Dad. 'Bounce?' She shone her phone at the gun. Dad's shaking fingers slipped in two more cartridges. 'Everybody behind me.' Faith pulled me back; I was as numb as a sack.

I heard myself bark *Run.*

The part of me that barked wanted the dogs to get away.

With the third blast, Jameson was knocked to one side. Headless, Big Boy still scrabbled at the gate trying to climb over it. Faith picked up the aluminium step ladder that had been left out in the rain, and swung it at what was left of Big Boy. He kept trying to bark, a kind of coughing sound. Faith pushed him again with the ladder and he spun away. He kept spinning in circles.

Bang. Petra looked up as though startled. The blast had exploded some of her rib cage. She shivered and dropped to her knees. She fell at once – maybe she'd not had the bug as long as Big Boy, so it hadn't taken her over as much.

Two more blasts in succession, each shot accurate. I remembered that before his conversion to virtue, Dad's first job had been in the Army. Schizo yelped as he was flung up into the air. He landed in a heap all angles like a collapsed tent. Jenny was the last. She had turned to run and the blast caught her rear end and blasted through her. She settled with forward motion like an avalanche of broken dog.

Faith flipped up the latch. Mr Keppel snatched up the rake that he'd dropped and pushed the still spiralling corpse of Big Boy away from us. Big Boy still didn't give up trying to find us without scent, without eyes. Mr Keppel swung the rake like a club and knocked him off his feet.

Me, Dad, Faith and Bounce gathered up poor Tom. I had his right leg which meant I stared into the face. There was no scalp above the eyebrows – they had been gnawing at his head. The grimace, the narrow eyes, looked like a frozen wild laugh.

'Get him into the shed,' said Dad.

Bounce: 'Shed?'

'I'm sorry. We can't lay him out in the house.'

'Get him back home!'

'We need to call an ambulance,' said Dad.

Bounce started to pump out hard, unforgiving sobs.

The shed had been built right after the world war by Mrs Tulp. It was tin, old tin at that, with ivy covering much of it. It looked like a great green shaggy beast.

Dad had replaced some of the old corrugated sheets and a couple of the main uprights, rooting them into a new concrete floor. After we lost our tools twice to thieves, Dad put in a new lintel and a big strong door with deadlocks. As there were no windows, he'd put in power. Dad snapped on the light and began to clear some plywood scraps from the workbench.

'Francis,' he said to Mr Keppel. 'There's a tarp up in the rafters.'

I went out into the garden, to make sure the fence gate was closed. I couldn't see Big Boy in the gloom, nor any remains of his head on the ground. The other dogs lay twitching beside the smouldering bonfire. The smoke looked like fog, and smelled like a whole building had burnt down. There was also that chemical smell, acrid, stinging but rotten at the same time. But nothing now of dog.

'I'm sorry boys,' I told the mist and smoke like they were ghosts. I turned around and walked back, and I saw something hulking and round in the lane at the top of our drive. At first I thought it was a car.

Then, with a clicking sound it started to run towards me. 'Dad!' I shouted. 'Dad!' I ran towards the golden light, the open door. I got in, and flung my back against the door just as something huge and thunderous slammed against it, knocking me forward. Faith jumped and shoved her shoulder against it too. 'Lock it!' she shouted. We got the door shut, but couldn't see the key.

Like a ram raid, a car driving into an entrance, the thing bashed into the door again, knocking both me and Faith back. A stench of death and that minty smell stung my nostrils. 'Oof,' said Faith and turned her head. Our elbows rattled as it flung itself against the door again. Dad shouted, waving the gun, but Mr Keppel and Bounce, stupefied, didn't get out of his way.

Dad put the gun down on the table, pushed past Keppel and Bounce, and leaned into the door with both hands.

Boomph! Like the sound of an explosion. The whole shed shook.

The three of us tried to hold the door. The key was not in the lock. 'The floor. The floor, goddamn it,' shouted Dad. Finally Mr Keppel moved, knelt, scooped up a key ring, hesitated, then put the key in a lock. All of us pushed, Bounce included, and Mr Keppel flipped the key.

The door was holding. Dad took out the keyring and stretched up – there was another deadlock higher up the door.

'What the hell was that?' panted Mr Keppel.

'Charity,' I said.

Three hundred kilograms of Large Black launched itself against the door again. There came an enraged if ragged squealing, and the sound of digging and snuffling along the lower edge of the door. Stench seeped into the shed.

Dad reached out his hand. 'Phone, Teddy.'

He speed-dialled and for once we had reception in our garden in a valley. 'Are all the windows closed?' Dad asked Mom at once. 'Lock the doors. Right now. Charity is in the garden. Yes. Charity. Alive might be the wrong word. French doors too? Look, can you get the sofa on end against the French doors? To keep her out! She's got us trapped in the shed. Windows, doors, all of it blocked. Go, go, go. Call me back.'

He keyed in again.

Boompf! Now the rear of the shed shuddered.

'Ivan, this is Mike. I know what the third pouch is for. Shush Ivan. No. You listen to me. Remember you said it was if the material in pouch one was undifferentiated? Almost like a stem cell? Not *almost* Ivan, more like it *is*. It grows anything. They heal; they heal so fast, it takes about two hours, so not a stem cell, no, something else. They heal any which way. Did you see Teddy's video of the fire...? what was it? A dead dog, Ivan, coming back and attacking us... What?'

Dad went very quiet. His shoulders sagged, his eyes rolled up to the ceiling. We heard rain clicking on the plastic skylight. Then grunting along the bottom of the door. 'I'll need to get back to you,' said Dad.

I caught a rotten smell again, and this time from out my chest came a low, deep involuntary growl: *Bad Food.*

Dad picked up the gun, thought a moment, then passed it to Faith and jerked his head towards the door. She nodded once, and said to all of us. 'Stand clear.' She stood with the shotgun pointed at the door.

Dad called Ivan again. 'Have we done the heat tests yet? Well, do them in an autoclave. I don't happen to have an autoclave. Sorry if I'm a bit rude Ivan, but people are being killed. One of those dogs is still walking around without a head, that's why!' And load up Teddy's video onto social media.'

I think he hung up.

Dad said, chuckling with sad eyes. 'That woman in the field loaded us up onto Facebook and Instagram – mad vegan burns sick dogs alive. Ivan says that we're a Twitter storm already.' He shook his head looking weary. 'Well, I wouldn't believe it either.'

He stared a moment and then his phone went. 'Yes, we're all okay, but Charity is trying to get in. I don't know why. Everything locked? Take some food and water where there's a strong signal, upstairs maybe in the bathroom. Because that door locks and there's a window so you can get out onto the laundry room roof if you have to. Yes, Teddy's okay. Look please ring everyone in the village you can and tell them. Tell them the animals attack.' He went quiet and nodded. 'No. Don't mention that or they'll think you're mad. Also, we're about to be hit by a wall of Disgusted from Knightsbridge. Ring everyone please before we become Persona Non Grata. Yes, we ARE all right. We've got the bird nuts to eat.' A trace of a smile. Then he said, 'Love you.' For just a split second I wondered if the entire phone call had been to Ken.

There was nowhere to sit. Mr Keppel leaned against the neatly stacked logs. Bounce had a hip edged up onto the workbench and a hand on Tom's boot, which she kept stroking. Mr Keppel had put the tarpaulin over Tom, but Bounce's back was still towards him.

'We had a beautiful life,' she said, mostly to his boot.

Bomph! And a snuffle. I wanted comfort and without knowing it, I began to call for Little One. Something in me began to wheedle out the Plaintive Meow.

Faith jabbed me with a finger. 'You. Quiet.'

It was a bit like waking up – I came to as it were. But I remembered my cat; remembered that Little One never went into the shed through the door. She could slip in through gaps in the old tin.

'There's holes in the tin. Dad, Charity's going to find one.'

We could hear trotters scraping earth and circling the shed. 'Move the logs,' Dad said.

Keppel and Bounce looked at him slack jawed. Dad started to lift the firewood away from the walls. Mr Keppel turned to help. Both him and Dad, pumping up and down from the waist, piled up logs into the centre of the narrow space. I jumped to help.

'You're too small,' Dad shouted.

I ignored him and started trying to lift logs. 'I think Little One used to go to that corner,' I said. It was right where the logs were piled highest.

Bounce tried to hop down from the table. Faith shoved her back. 'I'd keep out of the way,' she said, then jerked her head at Mr Keppel. 'Frank, keep out of my line.'

He chuckled. 'Damn right.'

'Keep it that way.' She raised the shotgun to her line of sight.

Dad grabbed my hands. 'I pass them to you, you pile them up.' He scooped up an armload for me. I started to sardine them together in row down the middle of the shed.

There was a screedling sound – metal being torn. Above the line of logs, tin was being peeled back, seized by yellow teeth as long as my finger. The stench, a mix of death and chemical hazard was so strong it tickled my throat and my made me want to vomit and cough at the same time. Charity was growling, more like a dog than a pig, and a corner of tin was rocked and lifted. I hoped her teeth would break. Dad grabbed hold of me and pulled me back.

'Gotcha!' said Faith.

The tin rang with the sound of a gunshot. Wood chips were flung like confetti; they caught the light and I couldn't quite see through them, but there was a shriek from Charity and her head no longer filled the gap. I heard Faith reload and, silently this time, Charity flung her weight against the hole. It bunched inwards. Faith fired again and this time I saw teeth explode. The gap was suddenly empty.

With a slam and a rattle, the tin next to the hole bellied inward like a fist had punched it. Some of the wood stack went flying towards us. A new huge dent had the rounded shape of a pig.

Faith barked a hard laugh. 'Shoulda left the wood where it was.'

Dad nodded. Keeping his distance from the gap, he started flinging logs every which way to cover the open hole. Mr Keppel joined in; Bounce hopped down off the table to help. Suddenly, like a boulder had been catapulted against it, the back of the shed was rammed. Dad's big old multi-drawered chest was in the way and it juddered forward. The pig squealed.

'Why are they attacking?' asked Mr Keppel.

I thought he was stupid. 'Because they want to eat us.'

That brought Bounce round. 'Why?'

Faith chortled. 'Animals don't like carrion. We're the only fresh meat for miles.'

'Why do they always go for the head?' Dad asked as if to himself. I thought of my row of Frankenstein stitches.

Mr Keppel said. 'At least we don't have to worry about the dogs any more.'

We were there for the night.

Charity kept snuffling around, but seemed subdued. Dad kept checking with Mom. She had indeed locked herself in the bathroom with cold quiche and tap water. An awful lot of phone numbers in the village were not answering. She'd also texted the What's App group that had formed around the Village Zoom. Muggy Day texted back that Witney had gone into lockdown too.

Ivan rang Dad but all Dad said was, 'Sorry Ivan, you're breaking up. Could you text that?'

Then Dad asked us, 'Does anybody have a phone charger?' None of us did. We'd soon be without communication.

Things had gone quiet; the banging had stopped. Had Charity gone away? We'd just about made up our minds that we could dash to the car and drive the few yards to the front door.

Suddenly squeals erupted. I don't speak pig, so I didn't understand, but the sound was first enraged and then pained.

We heard dogs barking.

Ours, ours, ours. Furious snarling, growls and a sudden ripping of flesh.

And another kind of barking, deeper, ragged followed by a doggy yelp that sounded stretched like a rubber band, deeper somehow. It was a submission signal, *You win. You top.* Something like that, but it was only sort of dog-like, as if Winston Churchill had learned how to bark.

Was Charity speaking dog?

She squealed again, and then the squealing trailed away in the direction of our drive.

Then claws started scratching on the tin all around us. Ivy grew up over the entire north side of the shed, and the scrabbling focussed on that. Then a thump on the tin roof as something landed on it. Claws scraped on the corrugated tin.

'Might be pigeons?' said Bounce.

'Not at night,' said Faith.

I could hear a growling and realized it was me. Then I barked: *Pack pack pack.*

Foe foe foe came the reply from overhead.

Hunt.

Bounce angled up her phone's flashlight

Good food

Dad took the shotgun and pointed it straight up. The plastic skylight was in two halves, each with one edge bolted to the crest beam. We began to hear a gnawing along that edge and a dog whining.

Here Here.

The gnawing sound focussed all along it.

'The plastic could split,' said Dad.

'How did they know it's there?'

'They see the light coming up through it,' said Faith.

'Smell,' I said. 'Deodorant and soap.'

Dad got out his phone, keyed in and greeted Ivan. 'The dogs are back.' He glanced at his watch. 'About an hour and a half, maybe two hours. Yeah, full-on gunshots. Oh great. Oh wonderful.' His voice was flat, deadpan. 'We'll be spared that then.' Amazingly, Dad chuckled. 'Yeah. That's about it. That IS about it. I'm – uh – I will have to save on the battery so my phone will be off for a while. Thanks Ivan. Get the news out can you?'

He stared at the darkened phone. 'So the autoclave leaves the marsupium undisturbed. It seems to continue to heal and reduplicate the material in the pouches. So. We needn't have bothered trying to burn them.'

'Ah. You could burn em down proper, just ash,' said Faith. 'Always look on the bright side.'

'The marsupia would still be alive in the ash.'

'Yeah but it couldn't walk.'

Mr Keppel ventured. 'You could treat the ash like atomic waste. Seal it in glass. Or big containers and drop them into the ocean.'

'Great,' said Dad. 'We could make zombie sharks.' He stared into space. 'And we'd have to burn every single animal on the British Isles.'

'We could volunteer to be nuked,' said Mr Keppel.

'Not a bad idea,' said Dad.

The skylight plastic crackled. Light caught a split in it, and the growling got louder.

We all froze. Without saying anything, Dad went to his big chest and pulled open a lower drawer. It was full of different cables. He inspected one about a metre and a half long with a plug at one end and twists of naked wire on the other.

'I'm going to electrify the tin,' he said. He switched on his phone's flash and then reached across Tom's covered body to switch off the wall sockets. The light went out but Dad turned on his phone. He plugged in his cable and checked for distance. The end of the cable easily reached the tin.

He went back to his chest, rootled around another drawer. The dogs overhead began to whine with excitement.

Food food food, one of them yelped.

'Faith you might want to have that gun ready,' he said. He pulled out insulation tape and wrapped it around the end, just to tidy up the naked wires, and then made a safety grip for himself about halfway down the cable.

'The rest of you stand in the middle.'

There was another thump on the roof, and more anxious nittering.

'Make sure you're not touching the walls. Or anything that's touching the walls. The only thing you should be touching is wood or concrete. Excuse me, Bounce.' He pulled Tom further away from the wall, and slid him along the table, away from the socket.

The Boys overhead began to squeal with excitement. I saw a snout and tongue under the raised edge.

Hunt

Good Food Good

Bite

They were still my Boys. We had played ball. Something in me that I could not control barked: *Warning warning*.

One of them snarled back at me: *Other*. They were my Boys no longer.

'Here goes,' said Dad and flicked on the socket switch. Our lights came back on. Leaning back, Dad touched the wires to the wall.

Pain pain pain the Boys all chorused. Their feet ran in place for a moment dancing on the tin. Ivy leaves rustled as they ran across them to jump; they howled and yelped and made other noises with ruined throats, sounds that twisted and seemed to run backwards. In all that vocal mess I thought I heard one word. In English.

Stop.

I had heard a dog say plainly, 'Stop.' But then I was an imaginative child.

We could hear their howling flow down from the shed and retreat into the field. The barking turned into whimpering and whining. *Pain Hurt Love*. We waited.

Silence. Then claws scrabbling up the ivy again.

Dad waited. A thump and one set of claws. Then another set brush-drummed the tin. Faith had the gun ready. Dad sighed and brushed the wire against the wall.

A fresh wail, yelps and a wrenched howl: *Pain.*

The cries made an arc of sound down to the ground. A shared yelping and whining spun around itself. It seemed to spiral away and out towards the field.

It was a long, dark night.

From time to time we'd hear panting or catch a gust of rotten meat or chemical mint.

From farther away, from the fields there came triumphant barking. *Good food,* the dogs said. Another sound seemed to bristle on my skin and work into my bones, a sound that meant *rabbit.* One of them had caught a rabbit. One that was alive.

Faith said. 'You want a kettle in here, Mike, for tea.'

Bounce started to talk about Tom – how they met at a dance. She was a Witney girl, he was from Huntbridge. He started earning money as a teenager. He and his brothers would go house to house, killing people's pigs for them. They'd haul a big tank of water and boil it up to soften the bristles. 'That's how he knew butchering before he had any training.'

Faith pitched in. 'At the Hastings, I was my job to hold the ewes while they was tupped. So I'm holding this ewe, see, but she wriggles free just as they let the billy go. Well, he's so hepped up he runs into me and does his business all over my duffle.'

Bounce managed to laugh. 'Spent force was he?'

'It was wash day, I can tell you. For a week. Life in the countryside, eh?'

Faith began to sing the most amazing song.

Cats on the rooftops
Cats on the tiles
Cats with syphilis, cats with piles
Cats with their arseholes wreathed in smiles
As they revel in the joys of copulation.

If Mom heard our laughter, she must have thought we'd all gone mad. From time to time came the sound of snuffling or claws on tin. One of us would touch the wire to the metal.

A different kind of barking seemed to lollop from the north, down our drive. I recognised the accent.

'Those are Dorothy's beagles,' I said.

There were snarls and yelps.

Ours ours ours
Food
You top

Dad had bought Mom a small chainsaw, no longer than my forearm. It was dainty, powerful and bright red. The Bijou Chainsaw, she called it. Dad snapped off its battery and plugged it in to charge.

We started to hear whispering, almost human. It went on for some time. Dad looked at the two generators and went to the tool rack. He passed Mr Keppel and Bounce an axe each.

More claws, snuffling and the kind of honking sound beagles make mixed with our Boys. Greyhounds are so much more refined.

Mr Keppel put the wire up against the tin. Dog agony – howls, yelps, whines. And for the first time something suspiciously like laughter.

We all agreed – just leave the wire touching the tin.

Faith passed Dad the shotgun. 'Take turns watching.'

Dad's eyebrow arched.

'You're younger than me,' said Faith, and climbed up onto the logs. 'Wake me at two.' Mr Keppel pulled the worktable further away from the wall. Bounce climbed up onto it and lay next to Tom. I saw that she didn't close her eyes but stared ahead. Dad left the lights on.

We waited there until first light. Bounce's eyes stayed dry and open.

Ten

At 6 am everything outside was muggy and grey.

Faith pushed her way out first with the gun, scanned the lawn, looked up at the roof and waved the rest of us out. We were armed with the Bijou Chainsaw, an axe and a pitchfork. For some reason I was reminded of *The Wizard of Oz*. Lions and tigers and bears – oh my!

Dad had said we would drive to the front door, but now, in daylight on open lawn, the distance looked remarkably small. We ran still carrying the garden weapons. Mom threw open the front door, pulled us in, slammed the door shut behind us, and fell on us all, hugging us, weeping when she saw me. 'You okay, Teddy-Boy? You okay, darling?'

Dad shuffled forward towards Bounce like a schoolboy caught doing something wrong. 'We should ring. The uh shed is probably…'

'I'm taking him home,' said Bounce. She drew herself up, face rigid.

'We can call to get…'

She cut him off. 'I am taking him home.' The same exact words, the same intonation. Dad nodded.

So out we went again. Dad watched over us with the shotgun as we all carried Tom. He'd gone stiff, like Little One had done, a rigidity that seemed to make the body smaller. Someone had grabbed an old hat of Mom's and pushed it onto Tom's head so that the worst of the damage was hidden. We loaded him awkwardly into the back seat, which he occupied, stuck in a standing up posture, that smile still on his face.

Mom drove the car with Bounce in the front. There was no room for anyone else. The rest of us walked along the lane as if on glass, looking at the banks or clusters of ivy, Dad with the chainsaw, Faith with the shotgun.

Bounce had us carry Tom into her front room. 'That's his chair,' she said. She got us to lower him into it and she tried to make it look like he had sat down himself, but his hips had set. He was more propped up against the back of the chair than sitting.

'That's his teacup there. And that's his whisky glass,' she said, arranging them. I had never seen grief before and I wondered if maybe Bounce had gone crazy.

Without a word, Mom waved me out of the room. 'I'll knock on the walls, make sure you're okay,' Mom said to Bounce, 'If you need anything just phone. Lock your doors. Lock everything.'

'A bit late,' said Bounce in a small voice.

We all fitted into the car for the short drive back along the lane, and no one was surprised when Dad locked the doors. He swung the Kia around so he could back it up to the shed. 'Right everybody,' he said. 'All the tools from the shed, into the car. Quickly. And keep an eye out.'

'The generators?' asked Faith.

'Those especially, both of them, and the fuel,' said Dad. 'And be quick.'

Dad spent the morning hammering DIY.

He was turning my room into a fortress. I was no use at it but Faith was fabulous. She and Dad drilled a hole through my bedroom wall and turned the cold tap in the bathroom round so it went into my room.

A generator was put in my bedroom as well, with a makeshift duct for fumes going up through the trapdoor into the loft. Mrs Tulp's old linen closet was in my room. Dad emptied it of sheets, old papers and my books to stow tins and dry foods there, including powdered milk and coffee.

Mom kept asking why we didn't just get out? 'Look, we've got your car and my car, we could get everyone into both of them and load up all this food and just drive away.'

Dad's answer was simple: we carried the marsupia. 'We're in lockdown for a very good reason. Unless we want to spread the thing through the entire South East?'

Mom's eyes were closed, her mouth drawn inward, but she nodded.

We carried the kettle and the toaster upstairs and then the two-ring hob left over from when Dad had rebuilt the kitchen – that was pushed under my bed.

Dad said to Mr Keppel, 'You're welcome to hole up with us. A bit crowded, but better than being on your own.'

Mr Keppel agreed. 'I don't have anything like this.'

Our phone began to ring. It kept ringing. I heard Mom say downstairs, 'He's not here. Look we have an emergency and I'll thank you to keep off the line.'

Dad was perched on the roof of the lean-to, unwinding barbed wire across the windows.

Faith said, 'You'll not be able to keep everything out. You had rats before. Gnaw their way through anything. Mice. They're like octopuses, they can squeeze through cracks.'

'Thank you, Faith.'

Dad jumped down from the roof and unwound barbed wire around most of the house. It looked like trenches in World War One. He came back with more screwdrivers and something sealed in plastic.

'You're putting a lock on the door.'

'That's what I'm doing, Faith.'

'You reckon the zombies will knock politely first?'

'Don't they always?'

'When they come to tea? They like their cream and scones, but they break down your door first. Just good manners for them.'

'Not this door.'

'We're the cream and scones.'

'Thank you, Faith.'

Dad took the shelves from the oven to make a grill over my bedroom windows. He hammered our baking trays flat, drilled and then screwed them to the back of the door. Faith dismantled the folding ladder to make metal braces, which she and Dad screwed to the doorframe to hold it together.

Dad had been around. 'In a bush fire, you should never back yourself into a room you can't get out of. Thankfully, this isn't a bush fire.'

'Bonfire of the Vanities,' said Faith. It was the title of a book about high finance, big men making money by thieving, destroying the system that made them.

'Teddy-Boy,' said my Dad. 'Can you fix all these bolts for me? There's other things I've got to do.'

'Okay.'

Mom waited anxiously at the bedroom door. By then the cloud had burnt off and it was sunny. Outside the window a pigeon made a rootling sound. Mom said, 'There's something on the news, I really think you should see.'

Dad nodded. 'We've gone viral, right? Vegan burns dogs alive?'

'Yeah. They want to interview you.'

Dad laughed. 'Not doing that again.'

'There's calls to prosecute you. And more, a lot more. It's all going off, Mike. This whole thing is exploding. All of Gloucestershire and all of Oxfordshire is in lockdown now.'

'I need to keep going with this.'

'And something totally bizarre has happened in Witney. It will affect us.' She raised her voice as he eased past her. 'You really need to see it.'

'I do, but this first!'

Faith took Dad's drill from me. 'I'm better at bolts, Little One,' she said. 'You go help your Mom with our lunch.' She gave my back a little push. Downstairs in the kitchen, Mom gave the wall we shared with Bounce a thump. A few seconds later, Bounce thumped back. When we'd first moved in, we had a tiny cupboard in one corner – it was actually under Bounce's stairs, which meant we not only heard footsteps, but every word in her kitchen. It was all rebuilt when we discovered that cupboard was part of a huge rat run.

Mom put her mouth close to the plaster. 'You all right, Bounce?'

A bit too long a silence, and we heard Bounce say, dimly. 'All right. Thanks. Don't worry.'

'We're making lunch,' Mom shouted. 'Want some?'

Bounce didn't answer

We took some tinned cannelloni beans and tried to jazz them up with the usual tomatoes and curry paste. All a bit feeble. While we worked we listened to the radio.

The radio news was mostly about the scandal of the Minister for Transport, Owen Wavering, being airlifted out of the lockdown area. There were reports that the Minister was suffering effects similar to a stroke, including loss of speech. The political correspondent aired her views on how this would affect the government's popularity and quoted a poll.

The lockdown area wasn't just bigger – the kind of lockdown had changed. All travel for any reason except medical emergency was banned. Police were being redeployed to enforce the new rules using powers from the last lockdown to detain anyone breaking them.

'Calls are growing to prosecute an Oxfordshire man for burning his dogs alive in an effort to quell the new virus. The man concerned works for the Well Being Institute, and a spokesperson for that organisation said the that every effort had been made to ensure the dogs were put down before being burnt. Meanwhile, reports of attacks by animals have overwhelmed police and emergency services in the lockdown areas, with reports of attacks also coming in also from the Midlands and areas around London.'

The phone kept ringing. Mom let it ring. Dad had no intention of doing another interview.

She knocked on the wall again. Bounce did not answer. The beans steamed.

'Right,' Mom said. She stood at the bottom of the stairs and shouted. 'You're coming down and you're eating some food and watching the news. Now!'

Faces dusted over with ground plaster, Faith and Dad trooped down the stairs for beans, and Mom made them watch the news. Sure enough, Cass Posthern's video was being featured and credited. There was a snatch of Ivan outside the WBI defending Dad. But the tone of the piece was not all hostile.

We were the link to the next news item. 'Certainly something very unsettling is happening in West Oxfordshire as our correspondent Andrew Chukwunonso reports.'

And there was our local shop owner looking rather merry with his new gig, reporting from a town in lockdown. I vaguely remembered that one of his two sons worked for the BBC. Mr Chukwunonso was an old man, but he did not look old for the camera – his eyes twinkled and his smile dazzled. Light reflected on his shiny forehead – like everyone else, he was feverish.

'The small West Oxfordshire market town of Witney was startled earlier today by a report that meat in a butcher's shop was starting to move by itself.'

They ran a phone video. It showed, at an awkward screen angle, people standing outside the store. They squeal and back away. A man in a wheelchair howls in panic, and an older woman shouts, and flings something from his lap.

'Customers first noticed beef on display outside the store beginning to shift about 10 am.' The elongated, phone-shaped image shows cuts of meat shrugging their way along the pavement.

Cut to Mr Chukwunonso interviewing a Witneyoid, a bone-thin man in his 40s trying to look 20 with dyed bronze hair and tattoos crawling over his collar. 'We were a bit startled looking at the meat, you know to see it was still moving. Then this steak or something jumps onto my leg. I don't know what it was trying to do, but it seemed a bit odd.' He chuckles, embarrassed.

Cut to a red-faced man in a straw boater – the proprietor. 'We source all our meat fresh from local farmers, so I'm not sure what's happened. The meat had not been frozen, and certainly, should not have been able to move.'

Mr Chukwunonso smiles. 'This is the second such astounding incident in the locality. On Wednesday, in the nearby village of Oldminster, a frozen deer carcass appeared to come to life.'

And there on national television is my video from The Ram's Head. It shows the headless deer thrashing its way out of the kitchen, and cuts to it running across the field.

It's credited to the Well Being Institute.

'And this a cooked whole chicken,' says Mr Chukwunonso, back on screen. The camera swings down to the pavement. There is a whole chicken, its back roasted golden and sprinkled with herbs. People are gathered around it and scream whenever it moves, lumping forward on wings and footless drumsticks.

'Watch,' says Mr Chukwunonso, and lowers his hand towards the gaping hole where the neck had been. The chicken leaps and envelopes his hand as people laugh and applaud. The chicken clenches and coughs, mumbling his wrist.

Mr Chukwunonso holds it up for the camera, laughing. It shifts around his hand. 'It used to be we enjoyed eating meat. Now meat enjoys eating us. This is Andrew Chukwunonso, from Witney, Oxfordshire.'

(Video is immortal. It is always in present tense. Video is as undead as marsupia.)

We all sat in silence afterwards, our beans cooling.

'Well,' Dad said finally. 'That will go around the world.'

'It's local news,' said Mom.

'As a visual, it beats Keir Starmer addressing Parliament,' said Mr Keppel. 'Though I can see the resemblance to the chicken.' He'd been a journalist for *The Telegraph*.

Faith grunted. 'Nobody'll be touching meat for the foreseeable.'

The tumblers of my world spun and clicked into place. The safe opened. We were in a new world.

'Bounce isn't answering,' said Mom. 'I'll take her some lunch.'

Faith stood up and pointed at Dad. 'You stay put,' she told him. 'I'll go with. And I'll take the gun.' She waited at the door while Mom microwaved a bowl. 'You drive,' Faith said. She and Mom darted out to the car.

Dad stayed slumped on the sofa, covering his eyes. 'I'll have to wire in the generator,' he said, wincing. 'Teddy-Boy I need you to help me pull wires into the downstairs cupboard. Oh! I need to make a switch so we can switch to generator power.'

'Switch upstairs,' said Mr Keppel. 'Or we'll have to go downstairs.'

'I'm really doing it to make sure we can keep the cars charged. Right.' Dad sat forward and blinked as if just waking up. 'Come on, let's get lunch washed up.' We gathered up bowls and spoons.

We were still washing up when we hear the squeal of brakes in the drive, and the front door bursting open. Mom was sobbing. Dad ran into the hall. Mom's hand was over her mouth and her cheeks were wet. Faith was standing in the doorway, backs to us, shotgun raised.

'Bounce is gone,' Mom sputtered.

Faith spun around smartly and slammed the door behind her, while breaking open the gun. Her face was grim. 'They got her,' she said.

Dad hugged Mom; she rested against him for a moment and pushed him away, lightly. 'Bounce was sitting next to Tom. Neither one of them had their heads.'

'The big glass doors were left open,' said Faith.

Mom looked straight at Dad. 'I think she left them open on purpose.'

Dad went upstairs to wire up the generator; our landline kept ringing.

Mom would pick it up, and after a moment, push the off button and put it back in its cradle.

'It's supposed to be unlisted,' she muttered. 'I'd unplug the phone but I don't know if it would affect our broadband.'

'It's got two separate plugs,' I said, but she still didn't do it.

It rang again. She snatched up the phone. 'Look this a community in crisis here. People are being killed! We need to keep these lines open. My neighbours have been killed. No, I will not tell you. You know darn well if you don't hang up the connection stays. Can you please hang up. No you cannot have an interview. Stop squatting on our line.'

Dad called for me, so I crawled under the staircase, where the fuse boxes were. Dad shouted down. 'I'm pushing the wire down now. Can you see it, Teddy-Boy?'

Both Mom and Dad were suddenly using this new nickname for me. I hated it. I think it made them both feel like I was older, more of a tough guy – or maybe they thought it would make me feel like that.

So I shouted up the stairs. 'Could you not call me that?'

There was a silence. I shouted again. 'It's not last century.' (I'm not sure what Teddy Boys were, except they imitated Elvis years before my father was born.)

Dad trooped down the stairs. His face was pulled awry by a smile but his eyes were amused and sore at the same time. 'Okay. Do I call you Edward?'

Something in the smile made me smile too. 'Just Teddy will be fine.'

'Okay, Son. And could you pull the wire through for me? Don't worry, it's not live.'

I ducked back under the stairs and saw crinkly bits of metal and blue, brown, white rubber peeking like mice through the drill hole. Finally I was able to pinch it with my fingers and pull it through into the cupboard.

The phone rang again. I heard Mom shout at whoever it was.

Dad's feet thumped the stairs and into the kitchen. He snatched up the phone.

'What do you want? Okay. I'll give you a statement. Here's a quote. Marsupia are a life form that we knew nothing about before this and are still learning about. Outer space?' He chuckles and shakes his head. 'One possibility is that they've been lurking for some time in animal burials. What we do know is that they appear to survive on any surface, full stop. That includes being frozen or even being burnt – and yes that's why my dogs recovered in the fire. In fact it could be that heat, even extreme heat, speeds up the process of healing.'

He sputtered. 'Yes, they attack people. They *kill* people, they've killed three or four of our neighbours. No, we don't know why. Like Rabies? Maybe more like we're the only fresh meat left.' Pause. 'The whole landscape stinks. Is there a cure?' Dad shook his head. 'I've just heard from WBI that the marsupia recover from being autoclaved – so honestly, I don't know of anything that could kill it. It has amazing regenerative properties. Animals appear to have died but then heal in ways we don't yet understand. Marsupia seem to be able to transfer genetic material between species, especially coding for nervous systems. This may account for the speech disorders we see in some people. If so we will have to rethink genetics, rethink much of biology, perhaps even rethink neurology and much of what we thought we knew about evolution. Marsupia-1 infect seem to infect all mammals, reptiles and amphibians but only some bird species – mostly water fowl as far as I can tell. Humans carry it and spread it. We're not the main vector, but a vector. They also give it to each other. Fevers and antibiotics don't heal it. Fevers may even speed up the illness progression. I don't know of a single case of a human or animal recovering. Yes. We should all stop eating meat, especially those who have not yet fallen ill. Is this the end of the world? Yes. Now will you please get off this private line. We are in immediate danger.'

Dad rolled his eyes and then blew out air in exasperation. Without a word, he rolled to his feet. 'They're still on the line,' he said, and went under the stairs to work on the wiring.

'No animals to feed, no weeds to pull,' mused Mom. She had nothing to do.

'And no vegetables to eat either after this summer,' said Faith. 'I'd say let's go shoot some pheasant, except that I don't want to see it walking around my plate.'

'We're going to get hungry,' said Mom.

'Yup. We are,' said Faith. 'Done here.' She went to the base of the stairs and shouted up at Dad. 'You want I come up there and wire in the switch while you do sommat else?'

Dad shouted something back, I went closer to hear.

Faith muttered under her breath. 'Bloody man. I ran me own house for forty years.' She stomped up the steps.

Mom looked awful. Her glazed eyes were still seeing Bounce. 'We'll have to leave them. There's no time to bury them, we can't risk it.'

I told her to go sit on the terrace with its big, locked metal-frame doors. I went upstairs to the bedroom kettle and made her some tea.

Faith, twiddling wires, could see the tumble of evacuated books on the landing. 'You'll still have plenty to read,' she grunted.

Mom's face seemed to be melting when I got downstairs. She was wiping it with a wrung-out looking paper towel. I gave her a hug and finally got her out on the terrace. I didn't know much about social media, but I'd joined Bluesky on the sly (It was a message system about oneself with added lies, self-importance and photographs). I knew enough to do a search for my Dad. There was masses of stuff, leading to more, all of it angry, incredulous. A lot of people said the government or scientists had made the whole thing up to increase their power. Another line of nuttiness was blind rage at anything New Age, meaning people like my parents.

On some Witney news group, a pasty-faced, plump, bearded man ranted. 'We had all this before with the animal rights demonstrators. They picketed that farm for years and followed rural workers home to vandalise their property. Now we find this supposed scientist, this vegan guy is burning dogs alive. We've had enough. We'll not stand for it.'

He seemed so confused and contradictory, that my eyes crossed. I couldn't begin to pick apart all his confusions. But he scared me. As much as the animals did. More so because he had no idea that he was an animal too.

Dad tested the generator. All the lights dipped; there was a chugging sound and what sounded like the whir of a fan; and then the lights came back on, the broadband and phones bleeping. I'm not sure how Dad did it. I never will know.

Then Dad cleared the garden.

I heard a buzzing sound and looked out the desk-corner window and saw Dad using the Bijou Chainsaw. He was cutting down the hedge of winter jasmine, old man's beard and other lovely plants that had hidden our front door. Faith stood guard over him with the gun.

I thought I'd done a good job keeping the garden for him while he'd been away. I saw then how overgrown it had become. Now we had a clear view of the drive and front lawn. He dragged the mass of cuttings off to one side. He backed the Kia up and unlocked the charging plug. We had to keep it locked or people would steal our electricity. The car was left, drinking in energy.

Dad came back in looked utterly exhausted. Mom was sitting hollow eyed on the terrace looking at blue tits on the feeders. He tried to call on his mobile, but growled and let it drop. He stood out of the front porch, held the phone up, dialled and then crouched over it. 'Hi. Hello?' He said. 'We're Okay. We're Okay. Can you hear me?' He stepped further out. 'Hello, it's me.'

He was ringing Ken.

Mom grunted, stood up and went to the front door. 'Sorry. Sorry, I don't want to interrupt, but should you be standing outside?'

He paused. He didn't want us to hear him talking to Ken. He could have just gone upstairs to get a stronger signal, but then Faith and Mr Keppel would have heard him talking to his boyfriend. 'You're right. I'll drive up to the passing place on the lane. I'll stay inside the car and call from there. I won't be long.' His Golf was parked under the apple tree. He backed up and then pulled forward. He signalled at the top of the drive and turned right. I caught his profile, focussed on the road, and then he disappeared behind the line of sycamores.

'You… you don't have to be angry with your father,' Mom said.

She slumped back into the kitchen chair, and took my hand. 'He never lied to me. Before we married. I knew what I was getting into.' She sat clasping my hands. 'So I don't blame him. For being who he is.'

'I blame Ken,' I said.

Her smile looked as though the whole weight of her face was pressing down on it. 'So do I.'

She sighed, a bit showy and stood up. 'But. We have your father now for a while at any rate. We have to make do.'

My heart sank even further. I'd thought maybe Dad had come back to us for good. Mom thought he had not; that he would go back to Ken. I clenched like a fist.

'Yeah we're Dad's bit on the side. It should be the other way around.'

He never came back.

Eleven

Mom cooked up lots of food to put in the freezer.

Faith got out the toolbox and asked for my help hanging an old thick door across the front of the staircase. 'Extra just in case,' she said. She was able to put in hinges into the thick wood. We were lucky. The door was a perfect fit, just where the staircase turned.

'Is your father back?' Mom asked, wiping her hands on a towel.

Something plunged in my chest. I looked out of the north window. In the driveway was our Kia but not Dad's Golf.

'Not yet.'

A little niggle of worry, became a quivering in our chests and hands that wouldn't go away. Mom walked in every five minutes to check the window. After about forty minutes, she just stood by the sitting room window, leaning out over the desk.

She went upstairs. I heard nothing. She came down.

'Maybe he went for food or petrol,' Faith suggested.

'There are six full canisters upstairs,' I said.

'Maybe he went to get some more cans?'

Downstairs, Mom was staring at her mobile. 'He isn't answering his phone. His phone is ringing and he's not answering it.'

Mr Keppel was asleep on the sofa. Mom touched his arm, then touched again. He blinked, grunted and woke up. She told him we were going to look for Dad. Would Mr Keppel be all right on his own?

'I'd rather come with you if that's all right,' he said.

Then our landline rang. Mom squealed and ran for the sitting room extension, and snatched it up. Her smile fell. 'Mr Day.'

Mom listened to him, looking more and more solemn. 'We can't really. My husband has gone out and we have to wait for him. What about breaking lockdown?' She listened, grey as a ghost. 'I suppose that does make sense. We won't be joining you just yet. I'm sorry, but we need this line open in case Mike calls. We do appreciate your telling us. Yes. Thank you. Yes. We will. No, that won't be necessary. Thank you.'

She stared into space. 'There's a caravan of cars leaving the village in twenty minutes. People are driving to Brize Norton airbase. They've turned a hangar into an evacuation centre for local people. Mr Day thinks it'll be protected by military. It's certainly safer than being out here in the middle of a field.'

Faith said, 'No police stopping folk then?'

There were supposed to be police at the top of the hill, turning people back to enforce the lockdown.

Mom said staring ahead, 'The police cars have their doors open with the engines running. And no police. No sign of them.'

Faith took up Dad's gun. Mom snatched up her car keys and strode towards the front door. Faith seemed to be chewing something, tobacco perhaps. She picked up the Bijou Chainsaw from the hallway dresser and passed it to Mom.

Mom eyed me. 'Teddy. I think you should stay here. Go up to your bedroom and lock yourself in.'

'No,' I said.

'Teddy we don't know what we're going to find.'

I had wondered what it had been like to be Bounce. Now I knew. 'I have to see.'

She looked into me and then nodded. 'Whatever happens you don't leave the car.'

'Neither do you.'

Mr Keppel reminded us. 'The front door is open.'

At least the Kia had a full charge. Mom had to wrestle with the steering to get it turned around on the drive. I told Mom, 'He turned right.'

'You saw him go?' asked Mom in a wistful voice.

As soon as we were out of the gate I began to whine and go tick-tock with my tongue. Animals were close by. And not far ahead at all, in the passing place, was Dad's Golf. I went still and cold.

We pulled up alongside it. There was no torn clothing on the ground. All the doors were closed. There wasn't even a window open, so he must have had a pretty good signal. Or maybe didn't.

Mom got out her phone and dialled. 'His phone is ringing,' she said. Suddenly, she flung our door open and got out to peer inside the Golf.

'Mom. Get inside,' I shouted. I was clicking even harder. She opened the car door. It wasn't locked. Pressing the lock button was a habit with Dad. The keys were still in the ignition.

Mom stood up holding his vibrating phone. 'I'll drive back,' she said.

We heard a revving behind us. A dusty van was roaring up the road, its side door open. A man, a bearded man, was hanging out from it, scanning the landscape. It slowed behind us. Mom hopped back into the Kia and tried to edge us forward out of the way.

I am reasonably certain that it was the man on Bluesky, the man protesting about our bonfire. We stayed in our car and watched the van do a three point turn in the next passing place about twenty yards ahead. Then it roared past us again, back into Oldminster.

Even forty years later, I curse my bad luck.

If we'd been three minutes later, I never would have seen that van. That van gave me hope that something else may have happened to my father.

When I no longer needed hope or belief, I realised that those men couldn't have had anything to do with Dad's disappearance. They were going up and down our lane looking for Beehive Cottage. Our postcode took in five houses on two different roads, and we'd never got around to hanging out a sign with the new house name. We were always getting everybody else's newspapers or post or tulip bulbs. The van sped off. If they were still looking for Dad, how could they have had anything to do with his disappearance?

'Mr Keppel could you drive the Golf back for me?' Mom asked.

'We'll probably find he's walked back home in the meantime,' said Mr Keppel. Mom didn't answer.

I was growling low. 'Get going for Chrissake,' said Faith.

So, the e-Golf went back under the apple tree, and the Kia backed up again by the front door to charge. We crowded back into the house.

I went straight to the landline and rang the police. I felt like the walls of our house, cool to the touch. I was very sensible and orderly.

'Teddy what are you doing?'

'Just telling the police that Dad's missing.'

Faith intervened. 'He wants to do something. Come on, Maggie, we've got upstairs to finish.' She placed two fingers on Mom's elbow and eased her towards the stairs.

It took twenty minutes to get through to the police. The shadows grew longer. Finally they answered. Mom came downstairs and stood over me.

I told them about the man in the van. I even remembered its registration number. 'My Dad's gone and they threatened him. You can find it if you look. He's the guy with the beard.' I gave them our three numbers to ring back.

The woman took all the details and then said. 'And I'm sorry about your Dad.'

I actually said, 'Why?'

'Because...' the woman paused. 'We've had a lot of missing people.'

'I'm going to find him,' I told her.

Mom stood over me. 'Teddy you can't get people into trouble with the police like that.'

'I saw him, Mom. You didn't. He was that Witney group in a video and he threatened Dad. That man in the van.'

Mom murmured something but it didn't come out clearly, and she enveloped me in a hug and kissed the top of my head. She just stood there holding me.

'I think we'll probably leave here in the morning,' she told me. 'When it's safer. It's getting a bit late now.'

'No,' I said.

'What?'

'I'm not leaving Dad.' That was all I knew, that certainty. I wasn't going away until we had found Dad and brought him home.

'I don't know what to do,' said Mom. Both palms were pushed into her eye sockets, rubbing them.

'You should sleep,' I said. 'It's going to be a long night. Come on. Have a nap.'

'There's food and water upstairs, everything.' She meant we'd done all we could.

'Come on, we should all rest.' I thought about getting her back onto the terrace so she could see the birds and the feeder. Then I imagined Charity slamming herself against the glass sliding doors. I got Mom upstairs in her own room. I got her to lie down.

'Just a half hour's kip,' I said.

I slipped downstairs. The Bijou was still in the hallway, its battery charging. I picked up and silently as a cat I slipped outside and eased the front door shut.

Thinking back on it now, I was not entirely lunatic to go out to find him.

Animals can't lie. Their communication works. Their instinctive barks and rattles happen without conscious thought, and the sounds shoot straight into the depths of other brains.

The sound of my barks and squeals changed.

They ceased to be warnings or pleas. They became bursts of snarls, alternated with high piercing cries.

I was casting a quarantine in sound: *keep off my land.* (or *get out of my way*)

I had complete knowledge – my life would not move on, could not move on until I knew what had happened to my father.

I was angry. I was angry at the earth and the grass and the pathogens in the air, but more than anything else I was angry at myself. I had made a stupid mistake. I had been wicked.

I'd let my Dad go thinking that I was angry with him. Maybe even hated him. I'd let him go without telling him I loved him, that I respected him as much as any person on the planet.

I hadn't valued the china bowl and then I'd let it drop. So I was trying to glue it back together.

It wasn't a long walk to the passing place.

There was no sign of a struggle. No tracks, no blood, no shreds of clothing.

I had a choice. I could go look in the barley field north of the lane and head towards Dorothy's beagle sheds, or I could scramble over the wall into the field next to our dog run. That field had been pastured, so the grass was short. If there had been a body in that field, I'd have seen it already.

I scrambled up the bank and through the sparse old hedge and into the barley field. A low trembling growl came out of me the whole time. I thought of the way Faith kept guard, and so I walked in slow circles scanning for the threats all around me.

The barley had not been harvested. The hill rose up all the time, gently. I trooped upwards through the tall, long-haired grain. I'd never been in this field before. Dorothy's house was hidden by trees, but the upward slope meant I was soon able to see her roof.

The long blades were damnable. Dad might be lying among them. So might Dorothy's beagles or what was left of the Boys. I buzzed the Bijou to warn them, and turned and looked down the slope.

I'd left a clear, trampled trail through the barley. Someone running or someone being dragged would have left even more of a wake. Dad had not come this way.

I followed my own track back down to the base of the field and walked east along its lower length. I came to the small depression along which the floodwater flowed from the high ground every time it rained. A good place to hide. A good place for an ambush. I could see no trail to it. I walked to its mouth, then stepped down onto the delta of gravel where the gully emptied itself onto the lane. My hiking boots clumped back onto the asphalt.

The other side of the gully was a copse of trees. Once there'd been six huge beech trees. But they had to be cut down: drought and flood and age had weakened them and they had threatened to fall onto the lane.

I stood up on the stone wall to get a better view. The legacy of those tall trees was that they had shadowed the floor of the copse so little else grew. The harsh summer had baked most of the undergrowth away leaving only saplings, ground ivy and nettles. It was fairly open and I could see there was no Dad. So I jumped back down from the wall and then, from behind, something snarled at me.

A really savage sound was torn out of me, a furious yelp-and-snarl. *I'll kill you.*

I saw a fox, limping, weaving unsteadily out of the wood, with a delicate greyhound by its side. A greyhound and a fox running together?

'Fuckers,' I said under my breath.

They turned in unison like it was a dance. They walked in step, their milky grey eyes on me. They grimaced like dogs, fang-baring.

Except that both of them began to chuckle. They laughed like human beings.

They began to lope towards me.

Ho ho ho ho.
Ha ha ha ha.

I buzzed the chainsaw and climbed onto the wall so they couldn't jump down onto me. The loose old drystone slid and clinked under foot. The fox looked ginger-red against the ivy.

There was a distant sound like a murder of crows all taking off together and both the dog's and the fox's heads exploded into grey-black, stinking mist. They must have been struck through by a single shot.

They staggered on, but I knew they couldn't see. The greyhound was fumbling against the wall, not able to climb it, so I jumped down into the lane and backed away.

'You daft Bath-bun!' Faith shouted.

She was walking up the lane with the shotgun. She'd be a minute or two catching up to me.

I went up the hill where the undergrowth was thicker and turned the saw on the saplings and nettles, sending up a fog of chips and leaves. I kept expecting to see Dad's jeans or tartan shirt. Nothing, of course, there was nothing. He had not been taken by any animals. I was convinced of it. He'd been taken hostage by those idiots in the van, that bunch of misguided oiks.

I jumped over the wall back into the road. Faith had caught up with me.

'He's not in those fields.' For some reason I was smiling.

She looked grim. *You're a right idiot.*

I still kept my smile. 'There's a chance that those people took him.'

'Don't fool yourself.'

'How did you keep Mom inside?'

'Told her the truth. Rescue teams always feed the mothers first. The mums go on to help the kids and the Dads. Lose them, you lose everyone. So if you think your father's kidnapped, we can go back to the house.'

We stared at each other. 'I want to check some more,' I said, my voice going small.

'Your poor mum. I can give you fifteen minutes,' she sighed.

'Then what?'

'I'll saw your head off and tell your mum the dogs did it.'

Across the lane from us was a track running down towards the river. A metal gate was chained shut across it, with strands of barb along the top.

It would have been a beautiful evening. The temperature had actually dropped a bit. A bit of high pressure. Clear blue sky and a bit of a breeze. It would be light until nine pm and right now at seven o' clock, everything looked orange, blessed.

I started to climb the gate, careful of the wire. Faith said, 'That's overgrown.'

I hopped down. 'Uh-huh.' *I guess so.*

Faith nipped over the gate in less time. 'It takes hundreds of people to find a body you know. They divide the ground up with numbers and then beat the bush.'

Faith was right, the lane was overhung. Elders and willow saplings crowded us and the grass was brown and high. I hadn't noticed it before, but the track curved so I couldn't see what lay ahead. Nothing had been driven down it for ages. There were furrows made by generations of tractor tires, but even these were full of grass. I walked along the ruts. I began to growl a warning: *Ours ours.*

'Oh that'll scare them off,' chortled Faith. She was walking backwards, gun ready.

We had to duck under a fallen willow which meant I had to take my eyes off the track. I could feel all my sense of certainly leak away. I mean, nothing had dragged a body down this way. And why would thugs take him here? What the hell could have happened to him? Why did he leave the car?

My feet felt heavy and I stopped walking. All I saw was dried, dead grass, reeds and leaves. I growled a warning.

There was a growling back.

My heart stopped, but then I realized the sound came from overhead. High up over the hill on the other side of the Windrush river, a helicopter hung in the air.

'They'll be looking for them policemen. Maybe others.' Faith put a hand on my shoulder. 'Do you want to go back? They'll do a better job spotting your Dad than you will out here.'

I lost heart. I nodded yes. Faith tried to keep her hand on my shoulder, but I turned around. I walked backwards, while she walked facing front, and we made it back to the lane and the house together.

Twelve

I got in, and Mom was calm, controlled.

'The police called,' she said. 'Their cameras show your van went down the B4047 and turned into the village. He lives in Witney, the owner. They'll follow it up.'

She gave me an odd, firm look with a downturned mouth. 'So you were right about that.'

'Sorry, Mom. I had to do it.'

She enveloped me in a hug.

Faith said, 'He's a good lad. Just needed to give it a go. Get it out of his system.'

I had not got it out of my system but I didn't say so. I called myself a wimp, and promised not to wimp out the next day.

We ate the same batch of beany slosh with tinned tomatoes and too much curry. 'Delicious! Really delicious,' said Mr Keppel. Again.

We watched the news. There were now fifty people missing. They didn't mention Tom and Bounce or Dorothy. They weren't missing, they were corpses in their own homes. That meant there'd be more deaths they didn't know about.

'Among the missing is a man who spoke to BBC Oxford recently, Dr Michael Spaulding. His abandoned car was found near his house. Dr Spaulding was one of the first people to warn that animals infected with Marsupia-1 attacked people. Also, all four of the officers assigned to enforce the quarantine zone around the village of Oldminster have disappeared, with their protective clothing found badly torn.'

They talked about how most of the village had escaped to Brize Norton. Mr Chukwunonso, still making a new career for himself, showed up again interviewing our Squadron Leader inside what looked like a sports facility. There were bunk beds and people's bags. In the background were the echoes of shouting children. The Squadron

Leader said, 'We're getting in food, basic stuff, but it's better than nothing.'

'And you knew Dr Spaulding.'

'Yes, lovely man. Terrible shame about the controversy. He was doing a lot to keep the village together.'

I said, 'Dad's not dead.' Nobody responded.

'We should have gone with them,' Mom said in the tiniest voice.

But it was getting dark, so we retreated upstairs.

We wanted to make sure we had everything we needed while it was still light to see. Mr Keppel remembered that we hadn't taken any salt for the food. We locked the doors and piled furniture back up against the French doors and terrace windows. We left all the lights on – better to see. I didn't want to still be downstairs when it was dark; I didn't want to see the motion-detector light flick on.

Upstairs, in my fortified room, I could hear scratching in the walls and claws scuttling in the loft. As always, I hoped it was birds.

Then out of the corner of my eye, I saw something flit across the carpet.

If you only think you've seen a mouse – you've seen a mouse. That's what I said. Faith helped me move the bed, and I saw something else flit past.

'If you see one mouse, there's ten more,' said Faith.

'They're in here with us,' I said.

'What I been saying all day.'

Without meaning to, without having to think, I started to make a screedling, neeping sound. Of course, I'd been exchanging marsupia with bedroom rodents these many months. So I was mouse-boy as well. No wonder I almost always had a fever. Mom stared at me hollow-eyed.

I was still in my hiking boots so I stomped and caught it. I stood on one foot and ground down. I heard a crunch. My neeping changed tone. Maybe it had a note of triumph. I scrunched down again.

Then I lifted up the boot and grabbed the thing by its tail.

How supernatural was it that the mouse was still wriggling and biting? I had plainly flattened its ribcage, but its furious head was intact and it was snapping and biting. Its front paws scrabbled, but the back ones hung limp. We had the kitchen knives with us, so I picked up the breadknife and on my night table started sawed the mouse in half.

'What are you doing?' Mom shouted. 'That's for food!'

I cut through it. The back half, limp-legged stayed still; but the top half tried to scuttle away. I grabbed it, put it back on the table and cut off the head. The head kept biting. The front legs kept trying to run, pumping air.

'Nobody should sleep on the floor,' I said.

Faith chuckled. 'Nobody's going to sleep at all.' The outside detector light had not gone on, so I felt safe scooping up the shrugging remains, leaving the room and flushing them down the loo.

We lifted up the beds, but the mice had all retreated into the walls. I had some lunatic idea of mixing pollyfilla with ground glass and bits of tinfoil and filling the cracks with it. Like we had any time.

The motion light flicked on.

We could see it through the upper floor hall windows. Faith calmly closed my bedroom door and locked it. Mr Keppel checked the window locks.

'Everybody got everything they need?' Mom asked. We had all the chargers including for the Bijou, lined up neatly on my chest of drawers. Also flashlights and boxes of ammo. The shotgun leaned upright in a corner, Mr Keppel's axe next to it. Mom had no weapons. She had a big brown leather case with all our documents in it.

I heard claws on stone coming from outside the back door. Faith, Mom, Mr Keppel didn't react. Hadn't they heard it? The growling rose in my throat; I became a snarl, then a sharp warning bark. Then I heard that odd whispering sound, and a sudden squeal. I thought: they've just learned what barbed wire is.

Then I heard a metal scraping sound, very faint. Like they were pulling the barbed wire back. I heard another, gentler pattering sound.

And then I honked like a duck.

Faith laughed aloud. 'Attack of the Killer Ducks.'

I had to laugh too, except of course it was probably true.

Something scurried across the floor, and I jumped. I arched through the air, landed on all fours, and caught the thing in my mouth. Mom yelped. I snatched the mouse out of my mouth and crushed it in my fist. I felt it quiver, jerk, struggle. I pushed harder, but I knew it would never be safe, never be still. Worse, a chemical taste permeated my mouth, sharp tingling but also shit-solid death stench. I whimpered, then wiped my tongue on my sleeve. Grey goop stained the cloth.

We had everything in that room we needed except for mouthwash. I snatched up the hammer, gripped the mouse's tail and smashed the thing on the carpet, over and over until it was as flat as a pizza crust. My eyes were watering, my gorge kept rising, I couldn't let myself swallow.

The mess kept moving and shifting, seething like soup on the hob, catching the light, even bubbling slightly. The blood had gone grey.

Faith asked. 'Who taught you to hunt like that?' But both of us knew the answer. It was a rhetorical question.

What the hell were we going to do with these remains? I flung open the bedroom window and tossed out the mess.

My mouth still tasted of death and decay. There had been no smashing sounds from downstairs. So I unlocked our door. Mom shouted at me. I spun out into the bathroom and grabbed some Listerine. Then I saw the bathroom garage bin with its swing lid, so I grabbed that too, and nipped back into my room and locked the door.

'Don't you *ever* do that again!' Mom shouted.

I gargled and spat into the bin, then gargled again.

That's when we heard a great *thump* downstairs. Something heavy was slamming into the terrace doors, that wide expanse of sliding glass. We could feel the glass shiver in its frame.

Something snorted then squealed and there was another thump.

'That'll be Charity,' said Faith.

A three-hundred kilogram pig was hurtling itself at the double-glazed, metal framed doors. *Thump*. Squeal. Snuffle. *Thump*.

Another sound twisted its way out of me. I actually felt some new kind of air passage open and divert, like I'd grown a fish inside of me and out came a new sound, a long ear-splitting piggy squeal. *My place! Go!*

Another shadow flitted and I jumped, managing to catch the mouse with my front paws. I was an expert mouser. Distracted, I bit it in half. My mother screamed, 'Are you crazy?' I used the Listerine, then the hammer to make sure the mess couldn't move then dumped in into the bin along with my fresh-mint spit.

Thump. Crackle. Glass was beginning to splinter.

Another thump and then a squeal of pain. Charity had been cut.

Thump again.

Thump followed by a sound of cascading a bit like falling rain, a shower of glass.

'They're through the terrace doors,' said Faith.

They'd kept silent until now, but the dogs started yelping with excitement, snarling with victory.

And then in a voice bigger than any dog's, like bellows were pumping air through a church organ, there came a long sustained croon. *Ours.* Charity the pig was howling like wolf.

I went to the window, but you couldn't see the back terrace from my bedroom – the lean-to was in the way.

I heard multiple yelps, almost felt the dog-bodies hurtling themselves like missiles at the glass.

Charity's voice thinned out to a piggy squealing of pain. She'd must have cut herself. She was probably shedding strips of rotten meat. Her blood would be grey or a congealed black. She was made of nerve cells and I know now that made the pain of being cut worse. I thought I heard her divided feet clatter away from the sliding doors on the wooden terrace steps. Had she fallen back?

Then a flood of sounds from downstairs, soundwaves coming to us up the staircase and through my bedroom door – an eager yipping, and a slipping of claws on tiles. The greyhounds were in the house. Then like a John Jorrocks jollity, a pouring of braindead-beagle yelps.

House said the beagles.

Treats!

Then a chorus of addled quacks. *Dry dry.*

Can't swim!

Ours!

The ducks growled. The idea of them being savage hunters waddling up the steps set both me and Faith off laughing. Our eyes caught each other's; we shook our heads. I couldn't stop myself quacking back: *No reeds.* That made both us of laugh more.

'Glad you find something amusing,' said Mom, sounding hurt and mystified.

Then from downstairs, a donkey hee-hawed. Muggy Day kept a showpiece donkey in his field and now it had joined in.

'Bloody hell,' said Faith. 'Old MacDonald had a farm.'

Both of us started to sing it. Well, there was really nothing else we could do.

Eee-yi eee-yi oh!

With a quack-quack here, and oink-oink there.

Another almighty crash. The next line of defence was the double French doors that divided the terrace from the sitting room. Each door was bolted top and bottom with a deadlock linking them.

The glass might smash but the wooden frames would hold for a while. The bolts would have to be knocked out of the lintels and the lock be broken open.

The thumping went on. Two great weights seemed to thunder through the fabric of the house. We could feel them ram the doors together, groaning or squealing each time. Like hammers, they seemed to have no will of their own. They flung themselves against the doors over and over. On the terrace, the dogs barked encouragement. Their claws scraped the terrace floor. The marsupia had taught them how to hunt together.

'No one left in the village,' mused Faith. 'We're all they've got to eat.' She picked up the gun and fed it two cartridges.

I checked the chainsaw battery. It was blinking green. I snapped it onto the handle, but only held the saw by the carrying bar, nowhere near the handle with its on buttons. I did all that while howling, snarling, barking as if possessed.

The dogs shouted back up at me. *Ours ours.* Part of me had no idea of my relative size or of their numbers. I was just ready to fight. Something in me growled back.

Mom suddenly screamed, high, loud, and agonised.

A mouse on her shoulder was eating her ear. I lunged, grabbed and pulled at the mouse, tearing strips of her skin. One last yelp came from Mom. I put the thing on the carpet and hammered it into helpless mash, then dumped it into the swing bin.

I couldn't believe the amount of blood pouring over my Mom's neck and shoulder. Ears are full of blood. It trickled down my mother's fingers and wrist in streams and all down her white shirt. We only had poxy little sticking plasters. We had no gauze bandages, but we did have t-shirts in the drawers. Mr Keppel tore a neck with his teeth and starting ripping the cotton into strips. Faith had the first aid kit open and was tipping disinfectant onto cotton wool (Damn, I could have just used that as a mouthwash.)

Faith dabbed Mom's ear; Mom tried to stop herself wincing and whimpering.

But nothing seemed to stanch the flow of blood; it pattered onto the carpet. Mom pulled off her jacket and rolled up the sleeves of her shirt. She wanted to save her clothes.

'Cold water clots,' said Faith glaring at me. 'Turn the tap on.' I wasn't used to having a tap in my room. Mr Keppel jumped forward and turned on the tap. There was a cough of air, and water seemed to explode all over the room, then soak a strip of T-shirt. Faith pressed the cold wet strips against Mom's head.

'My nice shirt,' said Mom.

'They do bleed, do ears,'

At Mom's feet, a mouse was sucking up blood from the carpet.

There was an odd rustling sound, low down.

Out of nowhere an avalanche of mice poured into our room. Twenty? Thirty? Mice poured out of my cupboard. They wriggled their way under the bedroom door. They clustered around the spilled water. Their claws scraped at the skirting board, trying to climb up the wall to the new tap.

I stomped them. Mom hopped up and down, her dressing trailing behind her ear. Then she grabbed a hammer and started to flatten them. Mr Keppel was cutting them with a big knife, but mice were all over his hands, which were now gouged and spilling blood. I pulled on gardening gloves and started seizing them by the handful. Too many to push through the grill out of the window. I stomped and mashed while Mom hammered. The floor was soon covered with a kind of furry, shifting soup. We hadn't brought a shovel. I started scooping up handfuls of seething mush and ramming in into the bin. Every time I pushed open the lid, some of it tried to seethe back out. Mr Keppel made a distressed sound and suddenly poured his beany dinner on top of them. I scooped up that with my hands as well.

Then, from downstairs came a splintering of wood, and a juddering as the locks finally broke. The beasts were through the French doors. The couch that had been upended against them fell rumbling onto the floor. What sounded like a river of dog claws poured into the house.

Ours ours ours

Hunt

I'm big

All around us was a kind of sizzling. Mice still did not like dogs. They became flitting shadows again, scooting under beds, through walls it seemed, injecting themselves through holes in corners. The mash we'd made bunched itself up, and like fat in a tilted frying pan it swept itself upwards, toppled the bin, poured out of it, and seethed under the door.

'They'll be back,' said Faith.

Mr Keppel was making frantic sounds, pouring Listerine over his torn hands.

Mom's hair was thick with clotting blood, and her face was splotchy. She had to sit down. Faith took her arm and lowered her onto the bed.

Beagles were tornadoing around the downstairs. Something – it could have been either china or glass – tumbled and broke. I heard a greyhound voice snarl something new in dog-talk, something like *Idiot* or *Fool* or *Cub*. I'd never heard it before. A clattering of breakage – the frail bamboo table had toppled, always top heavy with books.

Something large was clopping up and down the sitting room, hee-hawing and hauling in breath. Another piece of furniture fell with a kind of crumpling, probably the standing lamp in the corner with its old shade. The TV was next to it and something fell and shattered. The TV had been knocked over?

From directly under us, in the kitchen, came a spreading crash. Maybe dogs had jumped up onto the kitchen table, sweeping bowls and beakers onto the floor. Claws slipped and skittered on the polished wooden floors.

I could hear the greyhounds, snapping and snarling with an urgency that felt to me like it meant: *There, go there.*

Find find find

I heard a door creak open, I wasn't sure where. The sound seemed come directly up from the stairwell. I heard something big tip over, hit the floor, and crack with a sound like plastic – probably the vacuum cleaner. (Vacuum cleaners were electric machines that sucked up the lightest dust only and left everything else. That meant you swept up first, vacuumed and then had to sweep up again. But you felt very modern and burned up electricity doing it.)

That meant the dogs were in the cupboard under the stair. A metallic clang confirmed that. They had knocked over the leftovers of the cannibalised aluminium ladder that Dad had stowed there.

But why did dogs want to be under the stairs?

There there there! snarled the dogs.

Then I heard two snapping sounds and everything went dark.

'Power failure,' said Mr Keppel. 'What a bloody time for a power failure.'

'They flicked the trip switch,' I said.

Faith sniffed. 'Get the generator going. Fumes go up into the loft, let's hope it gasses them.'

Down below the dogs were thrashing themselves into a frenzy.

Got them got them

Won won won.

And a new sound, a hiss that sounded like 'Yes, yes, yes.'

'The fusebox has been tripped,' I said again.

A light came on. Mom was using her phone as a flashlight and leaning over Faith who was checking that the tank was full of fuel. Why didn't Faith get it? Why did nobody get it?

'You can turn the generator on if you want, but with the switches tripped, there still won't be any electricity in the house.'

'Naw,' said Faith.

'No circuits,' I said.

'How would they know about fuse boxes?'

'The fuse boxes were tripped. I heard the switches.'

I began to think of all the things that now wouldn't work. No water pump for a start. We had a header tank in the loft but after that was used, no water.

There was a sharp splitting sound from the staircase – Faith's temporary new door had been broken through, by something that sounded focussed and very hard – I think the donkey's hooves.

Up the staircase came the tumbling of many feet and a panting.

'We can't recharge our phones,' Mom said, and switched hers off.

'We have no broadband, so no wifi, no phone, no phone apps. The fridge will stay cool for about a day. Even the chainsaw will run out of charge.'

There was a sniffling and snuffling all along the lower edge of the door.

'Faith,' I said. 'Get that gun.'

'Frank,' said Faith in the dark, to Mr Keppel. 'Can you hold two spare cartridges for me and give em over when I ask?'

'We're still safe here,' said Mom.

From the landing I plainly heard more than one dog say, 'Door, door, door.'

'Did you hear *that*?' I asked.

Faith suddenly shouted in the dark. 'Bloody thing. Something bit my hand.' Mice were back with us in the dark.

I kept talking. 'Didn't you hear it? The dogs said "door", the English word *door*.'

'Teddy,' said Mom, in grief. She thought it was just my illness.

'Door door door,' said the dogs, in a hoarse, rhythmic whisper.

Mr Keppel said, 'In the name of God.'

Claws began to scratch against the opposite side of the door. Then the sound clustered around the wooden doorknob. I felt for it in the dark and grabbed hold. I could feel them trying to turn it, rocking it back and forth. Something just the other side of it growled, and I felt vibration through the wood. I imagined one of them clasping the round knob in its jaws and trying to turn it. Then the timbre of the sound changed – there was a smaller gouging and slipping. They were using their claws to try to grip it. They started to whine in frustration.

I yammered at them barking: *Ours ours ours.*

All of them, all the dogs, began to yowl the hunt sound.

Food food food.

Something threw itself against the door. Despite the oven plates and new metal frame around it, the only thing holding the door up were its hinges, old 1930s hinges. The metal plating would only make the door heavier. That weight flung itself against it again.

'Lean against the door,' I shouted. Faith and Mom jumped next to me. I took out my phone, and turned on the flashlight and pointed at the door knob. It shifted, strained against the lock. 'They know about door handles, too.'

Faith chortled. 'Given half a chance, they'll drive the car.'

The under-lighting from the phone turned faces upside down. Mr Keppel looked like a mad scientist. 'It's what your father was saying. This thing transfers genes.'

'Speech isn't in genes,' said Mom, coldly.

(Mom was right. Genes would only over time create structures that might be capable of speech. We know that, for a while at least, infected animals were storing brain tissue whole, healing it into their bodies where it became part of a neural network.)

Mom's voice set off a cascade of yelping and snarling from the dogs. It was Mom who had fed them every morning, and who was most associated with food.

Where is food? The greyhounds yelped. *You bring food! Give food!*

'It's the Boys,' she said with sadness.

Mr Keppel knelt down to look into my eyes. 'What's happening when you make those noises?' he asked me.

'They're not conscious. I don't feel myself making those noises. At least not in my head. But.' I almost felt shame. 'I think I'm growing new kinds of air passages to make these sounds. You know. Almost like a second throat.'

I may have been physically small, and I may have been easily frightened but I was not at all a stupid child. I was already pretty sure that was what was happening. 'The parts of me that do this are not conscious. I don't feel them at all. They just do things.'

'You better save your batteries,' said Faith. I keyed off the light, and the darkness, by contrast was even greater.

'They ARE going for the head,' said Mom. 'Maybe somehow they do get our memories.'

That set off a fresh set of howling, agonized demands mixed with aggressive growls.

The dogs were trying to burrow under the door. We could hear claws whirlygigging away at the carpet. Every so often, one of them still threw itself at the door – a dull boney clumping of shoulders and elbows.

Then from below came Charity's laboured wheezing, and a slow rocking up the steep staircase. Those steps had been too much for Mrs Tulp's knees, which is why she'd sold the house to us. Suddenly there was a louder *thump* and Charity bumped all the way down the stairs again, sliding and squealing. We heard a flat, gassy landing below, as if the pig were a set of torn bagpipes.

The dogs began to laugh. I don't think they were laughing at us, but at Charity.

It was odd wheezing laughter that sounded rehearsed and artificial, as if someone was making fun of the whole concept of laughing. Or was unused to it maybe. Or was simply surprised that they were doing it.

The dogs laughed and then howled dog-like then laughed again. *Ha ha ha ha, hee hee. A-roo a-roo.* As if just laughing were making them laugh more.

'My God,' whispered Mom.

'Ouch,' yelped Mr Keppel. 'Damn! The mice are still in here.'

Faith squealed and jumped. 'Yes, they are.'

I felt something trying to climb up my trouser legs. I kicked. Mom yelled. I stomped my heavy boots and stepped on something. A tiny neeping sound grew. I risked battery life to switch on the phone light. The floor was seething with rodents. The dogs kept laughing but now they were laughing at us. 'Ouch ouch. *Ha ha.* Ouch!' the dogs chorussed.

Mom said in a flat small voice. 'There's something at the window.'

Against the light pollution from the A40 and the B4047, something was silhouetted through the window, a small shape an elbow high.

I knew who it would be. I couldn't breathe. My heart was pumping. It was getting lonely, my being the only one who knew things. So I wanted Mom and Faith to know who this was.

I turned on the phone flashlight. Mostly the beam caught on the oven-rack bars. But plainly, sitting on the outside ledge beyond them, was a cat.

Once she had been called Ears, but those ears were gone, and her snout was bare of flesh, so there was a grin of grey gum, and long yellow teeth. But I knew who she was and my heart thumped, and I couldn't stop myself saying, like talking to childhood, 'Lit lit lit lit Little One, Little One. Lit Lit lit lit.'

There was a wheeze and a sound like air drawn backwards, and then the cat said plainly in words. 'Lit lit lit lit Little One Little One.'

Before she was quite finished, Mom cried out.

All I felt was loss. No fear. I gave the Plaintive Meow. Even before I was infected, I could make that noise. Really I was calling for my old life, with the beautiful animals and the bees and the garden and Mom teaching me history and math, and my bull of a father who would come on weekends. And for my cat. She had been such a good friend.

She answered with the same plaintive cry but I understood it better now. It had never been just a call or a pleading or something that said *I'm sad*. The Plaintive Meow had always meant this:

Safe.

Us Safe.

Then she slipped down from the window ledge onto the roof of the lean-to. She plumped down with aplomb. Insouciant. All those lost and vanished words, words for the elegance of a cat.

In that vanished world, a few years before this, a video had gone viral (A word which just meant it spread quickly among people like a disease.) The viral video had shown a cat defending a family child against a dog that was attacking him.

Cats know family.

Suddenly from downstairs there came hissing yeowls and then yelps of dog pain and dog rage.

Traitor.

Long low cat growls, and high furious, continual cat wails, more fearsome than any dog could make. I could imagine torn ears, slashed noses. I could imagine a blur of a cat running along curtain rails, then down the curtains, and onto backs that she slashed before jumping free.

There was a chorus of ducks, the alarm sounds they make when they waddle away from danger, and then the fluttering when they try to fly.

Little One yeowled: *Go. Now. Go.*

The sound thrummed inside my chest. I couldn't resist it. Triggered, I grabbed the Bijou Chainsaw and its battery cable.

'We go now,' I said, almost as though I was sitting back and watching someone else say it.

'What?'

'She's cleared them. We have to go now. I'm going now.' I really couldn't help myself. Humans offer each other choices. Animals don't choose. I unlocked the door and opened it.

'Come on,' said Faith. 'We won't last the night. Leave it all.'

Mom must snatched up the brown bag with all our documents. I can imagine her hugging the bag to herself. From the rattling sound, I think Mr Keppel was stuffing his pockets with cartridges. I know he also took the axe.

I started up the chainsaw. Mom cried aloud, startled, fearful of it. I pushed open the door.

Someone, Mom maybe, turned on their phone light. The landing was empty. Then, out of the bathroom limped a dog, Jenny I think because what looked like a puppy foetus had healed onto her backside. Its little head lifted up. Jenny's head was lowered, her grin embarrassed, the snarl continual. I rammed the chainsaw into her skull. The blade turned sideways and skidded out through a layer of tattered skin then ground to a halt in the wall.

'Give it,' ordered Faith. She took the saw from me, wrenched it out of the wall, planted a boot on Jenny's head and with a buzzing that took a count of three sawed through the spine. Jenny stood up, her head still on the floor. Faith kicked most of her into the bathroom, and slammed the door.

Mr Keppel had the gun now, and to my surprise he looked like he knew what he was doing. I thought he had fangs, then saw he had two cartridges between his lips.

The cat yeowled from below: *Go go go*. This time we all jumped, Faith took two steps at a time in the swinging phone light. As she landed, the saw started up again and she stepped into the dark. Mr Keppel followed and there was a bolt of lightning in the room – a shotgun blast that for some reason I remember as being silent. Through the arches into the sitting room, a donkey was hee-hawing, kicking blindly, hooves smashing furniture.

I thumped down the stairs on the old tan carpet with its loose tacks – *God don't let me slip*. At the foot of the staircase, my boots went into something's rib cage but didn't get stuck because the bones were fragile, scattering when I kicked, though I slipped on gunk. Mom somehow had my arm and pulled. I could smell Mr Keppel – aftershave, beany vomit, his sweat – right next to me. As I ran another blast dazed my ears, but I could still hear a piggy squealing.

I glimpsed Charity galloping towards us. Mom hauled me into the hallway. Keppel and Faith crowded the narrow doorway, blocking it. I saw an elongated skull, bare of flesh, still able to snap and snarl.

Someone had opened the front door; there was the grey dim light of the Witney sky. I heard the toodling sound of Mom's key fob and saw flashing yellow lights unfolding at the tip of the mirrors. She flung open the back-seat door, threw in her bag and pushed me. I think I saw her dip and fling away the car's charger head. She got into the driver's seat and shouted, 'Faith. Faith!' Alone in the back seat, I heard a squealing, and the sound of the saw.

We waited, listening to our breath.

Keppel came first, still with the gun. Without asking he high-hurdled his way into the front seat and slammed the door.

Then Faith came running out, still holding the saw. She cradled into the back seat. I realized that I had the charging cable and pack clenched between my teeth. Mom started the engine and the headlights came on. In a ghostly silence the car slipped up the drive.

'Sat on Charity's back,' said Faith. 'Cut off her head. Kept kicking, so I jumped off.'

Animals filled the garden, surrounding us. Ducks raised their wings, beaks open and hissing. Two muntjac deer were nibbling each others haunches, rather delicately as if it were a shy, friendly gesture. The bloody beagles came lolloping towards us from the rear of the house, dragging half their coats behind them like a striptease act.

A tiny black and white flash blazed into the ducks and dogs, tearing their flesh, making them jump back. A path was cleared through them before the shadow darted off towards the Mountain of Ash.

'Drive through 'em,' said Faith.

We heaved up and dropped down over meat and bone. There was a bad moment when the car wheels spun as if in mud. Then the tyres seemed to find gravel again, and the car jolted forward. It rocked its way out of our gate, turning left. We drove towards the village and suddenly everything seemed silent.

In Sandy Lane at the top of the hill, something seethed in the headlights.

It looked like a person walking upright; we saw gradually, that it was woman covered in a sheet of moles and voles, small animals of many kinds.

Mom stopped the car.

'Can't do nowt,' said Faith. 'They'd be up and over us too.'

The woman didn't cry out or run. She stood for just a moment and then, in the headlights, perhaps because of the headlights, she bowed and then started to dance. First she raised her arms, then did a music-box turning on tip toe, and a leap, as if she would stay in mid-air or sail up into the stars. It was a clear night overheard.

Mom turned off the engine but kept the lights on her, and watched, I think out of respect, until in mid-swirl, the woman's knees gave away, and she spiralled softly to the ground and was still.

Then we drove on, to God knows where.

PART FOUR
Albion Close

Thirteen

The Allotments was dark, no lights at all.

Not on Mr Chukwunonso's shopfront, not in any of the houses.

'Don't go to my place,' said Faith from the back seat.

'It's no trouble. If you need to get your things.'

'There'll be trouble stopping,' said Faith. 'It's dark. There's nothing in that house I'll miss. And I didn't clean it before I left.'

We had been thinking we'd drive on past the A40 to the air base. But the horizon should have been glowing with light. For the first time since I could remember that southern sky was dark.

'Go. Somewhere,' said Faith.

Mom pulled in opposite the ghost of the store. She got out her phone – the phones back then could show you all the numbers that had called you, and let you ring those. Then she waited, listening.

Suddenly even from the back seat, I could hear a male voice shouting down the phone. Mr Keppel sitting in the front seat snorted and woke up.

'Mr,' Mom began but then broke off. 'Is?' The voice kept shouting. Mom pulled the phone back and looked at the screen, then lowered it without saying goodbye.

'Brize Norton has no power. And that hangar – something's happening. I think they're being attacked. Mr Day just kept shouting "Stay away, stay away!".'

"Radio," said Faith. Mom snapped it on.

Witney had a thin-voiced radio station of its own. An older man with an Essex accent was speaking. 'Given this is a local emergency, yhe police advise that people stay in their homes and lock their doors. It's not clear why the power has failed. But sick animals are on the streets in the dark and they are attacking people. We're getting horrific reports of people being attacked in their own homes. We here at Witney Radio will keep on bringing you news and developments. Right now, we are listening to your stories.'

We were an opinionated people.

We thought opinions were like magic spells; they changed things through words alone. Amber or Fiona or Eddie or Jasper came on the radio, asking why the police couldn't just shoot the animals or why did it take government so long to act?

Why haven't the military on the base come to help? Where are the police? It seems to me, that this is a direct result of austerity.

To answer your last caller, it's more like all these immigrants coming in with diseases. I saw a Romanian by a caravan—

Excuse me don't you mean a traveller, a Romany?

Whatever, but the point is, he was living in a caravan with no facilities and a dog.

'That vegan in Oldminster saw what was going on. He tried to burn his dogs.'

'Yes,' said the announcer, 'and he's now one of the people who are missing.'

Mom turned it off.

Faith said, 'We can't stay in the countryside.'

Long pause, from all of us.

Faith explained. 'It's full of livestock, not to mention wild beasties. We've got to get out.'

'Where? Where can we go?' Mr Keppel's hands rose and fell helplessly.

Faith sniffed. 'Someplace where there's no trees. I'd've said that was Brize Norton, but it's gone.'

Mom stretched round to look at me, her face set. 'London,' she said, bunching up, her mouth twisting. I hadn't seen that expression on her face before. 'I'm part owner of a flat in London. It *is* my flat. Someone else is living in it right now. But it's not his flat.'

Her eyes were on mine, and I knew what was coming.

'Okay,' I said. 'I hope he likes it.'

'I don't care what he likes,' said Mom, and started the car. We drove the half mile through the dark to the on ramp for the A40 and headed east.

I was glad that we had driven out of Oldminster in the dark.

I didn't have to say goodbye. I didn't have to feel that the village with its fields and ruins and river would always now be stained with terror.

Instead I felt like I'd been packed full of pollyfilla that had got wet and then dried. I was stuffed to the point I couldn't move. I couldn't cry, I couldn't think.

It was summer and dawn dragged itself over the horizon at about five am. You wouldn't expect to see many cars at that hour even on the Witney-Oxford road, which was one of the worst in the country. Today there were no cars at all.

The fields began to look muddy brown. The sky was full of dust, a dim bronze colour. Already you feel the heat stored in the fields ready to glow again.

As we circled around the Woodstock Road Roundabout, Faith started to say something. As we left it, we saw three cows on the grassy verge. There was an access road where houses were lined up parallel to the main road. The windows looked too dark. The cows lifted their heads. When I tried to focus on their faces, there seemed to be something in my eyes. They began to lope alongside us.

But I was not making my warning noises. Didn't that mean we were okay?

'Speed up,' said Faith.

'The light ahead's red.'

'Go through it,' said Faith.

I heard a kind of clopping sound behind us but I couldn't move to turn my head.

'The cows are after us,' said Faith.

'Cows?' Mom sounded amused, like it was one of Faith's jokes.

Something rammed Mr Keppel's side of the car. He jumped with hooting sound.

'You betcha,' said Faith.

I once befriended a bullock who'd been grazing all summer in the next field – number seventy-two stapled to his ear. He liked to gambol and have his nose rubbed. I remembered how big seventy-two got, how heavy he was the day he trod on my foot and I realized I was afraid of him.

A beat to allow the world to change, and then Mom accelerated. She started to beep the horn over and over and roared onto the roundabout against the light.

There was no traffic; she need not have worried. Our car wobbled a bit, as it entered the main ring road.

'Can you see anything?' Mom asked arching backwards.

'Bessies don't like to run,' said Faith. She chortled. 'Hard on the udders.' She was looking behind us. 'Oops. One of the udder's come off. Bouncing on the road.' I couldn't tell if she was joking.

We accelerated away. And once again me and Faith started laughing. Mr Keppel roared and wheezed and cackled and rocked back and forth in his seat. We laughed until we wept.

We sped along a road that by-passed Oxford.

Main roads in those days didn't have crossroads. You could only drive in one direction at a time, and it was divided with barriers down the middle, with low trees all along it and down the central divide. At five-ten am, it was almost full daylight, but still not another car on the road.

Suddenly in the central divide, a woman leaned out of the bushes, waving her arms for us to stop, her mouth working. Mom slowed. We didn't know her, but we recognised the terror in her face – we must have looked the same running from our house.

'Make room,' Mom said to us and eased the car to a halt. She put on emergency lights that flashed to traffic behind as the electronic windows wound down. Mom shouted, 'Get in.'

The woman stopped, looked around, clasped a hand to her forehead and looked even more frantic. She shouted a name. 'My little girl,' she wailed. 'She was just here! Evie? Evie!'

'Get into the car.' Mom said to her quietly.

'Evie!'

A young kid was crying somewhere. The mother roared in anger and thrust her way back through the hedge. Mom started to beep her horn over and over. Faith said. 'Nowt coming behind.'

The mother burst through the bushes again dragging a little girl in blue trousers and orange sweater. The mother shook her and jerked her towards the car. 'I told you. Stay with me.' The child wailed louder. Faith darted out of the back seat, grabbed the child and hoisted her over the grey metal barrier. Clumsy, shaking, the mother folded herself over the divide.

Faith crammed into the back seat, pushing me into the arm-rest, lifting the child in with her. Jittering, the mother bundled herself in, saying thank you, thank you.

'Shut the door,' said Mom, anger flaring in her face. 'Shut—' But at that moment it slammed shut. The auto-stop coughed back to life and the car dragged slowly away. In panic Mom slammed the car into reverse instead of drive.

'My book,' wailed the little girl.

'You can't do that, Evie. I told you leave everything.'

The car jerked forward. I couldn't move. It was like I had to hibernate. It was like I was actually dead and dreaming all of this.

The little girl fondled her book which was very thick with a blue cover.

'Atsa lovely book,' said Faith next to her.

'It's my *Frozen* book,' said the little girl (*Frozen* was a movie for children, moving pictures, about not one princess but two. I'd never seen *Frozen*. In those days, everything was made spangled and rich for children.) 'It folds out,' the little girl said. She opened her book and cardboard fanned out into castles, with doors that would open, and a snowman who started to dance when you turned the page.

Her mother said again, 'Thank you, thank you so much.' Her voice was teary. 'There were no cars, nothing, nobody to help.'

'Were you attacked?' Mom asked as the car gained speed.

'The neighbour's dogs,' said the woman. 'I don't know what's going on.'

Mom said, 'With us it was our own dogs and a very large pig.'

The child pulled a tag and the picture of a palace of ice rose up as if it were growing from the snow-white paper.

'My goodness will ya look at that,' said Faith. 'Do you like girly things then?'

'Sometimes,' said the child, calm now.

The mother fluttered a hand to her chest. She was wearing just a black halter top and must have been cold at five am even in summer. 'Oh I'm sorry, I'm Dani McKenzie and this is my little girl Evie. Say hi Evie,'

'Hello.'

'I really don't know what we would have done. Thank you so much for stopping.'

Mom said it was nothing and introduced us. We all said hello. Well, I didn't. I was pollyfilla. 'We were saved by our cat,' I said. I felt like I was floating. 'Basically she saved me. Because she knew me from six years old and that made me a family responsibility. I know she didn't feel the same about Dad.'

Mom sounded bitter. 'My son's not himself. Got a bit of a fever.'

'We're all poorly,' said the woman. 'I don't know what's going on. It's manic. Dogs attacking people.'

I told her what I'd heard in the howling. 'The dogs are staking out new territories. Those territories are based on our houses. They understand houses and plots of land now. We're all they've got, so they are all rivals for resources. Which are us.' I thought that I was actually saying this out loud, but I couldn't be too sure, as I couldn't tell if my mouth were moving or not.

I kept on like the car engine. 'They're all exchanging signals and cries so all the animals are starting to sound like each other. They can talk to each other. And they can sound like us. So they must be growing new parts of their brains or something. Like I am.'

Nobody seemed to respond, so maybe I was dreaming. Or dead.

'And new throats as well. Maybe I've been eaten and I just woke up inside an animal's head.'

Mom said, 'Teddy. There's a little girl with us now. Her name's Evie. No need to scare her.'

Dani said, 'Evie didn't see nothing, thank God. My neighbour tried to run. I saw her dogs on top of her.'

I said, as a cold, clear statement of fact, 'They were going for the head.'

Mom got angry. 'Teddy. I told you. Quiet.'

'Sure Mom,' I said. *We'll be quiet enough when we're dead.*

Evie was looking up at me with solemn blue eyes. *I know what you're talking about.*

We drove east towards London on a thing called a motorway.

It was even faster than a bypass. So few roads crossed it that there were only nine junctions between Oxford and London. Those were the only places you could get off. You couldn't even turn around, but you could drive very fast – my memory is a hundred miles per hour, but that can't be true.

There was one problem going east. There were numbered exits eight then seven, then six. But if you were going towards London, for some reason there was no exit seven. You had to go all the way to junction six, to the foot of the Chiltern hills.

We drove into what was already a hot, baking day on an empty M40 – which even at five-thirty am would normally have had streams of traffic. In distance an escarpment loomed, blue with haze, the steep slope of Stokenchurch Hill. Ahead of us on the flat there was a kind of rumpled tangle. Something sparkled in sunlight.

'Accident,' said Faith.

'I see it,' said Mom.

We drew closer. Some cars were flashing rear orange lights (This was to show they were slowing the car down or stopping). Ahead of us, mostly unlit, was a mass of cars, unmoving. Breakdancing between them, moving in jerks and jolts or dropping down on twisted limbs and standing again was a herd of sheep with horses among them.

'Get off at the next exit,' said Faith.

'There isn't one,' said Mom, 'not til you get to the hill.'

A sheep trotted towards us, grinning. It looked stoved-in, its spine in a U shape. It could only walk sideways, its rear legs walking faster than its front.

A horse picked its way across the central divide. It had a beautiful brown-orange mane and a flattened chest about as narrow as its spine. What I thought had been white markings turned out to be its bare ribs.

A flashing car stopped, then backed up at speed towards us. Mom braked, fought to find reverse and couldn't. The reversing car roared towards us, then spun all the way around. Its front end swung in an arc, smashing into our left headlight and bumper. Someone screamed. The man in the driver's seat looked at us, looking frantic.

Mom went roared the car forward by mistake.

Dani shouted 'Turn around turn around.'

Mom U-turned the car to face the other way. Our car had something called autostop – which turned the engine off to say save charge. Mom had to fight to start the car again, calling it, 'This bloody thing.'

All the animals, the sheep, the horses the cows were grinning – their lips had gone. The car whispered and Mom accelerated away, gathering speed back along the motorway in the wrong direction. One tyre was scraping against metal, making a dragging sound and pulling the car to the left. Something thumped us and I heard glass crack.

Dani screamed 'You're going the wrong way!'

'The only way off is to get back to junction eight.'

'Get off the road.'

Mom was calm. 'We're on the hard shoulder. We're flashing. If oncoming cars have any sense they'll realize there's trouble up ahead. Teddy. Have you got your phone? Can you call the police and tell them. Tell them the motorway is blocked in both directions by a mass of vehicles that were stopped by animals?'

I thought: *Why is everyone so worried?*

We all enter the ecosystem as dust and protein anyway. If we're buried, the worms get us and the birds get the worms and foxes eat the birds. We become foxes, running free.

'We're all werewolves.' I said in passing.

'Better let me,' said Faith and took my phone.

'Oh Teddy,' said Mom in despair.

I listened without interest to Faith telling someone that we couldn't get through, it looked like the motorway was blocked. We were being chased by sheep and horses, farm livestock.

'They say the back roads are the same,' said Faith. 'It's happening everywhere. Cows and horses, big animals mostly. Dogs of course, dogs in packs.'

Another car drove towards us. Our lights were flashing; then theirs started too, we waved our hands up and down to warn them.

Faith was giving the police a running commentary. 'There's still people heading into it. You might want to warn them. We're playing dodgems driving the wrong way on the motorway.' Faith made a hissing chuckle. Then. 'The police hung up on me.' She made a surprisingly high hee-hee-hee laugh. 'Wouldn't be the first time they done that. You should have heard her voice. Playing dodgems. Hahahaha.'

Even Mom squawked as she hauled the car out of the path of a howling oncoming van.

'Is your house easy to defend?' Mom asked Dani.

'Well, the dogs got in. But its flood-proofed you know, high up off the ground on stilts.' Dani paused. 'It's a trailer actually. But it's got a flat roof you can sit on. We have a step ladder you can pull up after you.'

Mom suddenly indicated and the car wobbled. She swept off the motorway, leaving on the on-ramp, going the wrong way, beeping and flashing. We were all right all the way across the bridge over the main road and most of the approach, but as we rounded the curve, a car came roaring towards us. It flashed its lights and beeped its horn and I could see the driver shouting 'Idiot'. He was headed straight for us.

Just there, the real off-ramp merged on the left, and Mom veered onto the right side of the road.

'Well done,' said Mr Keppel, croaking.

Mom slowed down to thirty. She was panting, her mouth in a thin line. The car sighed its way through two roundabouts towards the Oxford Services. I knew them – they had a Waitrose and a Tesla supercharger.

Mom said in a small sad voice. 'I left the charger cable behind.'

Dani said, 'There's no charging point near me anyway.'

'I just tossed it away from the car and drove.'

Faith said. 'I don't hear anybody blaming you.'

'We'll run out of juice. And we need food.' Her voice was as pale as her voice, near tears.

Oxford Services was jammed with cars.

Cars had formed a circle around the chargers to wait – there was a row of them just to the right of what looked like a main entrance. I'd never seen cars used as fortifications before. They were like musk oxen around a fallen calf. A man stood guard on a car roof with an axe. Mom stopped opposite him. 'Have they come?'

The man worked out her question then answered. 'Yeah. But not since sunrise. It takes everybody half an hour to charge, so we figured we'd make a barrier. Form an orderly queue like.'

The main bank of chargers were further round to the east, but these were next to a canopy that was, I think, supposed to be shaped like a wave.

'I left my charging cable behind.' Mom covered her forehead with her hand.

'You can use ours,' said the man. 'If it will fit yours. We're not going back home, are we Kylie?' A good-looking woman with sun hat and shades leaned out.

'We'll still need the cable, Jason.'

'Well yeah, I'm just saying that we won't be needing our cable for home.'

Mom intervened. 'We're not going home either. And we wouldn't dream of keeping your cable.' The sun was still low, but fierce, right in our eyes. Mom shaded hers. 'I don't suppose there's somewhere here we could buy a new one?'

Jason was quite handsome with a gingerish beard and muscles running a little to fat. 'I think buying and selling is a thing of the past.'

Nothing I've heard since tolled the changes as simply as that.

Mom put the car in park. 'Right everybody out and we stick together. Faith, bring the shotgun.'

'We should save on ammo,' said Faith. She held up the chainsaw. 'Got the cable for this though.'

Mom jabbed me. 'Teddy, move your butt. I know you're tired but we need to carry things. Come on. MOVE!'

I stirred myself. I heard her open the boot and make a little noise of despair. 'No shopping bags.'

Mr Keppel limped round to the boot as well, and got out the jack and the tools 'I'll just straighten that panel, save the tyre.' He had turned out to be some use.

Mom pulled me along by the collar, but she was also, without quite realising it, leaning on me for support.

I felt as if my clothes had been coated in concrete which had set and dried. My feet shuffled.

'Fight it Teddy,' said Mom. She could see I was sick again.

What the hell do you know?

The whole world buzzed. My vision was a bit blurred. And I kept straining, not to see, but to do something that was not there. I was trying to smell food, trace the scent.

There was the beautiful wavy canopy that promised a shopper's paradise.

Little Waitrose
WELCOME BREAK

The signs outside seemed to glow. The expanse of pavement around us was vast. Why why why did people want to flatten everything? Just to walk on it? Maybe having only two feet meant they fell over more easily.

SEATING FOR 600 PEOPLE. said the sign.

Established 1998.

Faith grunted. 'Ended 2025.'

The glass of the sliding doors was broken. There was a constant whirring sound of automatic doors trying to open, jammed by the shards on the pavement.

At the doorway Evie made a whimpering noise. *I'm just a puppy don't hurt me.*

She was a nice little girl who also spoke dog, and there was something simple and neat about her. And she liked books. I took her hand. Deep and dark, something rumbled out of me, something big but totally unaware that I was small for my age, skinny, and scared. The growling was a warning to other dogs to keep away, keep away from our cubs.

We ducked through the broken glass doors into Welcome Break Oxford.

Everything in the sunlit, luxury forecourt designed for your ease and comfort was either shuttered or broken.

Just inside the door was The Little Waitrose, which was very little. It would have carried sandwiches, fresh fruit cups, hot chicken sweltering under glass, pot-o-noodles, aspirin, travel supplies and in one corner a selection of vegetables 'picked daily for freshness' that had been flown from Kenya.

Now it was empty. Glass underfoot sparkled like winter. There was a long smear of blood across the floor. Someone had cut their hand? Or maybe a body had been dragged over it.

Evie whimpered. I kept up a low growl. From outside came a clattering somewhere off towards the Krispy Kreme Donuts stand. I turned and barked. I shook Evie's hand. *The adults can't do this.*

It needs young brains.

Mom was overstretched 'There's no food.'

'Did animals do this or people?' Dani wondered.

'Same thing,' I said in a hollow voice.

We heard a shouting from outside. 'Get away. Get away.' It was Mr Keppel's voice. I turned and seemed to wade through mud. Outside, a Labrador, fat with fur in damaged strips, had hold of Mr Keppel's leg.

Jason on the roof was shouting, and the circle of cars started beeping their horns and flashing their lights. I knew it would not be long until more dogs arrived, drawn by the Labrador who was signalling.

Good food. Good food.

I dragged myself as fast as I could but for some reason my feet wouldn't get off the ground. So I shuffled, got closer, and with no conscious thought, gave a low threatening snarl. *Mine. Leave.*

The Labrador growled back but Labradors are big softies. I could tell its flesh would rot soon. So I came on strong, my growl saying *I am very confident.*

 Behind me I heard Faith start up the little red chainsaw.

I am more and more confident.

My pack.

I began to bark more, over and over, sharper and sharper. *I am winning. Go.*

Little Evie joined in with a high sharp bark. *We are winning. Go.*

Go go go go go.

The Labrador hopped and limped away. Softie. It left behind that minty stench. I could see the dog was all open and buzzing with flies around the backside. Flies would be doing a great job of spreading the marsupia.

Mr Keppel rolled himself back to his feet. 'Nearly done,' he said, shaking. He didn't say anything about the attack. He had somehow pulled enough metal clear of our front tyre.

Both Evie and I stopped the hound music.

'What the hell's happened to our kids?' Dani asked.

'It's the disease,' said Mom.

Faith turned off the chain saw and crouched next to the tyre. 'Good job,' she said to Mr Keppel.

'In Iraq,' he said, out of nowhere. 'You had to keep your car going yourself. I once changed a carburettor in a sandstorm.'

I was too buzzing to think to ask him what he'd been doing in Iraq.

Faith put a hand on my forehead. 'Teddy's burning up,' she said.

Mom also felt my forehead, tutted, sagged, shrugged. We were all sick. What could she do?

We all got back inside the Kia. 'Lock the doors,' Mom said. She got out her phone and dialled.

'Who are you calling?' Faith asked.

'The AA,' said Mom as if it were obvious. (The AA was a business that sent out vans to repair cars in trouble. You phoned them and they came. Unless of course you weren't rich enough to subscribe, you were at home, or you'd tried to commit suicide.)

Faith started to laugh. 'Good luck with that.'

Mom hugged herself, gathering in scraps of hope.

She keyed in the options and then pronounced her name, then gave her membership number. 'I'm afraid I've lost my charging cable. How long until you can get here with a spare? Yes, I know. The roads are blocked. Oh great, thank you. How long?'

We sat and waited. Mom turned on the radio.

BBC Oxford was saying that the John Ratcliffe Hospital had asked the public to only go to A&E in the case of life-threatening injuries. The facilities were overwhelmed. The Frank Churchill hospital complex nearby was treating people in their cars.

If you feel unwell please stay at home. Keep all doors and windows locked. It's difficult in this heat, but as you've just heard, Oxford is being overwhelmed by animal attacks.

Foxes had tackled and carried off an elderly lady walking her dog. A child was attacked in its bed by the family pet who'd been asleep in its room. A meat packing plant had been found empty, its doors broken down from inside.

We're getting reports of livestock blocking cars in both directions at the foot of Stokenchurch Hill. You are advised to avoid both the A40 and M40. Again the advice from the Oxfordshire Constabulary is stay at home, don't go into your gardens and close and lock all doors and windows.

If you see any animal at all, get inside as soon as possible. Domestic pets and livestock are especially dangerous.

We needed water.

I very nearly said that in dog – there is a water bark, but it's ambiguous. It can signal that you've found water and might bring thirsty dogs nearer.

I kept sniffing, but my nose had gone deaf.

Evie made a yipping noise. *Go hunting.*

I told Mom in words (I think), 'I'm going to get water.' Before the adults could stop us, both Evie and I ducked out of the car. Faith loped after us with the chainsaw. I looked back, and Mom was leaning forward with her hand over her eyes. She might have been asleep.

PIZZA EXPRESS was an independent building next to the main entrance. Its door had been kicked in and almost all the food taken, but in the back of a fridge I found some milk and four bottles of Italian mineral water and a packet of pre-sliced pepperoni. Meat. Evie and I fell on it. I snarled: *Me first male and bigger.*

I was no longer a vegan.

We went back to the car, and my mother said, 'Thank God.' Maybe because we were safe, maybe because we'd found water.

'We can refill these in the toilets,' said Faith.

We waited. The sun got hotter.

Cars came and went. Jason with the axe said sorry, but he really needed to get going. He waved goodbye and drove off with his cable.

After two maybe three hours, the AA man arrived.

The fourth emergency service. He jumped out in full protective gear and a clear face screen. 'Margaret Spilling?' he asked cheerfully.

'Spaulding. Yes that's me.'

'A spare charging cable for a Kia Neo, yes? Do you want both formats of that.'

'Both,' said Mom, blinking.

'Good. Don't let the face screen alarm you, it protects both of us. Just say if you can't hear me. Now. We've been asked to help carry out some tests. Strictly voluntary, but would you be willing to give blood samples?'

We all blinked.

'The Department of Health have asked us to help get an idea of the spread of the pathogen. All data are anonymous and kept in confidence by the Department of Health. I would remind you that are putting other people at risk by breaking quarantine. That's why you're of interest.' The clear screen meant I could see that he had goofy teeth. He took out a clipboard. 'Contact name and address?' Like he was signing us up for cable TV.

'We don't have a home,' said Mom. But then gave him the details of Beehive Cottage.

'Mobile telephone number?'

We gave him details and he printed out on a hand-held device, little labels which he wrapped around test tubes.

'Have you been attacked?' Mom asked him.

'Oh yes. Hold still. You'll be amazed how screwing up delicate wing nuts can train you to find a vein. Develops digital finesse.'

'By dogs?' Mom asked again, but he blinked in confusion. 'Were you attacked by dogs?'

'No. By an alpaca as it happens. Completely off its head. A lady had kept it for craft wool out by Abingdon. It had already eaten her. Her husband just wanted a lift away from the place. I told him that we only guarantee to get you home, and he was already home. But. Under the circumstances. I was driving through Hailey anyway so I dropped him off at his sister's. There we go. All done. You should have test results by text message in two days, but to be honest – nearly everybody tests positive.'

'So it's an epidemic.'

'Whoo yeah. Six-months incubation period, close personal contact not necessarily, spread by just breath on a surface. Are your children making animal noises?'

Dani covered her mouth like she was trying to block words.

'Well that's normal. Didn't use to be of course. The current thinking is that it's transfer of genetic material back from the animals into humans. Seems to do permanent damage only to kids. Younger brains grow into it, like. You all right to get home, ladies?'

'We don't have a home,' Mom repeated.

'I do,' said Dani. She repeated her address – 5 Albion Close.

'Well, in that case I'll be on my way. Would you mind filling in our customer satisfaction survey? Also for you today, these leaflets are about our special offer for continuing customers, holiday getaways. Though. To be honest, I don't think you'll be allowed to go anywhere. Ah. You're asked to report any new symptoms to the phone number on your printed receipts – fever, barking like a dog, marking territory by peeing, biting other people. Please stay at home until notified. The hospitals are full so don't even think of going to them. Now is there anything else I can help you with? Have a lovely day. The sun is still out. The birds are still singing.'

'And eating people,' said Faith.

'Only some species of birds. Not hens from some reason. Most songbirds don't seem to be getting ill. Carrion birds don't seem to get sick either. Aquatic poultry are the worst. You should see what the swans at Swinbrook did to the people holed up in the pub. Dreadful. Looked like a war. It's got a lot of history, Swinbrook you know. Mitford family.'

'Do you think you could just clear off?' said Faith. 'With our thanks.'

'I'm a bit scared actually,' said the AA man. 'My name's Oliver. Call me Olly. This is my number. Just call if you want a chat.' He looked around at the circle of cars and called out. 'Anybody else having a problem? I don't care if you're AA members or not.'

We left him there.

Fourteen

So what would they hide behind a row of trees along Oxford Ring Road?

A trailer park.

Dani gave us clear, crisp directions or we never would have found it: off the bypass at the Marston exit. 'Do a U turn please, yeah like you're going back onto the bypass. There'll be a left. Just here.'

Then a right, then a left, then a right, then a right, and finally we arrived at Albion Close.

The Albion Mobile Home Estate was a one-way loop that circled back on itself. It wasn't large – there were maybe twenty-two of the more permanent looking homes lining the main circle. They tried to look like they hadn't been hauled there on flatbed trucks. The homes were all painted the same shade of toned-down yellow, trimmed with hedges and hung with flower boxes. The one on the corner opposite had a white bird bath designed to look like a fountain.

Dani was jammed into a far corner with five other boxes on wheels. I think the proper name for these was caravans and not trailers. They'd been left at slight angles to each other and had no defined yards or driveways. Cars were parked at cross purposes on hot, broken asphalt.

Dani's place was flat roofed and small, with a tricycle left out front and what looked like a giant plastic pretzel.

'I don't live in Buckingham Palace,' said Dani.

Faith grunted. 'A Chihuahua could punch its way into that.'

'How did you know?' Dani asked. 'Horrible little things. I saw them off with a broom.'

Faith stretched out of the back seat carrying the saw and scanning for danger. Mom grunted trying to rock herself to her feet, and looked like someone had slapped her.

Dani was playing host. 'We've got a fridge full of food and the power's off. Pity to waste it.'

Mom suddenly sagged. 'We had a generator. I left that too.' Mom kept finding reasons to grieve.

'All of us left it, not just you,' said Faith.

Inside, the trailer was crammed with a two-piece fluffy suite. It was beige like a giant cat. There was just enough room to squeeze sideways past it. One wall was a flatscreen TV. Evie slept on a kind of shelf above the kitchen. The kitchen would have fitted into a submarine, but had cupboards, a stove and a fridge so tall and thin, you'd need an anamorphic lens to see it as a fridge (Sorry, I can't explain everything). Mom dropped onto the sofa and hit her head on a shelf. Mr Keppel was slightly stuck getting up the steps. Still sitting on the sofa, Faith was able to reach out, take his hand and drag him inside.

Part of me still thought Mr Keppel was dead weight, something that slowed the pack. I thought he put us in danger.

A sharp piercing shriek escaped me. It didn't sound like a dog cry, but it was. It was not a voice that dogs use with people. It was a sound that told old dogs to die, die so the pack could live. The sound was so loud and so terrible that Mom squealed and covered her ears. Almost as if she had understood it. Evie gave me a hug. I started to scratch the back of her head.

Mr Keppel blinked and stood up. He could stand up inside – he was both short and skinny. He'd been born in nineteen-forty and spent his childhood eating carrots. History repeats.

'Thank you for that,' he told me. 'I feel so much better. Like a bubble in my head just went pop. Quite my old self again.'

'What did you do?' Mom asked me.

'I told the dog in him to die. That it was no use struggling.'

Evie said, lisping. 'It doesn't work with people.'

'It does when they are part dog and don't know it,' I answered.

Dani and Mom just stared at us. I heard a buzzing, and I could smell cold somehow.

'Did you know that your fridge is on?' I asked Dani.

Somehow power had been restored to Oxford.

Out came the food, still cold. The ice cream was soft but chill.

Dani made a show of smacking her lips. She was good at keeping Evie amused. 'As Bert Simpson says. Life is short, start with dessert.'

We all had a dish of Cookie Dough ice cream, and it was like the real world had come back. Maybe things would get back to normal. (Bert Simpson was an obnoxious cartoon character. Cartoons were supposed to be sweet for kids, but this one was cynical for adults. So children enjoyed it even more.)

Mom fried up onions and mushrooms with bits of stale bread and ketchup. It sat on the plate looking bloody but it smelled of straw and other people's armpits. It was not as good as Cookie Dough ice cream.

What I saw in my head were other tins. My feet began to scuff. 'I don't suppose you have any Whiskas?' I asked.

'No, no we don't have a cat.'

'Any dog food?' I could see the tin's labels and imagine the meaty smell. I started to drool. 'Maybe next door has dog food?'

'The Chihuahuas are still there.'

Mom's face filled my vision. 'You will fight this. Whatever it is. *You will stay you.* You are a vegan. The one time you tried to eat beef, you threw it up. Dog food is muck. I wouldn't feed it to a dog, and I'm certainly not going to feed it to you.' She pushed the bowl of stale armpit at me. 'This is what we eat. You will enjoy it.'

I was too exhausted to fight, so I dug in the spoon and the stuff seemed to evaporate on my tongue and then boil back as something else. It became delicious too. It was the taste of home and family from the previous era, when Dad would call from a treetop that he was coming down to eat. My doggy brain went back to its corner, slumped down onto its blanket.

The trouble with being human again was that grief flooded in.

Home was gone. Dad was gone. Except that it was like I could almost hear him troop up the tin steps; like he'd gone out to get bird feed and had come back and was going to say, 'Teddy I've got a delivery in Bath next weekend, want to come?'

I kept thinking about how he'd disappeared. Maybe he'd escaped up a tree. He could climb trees better than any dog. Maybe he was still stuck up a tree. Or maybe he'd climbed down and got back in the house, was waiting for us. All alone and wondering where we were.

I ate the home-cooked food and a slow tear crept down my face. Mom gave me a hug.

Dani turned on her TV.

How they loved their news. Somehow their own lives were made more real by being reported on TV.

I remember a phone video of a dog pack running through a branch of Debenhams. That morning's A40 carnage was caught on screen by someone else's mobile. Whoever held the phone screamed as a bullock rammed itself against a bumper over over until it pulped its own head. 'Why isn't it dead? Why isn't it dying?' said the phone witness, sobbing.

Eventually the attack stopped and most of the drivers who stayed safe in their cars were able to drive out of the melee. Police then blocked the M40, and also blocked all A and B roads between Oxfordshire, Gloucestershire and Berkshire.

Mom looked glum. 'We couldn't get to London even if we wanted to.'

Didcot power station had been stormed by the RAF.

And blow me, if it wasn't Oldminster's own RAF Squadron Leader being interviewed again, looking embarrassed and amused at the same time (except for a livid gash across his forehead). 'Well, something had been eating through the cable. I tell you they must have got a powerful shock, because they chewed the wire through. And they must have gone on chewing while being electrocuted.'

'How is that possible?' the reporter asked.

'If you've seen these things, you can cut off their heads and they still keep coming. I mean there is absolutely nothing you can do if they come for you.'

He laughed heartily, the palm of his hand flattened across the gash on his forehead.

'Then how did you escape?'

He laughed louder. 'Military fire power. The bits kept crawling, mind you.' His smile was suddenly queasy.

What he didn't say was that the animals must have known enough to kill the electricity.

Long scheduled, the film that night was *Dr Doolittle* about someone who talked to animals. 'Turn it off,' said Mom, her voice icy.

I don't remember Dani saying we could stay. I don't remember there being any discussion about it. I guess it just seemed like there was safety in numbers.

Exhausted, all of us climbed up onto the trailer's roof, and pulled the ladder up after us. Across Oxford dogs howled, cats cried, all of them hunting. Things snuffled around the base of the trailer. I leaned out and saw scampering or prowling or crouching shadows. Faith, Mom, and Dani took turns watching. Mom handled the shotgun like it was a Ming vase

In the morning, I was jerked awake by a kind of dawn chorus played backwards, a disjointed range of creatures crying in distress, hunger, confusion, rage. From the top of the trailer, I howled at all the animals: *SHUT UP.*

And they did. I got five minutes silence, and that was enough to sleep more.

I woke up feeling clear headed. Everything felt stronger. My heels seemed to have carbon fibre tendons. My energy was back. Mom felt my forehead. 'The fever's gone,' she said.

Evie and I played with her *Frozen* book. A reindeer splayed out of the cartoon pages, and the sudden animal movement made me jump. Evie squealed with glee.

Dani wanted so much to make everything lovely for her. Dani kept making desserts – rice mixed with jam, fried bread with sugar. She dressed Evie up in party dresses, with cardboard tiaras. Evie was always in pink, and Dani was always saying, 'Evie you look so beautiful.'

Evie would wait til Dani wasn't listening. 'Are you still barking?' she whispered.

'I think so. But I never know when I'm going to do it.'

'Me neither.'

'It's like breathing, you don't have to think about it.'

Life was boring, but boring felt necessary. Mom cooked pasta with bits of tinned veg in it. The news kept saying that food deliveries would resume soon. How, with all the roads barricaded?

Pretty much every country in the world had banned travel by Britons. They'd had some practice with pandemics, so the airports were quickly closed and flights grounded. I had the impression some people enjoyed shutting out the Brits. 'So,' said one Belgian official. 'They will just have to stay to their little island and do the best they can.'

Underneath it all was an ache, as stubborn as an underwear stain on a long car trip. Sometimes I couldn't give it a name. Sometimes it was just one word, circling endlessly: *Dad Dad Dad Dad Dad.*

It was selfish of me. I wished I'd seen his dead body. Awful as that would have been, it would have eased me. I daydreamed that I'd walked through the fields that day, but that I found him. Twisted, gnawed but in his tartan shirt and working boots. I would have seen it. I would gather him up. I would cry. I would carry him home. Mom and I would look at photos. I could send him off to the next world, bury him under the lime tree with its hive.

I needed to know what had happened to him. I needed to know where he was. If he was going to stay silent forever, I needed to see that silence.

The need wouldn't go away. In the long airless baking sweaty days inside that caravan, the need just got worse.

People are events.

If you are cut off from people, then nothing happens. Each hot baking day swelled into the next. I got sick of filling in Evie's colouring books with her. I got bored of the Disney-princess DVDs which she loved with memorising devotion. With exhausting powers of concentration, Eve could recite all the dialogue along with the movie – and then select replay.

In self-defence, I suggested to Mom that we take up my home schooling again. We were still stuck on algebra. I remember the moment when I realized Mom couldn't teach it because she didn't really understand it. I turned to an online encyclopedia but it seemed more interested in telling me the history of algebra than in telling me how to do it.

So I went back to playing with Evie.

She was five years younger than me, and so she didn't trigger my fear of kids my own age.

This fear was my dirty secret, my greatest shame. My worst moments had come whenever Mom or Dad noticed it – a sideways flicker of the eyes. 'Is there a friend you'd like to come fishing with us, Teddy?' The answer had always been a shame-faced 'No.'

So I went back to Evie's colouring books, faking it a bit, but at least I was being of some use, giving Dani a break, so it made at least two other people on the planet happier.

Evie had a magic book where all you had to do was rub the surface of the Princess dress and the blue or pink would come through. I would have preferred Star Wars.

And sometimes she would whisper. 'You speak cat, too. I wish I spoke cat.'

'I like both. My cat was special.'

'I wish I had a cat. Why don't you speak more cat than dog?'

I shook my head. 'No idea. We had five dogs and only one cat? Maybe?'

When dogs barked we both looked up and I knew we'd both tried to raise our ears. I could hear her sniffing. I'd catch her eye and she'd grin. We both kept it disguised. We knew it worried the adults. We knew we were different from them, like we'd grown up in different countries.

In fact, we had. Well, more like in different worlds.

Dani liked being spelled on childcare, lolling her head back against the giant fluffy cushions. 'Thank God they get along so well.'

'We're very lucky,' Mom agreed but she looked worried. I'd turned ten in May and I was playing with a six-year-old girl.

At nights, the universe yawned open.

The loss of my Dad would not let me sleep. The night had teeth and it chewed me over and over like gum. Where was Dad? What had happened? How had he died? Why was the car door closed? Why was there no sign of a struggle? Why why why would he have left the car? Maybe he had been kidnapped by crazy people – we'd never heard back from the police. I got silly fears – did the marsupia mean he was dead and couldn't move but could still roast in the sun, feel pain, feel cold? Were dogs eating him and did he know it?

And I was mad at him. I had fantasies where I told him to stay away from my beans. 'We don't need you,' I'd tell him. 'Go back to Ken and stay there.' I hated him for leaving us.

It was the heat, the marsupia coming back again and again in waves of fever that did nothing to fight the disease. It was also grief – I stopped eating. I had no interest in food.

Most distressing of all, when it got too much I would just start to howl, over and over, howl like a wolf at the moon in that tiny caravan.

Mom's face would crumple and she'd take my hands and plead. 'Please stop Teddy, please just stop. Come back, Teddy. Please come back.' She hid her head.

The propaganda on TV was relentless. There was the THANKS FOR STAYING PUT campaign. STAY SAFE – CLOSE WINDOWS.

An Oxfordshire farmer had built a seven-foot wall around his cattle sheds to pen in his livestock. 'There's no point killing them. You can't kill them,' he said his eyes staring, looking slightly mad. 'You shoot them, nothing happens. And they come at you more like wolves than cattle.'

The cows glared balefully at the camera, heads down like they were going to charge, something manic in their eyes. 'I haven't fed them in five days. No water. They're still standing.'

'Are you starving them to death?' the reporter asks.

The farmer has a strange kind of calm about him. 'They're already dead. Something else is making them move.'

Finally someone had said it.

Television for me like someone telling you a bad joke, elbowing you over and over and saying *see, get it?* The same news items circulated round and round, with the same repeated snippets of film. The newscasters looked to me like puppets, miming friendliness when there was none, miming happiness or commiseration. But television did manage to open up the world in that tiny caravan. Radio would have told us more, but TV showed it, and some things you have to see.

The world had locked us down. All shipping was banned. There were shortages of nearly everything; superstores stripped, warehouses empty. People had gone and killed all the animals in a wildlife park. In fact, the Army was first called out to protect herds and zoos from people, rather than the other way around. Before marsupia, we'd all thought we lived in a David Attenborough film with animals threatened by us. (David Attenborough was a bit like a Zip star nowadays. Everyone knew him. He showed us lots of lovely films about animals and realized too late that the films were telling us everything was all right.

'What's going on in the rest of the world?' Mom demanded.

'Try Al Jazeera,' suggested Mr Keppel. So we got the news from Nigeria or Japan or Myanmar. It was a relief to hear about elections that the opposition said were fraudulent or of trouble between Qatar and Saudi Arabia. That sounded human and sane.

After two hours of news, Evie's mother would sigh and say cheerily 'Something else?' It was her house.

So we sat through cooking competitions, or shows where women in bikinis pretended to be attracted to men in swim trunks in order to win a prize. In the evenings, we watched murder thrillers with women detectives. As if people needed killing for a story to interest them. Nothing on TV seemed rooted in the earth, in what I knew of as the world.

'Teddy. Time for lessons,' Mom would say briskly. On her phone, there was still a whole network of teaching materials and plans. 'Ooh that's clever,' said Evie's mum. 'Could Evie join in? Would you like that, love?' There was a yearning in Dani's eyes. For whatever reason she'd been shut out of education herself but she didn't want that for Evie. Dani had no books but Evie had a whole shelf full.

Mom would try to get us to play maths games. She'd prod me to describe what I'd learned from solving the problem. 'To find a percentage all you do is divide by the bigger number.' She'd coax me, shaking my wrist. 'Come on. You used to love the problems. Teddy?' Couldn't she see the problems had no use now in the world?

Evie would nitter to calm me down. *Sleep. Rest.* She'd groom the back of my head when the adults couldn't see. We didn't want the adults to know we were dogs as well as people.

One thing that could sometimes rouse me, in which I could take an interest, was information about the marsupia.

YouTube, TikTok, Instagram were all full of information about what researchers were learning.

Basically, the marsupia was immortal.

On cold damp metal, in autoclaves, in deep freeze, in solutions of alcohol or bleach – the marsupia never became ineffective.

Yes, you washed your hands, and you got it off your hands but all you'd done was drain it down the sink and into the water supply.

There was nothing in the water purification system that could kill it. Old fashioned ceramic filters could sometimes catch it because it was so large, but the filters soon became clogged with a grey slime: a marsupia colony.

There were clever infographics showing the relative size of outbreaks in big red blobs and how it was spreading.

Basically, sooner or later everyone on Britain's mainland would bear the weight of it. The ground, the air, the water, Britain itself would seethe. 'Sssh,' I would say whenever those graphs showed up. The only programmes I insisted we watch were about the disease.

One day, Mom passed me her phone.

'This is Dr Szenas. He used to work with your Dad,' she said brightly. Like I didn't know who Ivan was. He was the guy who'd turned Dad into a useful idiot on radio and claimed credit for my deer video.

'Hello Teddy hello,' said Ivan, sounding boisterous. Mom had left her phone on speaker. I guess she wanted to listen in.

'Hello Sir.'

'How are you?'

'Fine Sir.'

'Are you missing your Dad?'

No. Not at all. He left us. He was gone already. So there's no difference.

'Yes, Sir.'

Sometimes I just curl up and cry.

'That's understandable. It must be difficult. Your mum tells me that you're interested in the marsupia.'

I leaned forward. My nose felt sharper. 'A bit.'

'Good.' He was trying to sound like a nice uncle. 'Do you have any questions?'

I wasn't feeling cheerful. I didn't want to be made cheerful, so I was blunt. 'How can a dog without a head keep trying to kill you?'

Safe in your little London lab.

'Okay. You know the marsupia have pouches.' It sounded like his answer was rehearsed if not outright habitual.

'That's why they're called marsupia,' I deadpanned. 'I believe.'

'The pouches carry gene sequences copied from many different species. Now a virus will hijack one of your cells and turn it into a factory for producing more virus. The marsupia do that as well, but they also copy sequences of genes from many different animals into host cells. Sometimes specialist cells from the brain.'

'Like a retrovirus.' *Go on, you can use big words.* The marsupia uses reverse transcriptase.'

Ivan tried to sound pleased. 'Good. Your Dad explained that? Good. So take an animal's leg for example. The marsupia might hijack nerve cells in the leg for sensing pain or for signalling muscles to move. Or even ordinary muscle tissue. And it makes these cells reproduce as specialist brain cells. Over time these join up to make new structures. Effectively the whole body becomes part of its brain. Of course the body still has all its other functions. Which is why infected animals increase in bulk. Your pig for example – we think by the end it would have weighed 375 kilos.'

'Their whole body thinks.'

'And they have new light-sensitive cells on their skins or structures for smell throughout the body. And there's what look like little islands of cerebrum. So who knows, maybe they can store memory there as well.'

'So it doesn't need a head.'

'Exactly.'

'Is that why I'm talking like a dog?'

He went all appropriate, his voice so soft and sad. 'Oh Teddy.' He sighed. 'Not exactly. otherwise…'

'I'd be a zombie too.'

'Partly. The marsupia doesn't kill people. Dogs communication appears to be hard wired. And it does look like the marsupia is able to cross into the brain itself, which is worrying, and it can transfer genes from other species there too. If the person is young enough, and the brain is still developing…' He paused. '… then they might grow structures based on those genes.'

'I'm growing a dog's brain?'

Silence. 'Well, we don't know how the tissue behaves in that context.'

I did.

'Can I get better?' I sometimes remember myself saying this with dull sadness, sometimes pleading, sometimes just pissed off. It's like I said it in many different lifetimes.

'I don't know, Teddy.'

'Brain surgery? You could cut out the new bits.' I was being jocose. He said nothing. *Nothing comes from nothing.*

I let him have it again. 'Is that how my cat is talking English?'

He said, like tiptoeing barefoot over broken glass, 'That isn't possible, Teddy.'

'Yeah well it's happening.'

'Cats don't have vocal cords.'

'Their larynx isn't that different,' I corrected him. 'At least, that's what Dad always said.'

'What else did your father tell you?'

'Animals don't have the structures in their brains to process words or sentences. That's the main reason why they can't speak. Though I seem to be growing a second throat to bark with, so who knows. Maybe cats and dog are growing voice boxes.' I felt I was being very witty. 'Maybe I'll start sprouting fur. Maybe they'll grow thumbs. We can meet somewhere in the middle.'

He made a dry noise that was an attempt at a chuckle. 'Okay.'

'But as my mom says. Genes don't contain language. They don't contain memories. They can grow into structures that can learn English grammar or about circuit breakers. But you don't inherit English and you can't copy it with reverse transcriptase. And *that*,' At this point I think I sounded quite gleeful, 'That means there's something you don't know, Doctor.'

Which was, for me, the whole point of the conversation .

I mimed being an arrogant adult. 'Such an imaginative child.'

'All that's very interesting, Teddy.'

'Isn't it.'

'Could you put me on to your mother, Teddy?'

'Sure.' I held out the phone to her.

Mom was flustered. She took the phone and put her thumb on buttons but couldn't turn off the speaker.

'Bright boy you have there Maggie. I have to say I'm worried about him.'

'Hold on, Ivan. Please. A *second*. The phone is on speaker.' She kept prodding it with both thumbs.

'He sounds a bit angry. Can you get him to a counsellor?'

'No, Ivan. We're in a trailer park by the ring road. Can we, can we talk later?'

'Or maybe you could get him here so we could look at him?'

I yelped with laughter and raised my voice. 'You want human guinea pigs now that the real ones are dying?'

He ignored that and asked Mom, 'Are you okay for food? What have you been finding to eat?'

Mom scratched her head. Her salt-and-pepper roots were showing. I hadn't realized she'd been dying her hair. 'Noodles. When we're lucky. Teddy keeps asking for dog food.' Her voice rattled.

'The government knows there's shortages. They're talking about airlifts of food. They'll announce it on TV and radio soon. Phone me any time, please. Day or night. Just call. If, if, if Teddy wants to talk more about what we're finding out that's great, just call. The lockdown isn't going to last much longer. There isn't any point. The infection is just about everywhere. So when – w*hen* you come to London, we'll arrange a visit to the labs.'

'Okay, Teddy?' he added, speaking up, knowing I could hear him.

I barked at him.

Those weeks at Albion Close all run together in my memory, so I'm not sure when I spoke to Ivan next – maybe after the first of the airlifts.

He rang up sounding dim and sad. 'Hello Teddy.'

'Bow wow,' I said in English.

'Teddy. You know we keep some animals here for study?' He sounded ill, shivery and feverish. 'There's new structure. Some of them are growing it, have grown it. We're calling it, for the time being, just here in the lab, a ventricerebrum. It's, it's...' He went quiet like a car running out of power. 'Uh. It's like a second stomach in which the masticated brain tissue is held. And the brain tissue being infected heals. It heals back scrambled, but we think some connections are still whole.'

Another long silence, which gave me time to think.

'So would it have the same memories?'

'We don't know.'

I'm sure I was the one who said, 'And the whole body is a brain so the stomach is wired into that. It's a second brain. Someone else's.'

There was a rustling sound. I think he was nodding yes.

'Many people's brains, all healing together.' I paused. He made a noise. 'If you count other animals as people too.' I pushed my belly. 'I don't have a second stomach,' I said.

But then I wasn't eating brains. As far as I could remember.

Ivan sounded shaky, distracted. 'The animals we aren't feeding fall apart. They just decay. The new structures are only in the animals we're feeding.'

'So you're feeding them human brains?' I was joking.

'No. That would be unethical.' He'd taken me seriously. 'The others are decaying, Teddy. If they don't eat they will all eventually just decay and die. This will end. All the sick animals will go. We're helping an Oxford lab with a vaccine programme you may have heard of. They think they'll have a vaccine and will be able to begin inoculating people within the year.'

'And the animals?'

'We'll try to save some of them. It's going to be all right, Teddy. This will end.' Then abruptly, like he'd been overwhelmed, he hung up.

A vaccine isn't a cure. And I wasn't sure I wanted to be cured.

Life wasn't so bad at Albion Close.

A stand of evergreen trees screened us from the bypass. A huge block of new-build luxury apartments did glower down disapprovingly from Park Way, but right behind Dani's caravan were the allotments. There must have been forty or fifty of them. At first we'd wave from the roof to the plump ladies in wide straw hats or dads with kids as they weeded and watered. For some reason, though I'd watered our garden and it had died, their vegetables thrived.

Things got worse; the gardeners stopped coming. Rather than let their produce go to waste, we stole it. It was that or starve.

By the end of our time there, we'd have expeditions to the allotments just about every other day, partly just to relieve the boredom. I would tote the Bijou, Faith would carry the shotgun and Mom and Dani the plastic bags. We'd come back with beans or courgettes that Mom would fry using rapeseed oil from Dani's huge bottles that looked like someone had used them to pee into.

Once someone shouted at us, someone with a right to be there, one of the straw hats. She sounded as posh as the Oldies – North Oxford, Mom later called her.

'I don't see anyone else here,' Faith replied.

'We work hard to grow these vegetables!' the woman raged.

'And we have kids to feed,' said Faith. 'And you're a fool for being out here without a gun.'

We went back rather than have a fight – but Faith was right. We never saw the woman again. The text messages and radio shows kept saying – stay safe, stay indoors. It was a devastating summer, and by the end we'd be lucky to get a half-rotten onion, a puckered cherry tomato or a shrivelled string bean. But it salved Mom's ache for vegetables.

One day, I heard Mom talking on the roof.

A cold hello from her. Then, 'We don't know any more than that. Mike just disappeared. We have to assume that, yeah. No Ken, we haven't. It's been hard. We're in Oxford now. The town. Staying with friends.' Everything she said was short and cold, not wanting to give information away. 'Well sorry, but we haven't always been able to charge our phones.'

I growled and stepped out of the trailer to listen.

'We're coping. No thank you, we're doing okay. You're in lockdown too remember.'

She started saying yes, yes, no, no and thank you goodbye.

I asked, 'What did *he* want?'

Mom leaned over the edge of the roof. 'More information about what happened to your father. I guess he also wanted to know we're okay.'

'We're doing just fine without him.'

'Just fine' Mom agreed.

Mr Keppel started taking an interest in our car, and involving me in it.

We'd open up the bonnet. Faith would be on the roof with the shotgun (I can't quite remember when we went shopping for cartridges, but we must have.) The car wasn't broken, but we'd spend all afternoon rehearsing how to fix it.

'The thing I love about these electric cars,' Mr Keppel said, 'is that there are fewer moving parts to go wrong. Back when I was your age, my father and I would spend every Sunday taking apart the carburettor, checking the fan belt. Once a month we'd check the pistons and the crankshaft. None of that with this vehicle. Just check the brakepads, do a charging test. There isn't even the need to check the oil.'

He sat Evie down and started to explain the car to her as well. She wore her blue trousers. 'I can't wear my good party dress,' she announced loudly to Dani, glad I think to be out of it.

'This motor simply doesn't get hot enough to need a cooling system,' said Mr Keppel. Evie nodded.

He paused, finger on his chin. 'What we should do is get spares. You don't repair an electric motor, you replace it. Brakepads, the same. Some spare everything. Yes.' He looked quite jolly. He had a broken front tooth and teeth a colour I'd never seen before. It wasn't unpleasant. It looked like elephant's tusk. 'We should stock up while there are still the parts.'

'I don't know if we can afford it,' said Mom.

'I'm happy to pay for it,' he said.

'But where will you get them from? Everything's closed.'

Mr Keppel rang our AA man. 'Hello Oliver. You're still there? Still alive?'

The AA man raided his own warehouse and showed up at Albion Close in his yellow van. Stayed for tea. Tea was one thing we still had plenty of, along with hot water. He sat on the edge of the trailer doorway and asked if he could live with us.

'I could sleep in my van,' he offered. 'It would be company.'

'We don't have any food,' said Mom.

'I'd keep your Kia in good nick.' Olly still looked hopeful.

'Teddy and I are doing that,' said Mr Keppel. 'That's why we ordered spares.'

The AA man looked like a marionette suspended by invisible wires that he could not control. 'I can see it is bit of a crowd. With the wee bairns to take care of. Mine are stuck in South London with their mum, so I don't know when I'll see them again.'

He kept talking for as long as he could. Finally he said, 'Cheers then. Bye.' He said goodbye for about fifteen minutes and finally got into his van and drove off into the dusk, still wearing branded yellow. Someone else whose world had gone.

'Dead man walking,' said Faith.

Could she hear the hound music inside people too?

That was how we got our car spares in the middle of lockdown. And for what feels now like a year's worth of afternoons, Mr Keppel taught us everything about electric cars and motors. He had Evie and me make our own crude electrical engine, wrapping wire around a peg. She squealed with delight when it started to spin.

That sunny time could only have lasted three or four weeks at most.

Mom must have read something on her phone or seen some YouTube channel.

She made a lantern out of paper and string with a little platform and she'd found one of those small round candles.

'Teddy. We're going to do a little ceremony for your Dad. All right? Just so we can think about him. And how much we love him. And how much we miss him. How we hope he went to a better place.'

Total pollyfilla. 'Sure,' I said.

'So we're going to light this candle, and the hot air will fill the bag and it will go up into the sky. And we can think of your Dad's journey.'

'It hasn't rained in two months. It will come down on the fields and start a fire.'

'It's a town, Teddy, we're in a town.'

'Great – it'll come down on someone's dry roof and start a fire. We can burn down half of Oxford.'

Her chin clenched. 'I'm going to do this. And we can think of that light, joining the stars in heaven.' Her voice broke apart.

'What blog did you read that on?'

She lit the candle. The paper glowed. She stood out in the yard at night and she wasn't frightened because it seemed like all the animals had gone. She held it out like she was going to launch it up into the sky, and angels were going to start singing or something, and the whole thing seemed so stupid to me that I erupted.

I don't know what noises I was making, but I attacked her and tore the lantern to pieces and I stomped on the candle. I left her still standing there with her face hidden in her hands.

Something clouted me hard on the back of my head. 'You little worm,' said Faith and grabbed both my arms and pulled me back around. 'You say you're sorry to your mum NOW.'

You can hit pollyfilla, it doesn't hurt. I could just about move my jaw to say, 'Sorry, Mom. I shouldn't have done that.'

'It's okay, Teddy.' She'd been crying. 'It was just an idea. I thought maybe, it would help. You know. To think about your Dad.'

'*He left us*. He wouldn't be here anyway.'

I climbed up the step-ladder onto the roof. I made the Plaintive Meow, over and over and over. But nothing answered. The silence had become total..

At first we didn't notice that there were fewer animal sounds.

In that hammering heat, the trees dropped their leaves, so there was no rustling in the air.

Evie and I would call, but nothing answered. There was no more network of barking between the trailers or the houses. At dawn from the roof of the trailer, we might see something without legs, without shape, a magi-mix blend of hide and bone, shrugging its way across the road. I began to have a third or fourth great well of fear inside me.

The animals were ceasing to move. They were going into the earth. As Ivan had said, soon there would be no more animals.

When we'd first come to Albion Close the most terrifying moment of any day had been climbing down from the roof and going back into the trailer. Would there be a predator inside it? When we opened the door, what might spring out?

'Well if the doors and windows been shut and nothing's broke a window, then there won't be nowt inside. Stands to reason,' Faith used to say. It became her job to open up the trailer each day.

We had heard prowlers at night in the yard, feet and snuffling. We'd see dim four legged shapes patrolling the Close. All that had stopped, we realized. We were becoming blasé. The worst was over.

The animals, we thought, were fading.

I could hear what the animal part of people said as well.

Mr Keppel grunted for no reason as he rested in the sun on top of the trailer. He was already sitting, so there was no reason to grunt.

He sat in the torn, folding chair, the sun burning him the colour of chestnuts, and he thought he was impressing me with the importance of education, of English grammar.

'Words are all we have,' he said. 'I learned this as a journalist. Keep your tools clean, keep meanings exact, you'll be able to think. You'll find truth quicker too. So many people these days can't. Think.'

Underneath the words, was a whine, a whimper.

My world gone.

He couldn't hear himself, so I helped him.

'Have words changed a lot?'

'Oh!' he said. 'No prepositions these days. Too many foreign speakers, and prepositions have to be drunk in with your mother's milk.

And verbs. We used to be able to pinpoint everything in time. *I was having one of my turns when Deirdre, having eaten too much hash fudge, brought me up sharp.* Now everything is present tense. Events from the eighteenth century are narrated in present tense. It used to be the tense of general truth. "The world is round". "French is spoken in Haiti." Now it's the tense of YouTube.'

A human whine sounds a bit like a violin. Or maybe, a violin echoes that unheard whine.

'When I was covering Syria I used to stay in a hotel in Aleppo. It was not a major posting back then, just a story from time to time about the Assad family, or relations with Israel, or maybe a bit of archaeology. The hotel had been a house in the souk, very old, rather grand. The souk was from the thirteenth century. Dark inside, all shadow with these blasts of sunlight coming from the skylights. Mounds of spice. You couldn't see the hotel from the outside. It was just another high wall with an arch, but inside it was a courtyard with verandas that went up four storeys. We'd have breakfast on the roof, eggs and spices and chopped vegetables and look down at the fountain in the courtyard. The owner was a lovely man, a friend of mine. Ali. I bought a beautiful tablecloth from Ali and I have it on my dining room table now. Or I did have it. I don't know if it's still there. And Syria now…' He made his hand burst open and made the sound of a bomb.

The little wheeze in his chest said, *Time to join.*

I got confused and spilled over into words. 'Join what?'

He shook his face. *What? What?*

'Sorry. Thought you said something else.'

I left him because I didn't want to hurt him, and I went down into the Submarine Kitchen, and there was Mom.

'Mr Keppel is going to die soon,' I told her.

She was bowed over the food, chopping our one onion. It was going to savour a mass of rice and nettles we'd torn from the roadside. It was like Mom was praying to the food, willing it to be enough. So it took her a while to look up and answer. 'You're a strange little guy, Teddy.'

'Get used to it,' I said. I walked out onto the baking driveway, the glowering sun and hoped I would disappear into it.

Evie was waiting for me, and took my hand.

Though I never forgot what Mr Keppel told me about words.

I'm not sure when, in that unending sunlight, but a helicopter made a pass and started dropping food parcels from the air into the allotments.

'Run Little One.' Faith gave me a shove. 'My old bones.'

So I and Evie scampered, Mom and Dani ran after us, shouting in panic. Evie and I jumped up onto the first parcel we came to, but it was the first one the neighbours came to as well and they crowded round. Evie bared her baby teeth and growled.

A male nurse from Kenya took charge. He was from a caravan in our corner. It housed four NHS staff. 'We all wait now, we all wait. We take turns yes, some for everybody.' He was a big guy. He looked at Evie and me growling and just chuckled. His name was Mustapha. 'You can stop growling, kids.'

Tinned meat. Tinned soup. Pasta. One tin of ratatouille. 'Isn't there anything for vegans?' Mom sighed.

She was from another world too.

I saw a tin of halal chicken-spice stew. I knew that halal meant something middle eastern. So I snatched it up for Mr Keppel. I saw a tin of dog food and slipped that to Evie, who hid it in the folds of her pink party dress. And then she grabbed another one and grinned. We didn't tell Mom and Dani.

I gave the spiced stew to Mr Keppel. He smiled a dreamy smile and turned it over and over in his hands, his eyes misty. On the roof that night Evie and I tabbed open one tin of dog food and scoffed the lot. We licked the tin and didn't cut our tongues.

Last thing that night I saw Mustapha get onto the hospital shuttle, greeting and laughing with the other NHS workers on board, and I had the weirdest thought. If Dad had to leave us for a guy, I wish it had been Mustapha. I'd have liked being in a family with Mustapha.

A few days later, Mr Keppel looked asleep in that chair, but I knew he would not wake up.

I climbed down the tin steps to where Mom was sheltering in the trailer and the first thing she said was 'Teddy! Why are you howling?'

Systems had been speeded up. Dead bodies drew animals, so the funeral system had changed. Mom rang a helpline she'd heard advertised on the radio.

A military van drew up about twenty minutes later with a grey body bag and assault rifles. The Army had taken over Oxford crematorium, just nearby up a small road from the Headington Roundabout. I remember that the road had a twenty mph speed limit in case of funeral corteges. The Army said we could attend the cremation if we wished.

Mom paused. She glanced at Faith.

'He weren't family,' said Faith.

'He was. In a way.'

'Not much of one. Dear old fella, mind you.'

Mom wasn't going to risk it. She told the Army officer, 'We didn't know him that well. His name was Joseph Keppel. He was our neighbour. His house is in Oldminster. Sandy Lane, Witney. We don't know his next of kin.'

'We'll deal with all that. So long as we have a name.' The woman was some kind of Army personnel with a tablet, and she punched in data with a gloved finger. 'Your assigned slot will be three pm this afternoon. Is that all right? If anyone would care to come and say a few words?'

'Can we say them here?' Mom asked. And for some reason she could recite the King James version of Genesis, only she called it *Bereshit*. She stopped at the bit about dominion over the animals.

'Guess we blew that,' she murmured.

'That was beautifully read. Well. Recited.' The Army person shrugged with a suddenly soft smile.

'I was an actor once,' said Mom.

And Mr Keppel was driven away.

'He kept the car going,' said Faith. The ultimate tribute.

By then even the insects had stopped buzzing. The silence swelled like a balloon. So did the smell. The smell was so bad that it began to occupy all your thoughts. It was as though every single thing in the countryside had died.

And it just about had. We thought it meant that all the animals had gone, finally rotted away.

Ivan was on TV, saying as much. He had become some kind of celebrity. The marsupia worked to heal, but it couldn't ultimately heal death itself. 'We're not getting any heat signatures,' he said. 'Before we could see the animals just glowing with fever, moving through hedges or along roads. But now our surveillance doesn't show that. It doesn't show anything.'

'So are you saying,' the announcer asked, 'that the worst is over?'

Ivan nods yes and smiles even though his words say something else. 'We have to wait and see.'

Mr Keppel had made the right choice. He took himself off before things got really bad.

Fifteen

Evie and I wanted more dog food.

We knew Dani's neighbour across the road had had dogs. But they were silent. We listened for dog music; we liked it; but we'd heard none. We were fairly sure that all animals were dying, or more accurately decaying into helplessness.

So we got the idea of telling Dani and Mom we were going to climb up onto the roof – and then sneaking out to hunt for tins in the big trailer on the corner.

Its front was on the main loop of Albion Close – a superior kind of mobile home. It was sprawling, dolled up to look like an American ranch house with an added porch-patio now full of unswept leaves. The aluminium door had been left unlocked.

Inside, the place smelled putrid – old vegetable waste, poo, and that chemical smell.

One of the owners was still there, sitting on his sofa, with a mouldy cup of coffee on the table. His face had flowed then hardened like brown candlewax with teeth. Everything above his eyebrows was gone; lower down his chest, he'd been stripped to the bone. He was still wearing checked shorts.

I heard a yipping and growling, and jumped, but then realized the sound was rumbling out of Evie and me. I settled down to laugh at being scared, and then I thought: *what are we yipping at?* Evie and I must have had the same thought because both of us began to bark: *We strong. You weak.*

I started up the Bijou Chainsaw.

Then from out of the toilet, the two dogs hobbled.

That's when I saw the axe lying on the turquoise carpet almost behind the owner's chair. Before he'd bled to death, the owner must have axed the dogs. A knife could never have done that much damage.

Both little Chihuahuas had been chopped up, maybe not exactly in half, but into pieces.

The two dogs had healed together. They had six legs, one broken, one turned backwards and two heads, one much higher than the other.

The worst of it was that one head had no eyes. In a socket was a mouse. The light caught on the mouse's black and living eye; it glinted, looking right at us.

Evie and I barked and snarled, and bounced up and down in rage. The dog(s) stayed silent. They stared in silence. Those tiny little rat-like things would have thought they were as big Alsatians, as big as elephants.

Still silent, still not talking, they trotted towards us, teeth bared like they thought they could swallow us in one mouthful.

I hit them with the Bijou. They were like badly pressed doner kebabs. The chainsaw not only sliced through them in a cut; it sent leaves of them spinning across the room and into our faces. I pulled away in surprise and the backstroke made them almost explode.

No blood, except for already congealed gouts of fungoid ooze. One of the heads was trying to bark but had no air. Its mouse was trying to escape from the eye-socket, little claws scrabbling, but it was rooted by strands of something growing into its back. I stomped on it and it burst like a mouldy tomato. More stench.

Rattling footsteps on the metal porch and Mom called in panic 'Teddy? Evie?'

'Stay out, Mom,' I told her.

A Chihuahua torso with a lopsided head was still trying to work its way towards us on two legs.

'Teddy?' Mom ducked into the room.

'Stay out.'

'What are you doing here?'

'Trying to find more food,' I said which was true. I let go off the safety and the saw stopped.

Mom saw the kebabs on the floor twitching and called on God. And I think she meant it.

'Look at this,' said Faith. She kneeled down and saw the smashed tomato of a mouse, still linked by tendrils like the roots of spring weeds. The tiny body was being dragged back towards the head, which had been ripped from any body at all and had lost its lower jaw. The pouch of fur and bone that had been a mouse was jerked back into the eye socket. Its one eye still gleamed. Then without any guts and only two limbs loosely connected, the mouse began slowly and laboriously to walk the head forward, its tiny feet sticking out from under the jaw, hauling it as unsteadily as a wheelbarrow.

Faith stood up, knees clicking. Dani covered her mouth and said, 'I'm going to be sick.' I got out my phone and videoed it.

As we watched, the two torsos, those limbs, even the two heads slowly drew together, shrugging, side-winding, hiccoughing, twitching their way closer to each other.

The mouse-driven head jammed itself against a rear end. Little nerve-like roots wriggled out between them. The head began to attach to what looked like the remains of the anus.

'Teddy, Evie, come away please. What if you get sick?'

'I'm sick already.'

Faith said, 'In an hour or two whatever that is will be walking about.' She barked a laugh. 'I don't know how they'll tell which end is front.'

I said, 'I just hope the man on the sofa doesn't stand up.'

Faith's mouth went thinner – it was how she smiled. 'That'll be phase two.'

Dani said, waving her hands, which had been over her nose, 'Let's just get out of here. I mean, away-away.' I think she meant, away from Albion Close.

'Nowhere to go,' said Faith.

'There's the moon,' I said.

'Oh this lot will do all right on the moon, it's us who won't be able to breathe.'

I said back to Faith, 'I never thought of it before, but Zombies would be really useful in a space programme.'

Faith went back to what Dani had been saying. 'Nowhere to drive. And we couldn't just lock ourselves in the car. Glass breaks. The only place we got is the roof.'

Faith paused, looked at the healing ball of dog, and then blasted it again with the shotgun. 'I don't care what they tell us, those things aren't going away.' The mess looked more like a cuttlefish than a dog now. With a moist kind of sound it started to snail its way back together again.

As we left, Evie said in a tiny solemn voice, 'They didn't say nothing.' She meant the Chihuahuas, and she was right. The beasts weren't signalling any longer – no barks or clicks or growls or meows. They didn't need them. Like the bees, their tails all pointed in the same direction.

Faith.

I think she had a military mind that she'd never had a chance to use. I saw her back in the caravan, old knees cushioned on a pillow, emptying the cupboard under the sink.

'No point taking pasta or rice,' she said to herself.

'Take it where?' I asked.

'Onto the roof. No way to cook it.'

She started to separate tins and cheese. I uploaded my dog video to Ivan, mostly out of a kind of anger. I wanted to shake him up. Then I rang him, and it was his usual smooth line – nothing to worry about, the military are surveying, there's no heat signature, everything's getting better. I got one good line in: 'Would dead animals have a heat signature?' Ivan chuckled as always, offered good will and rang off.

The rest of the family were on the roof. The big beach umbrella was up, our only defence against sun and rain. Evie was laid out under it in her toy sunglasses, playing at being a TikTok star (TikTok was social media, running videos, but basically there is almost no way to describe it now.)

She was having fun. 'This is Evelynne McKenzie and I'm here in fabulous Las Vegas, California. We are by the pool of the luxury Desert Sands Hotel and I am working on my suntan. Later this evening I'll be reporting from the important fashion show from Versace and Fatface.'

Overheard, helicopters sounded like they were beating rugs. We'd grown used to them circulating all the time, dropping food or flying overhead at night beaming down spotlights. It was like we'd been occupied by foreign troops.

Mom was looking at her screen and scowling. 'I just got one of those texts. You know, from the Council? They're telling everyone to get home and stay inside.'

Dani was half asleep. 'They're always telling us that. Fat lot of good.'

'They don't usually send out texts about it.'

Something made me ask. 'Is your phone charged up?'

'Yeah, plugged in all last night.'

I'd used the Bijou, so I went downstairs to plug in the battery pack. The little green light came on. So it still had charge. I saw all our other phones charging in a row, all charging.

That was when my phone rang.

It was Ivan. 'Has a civil defence message come up on your phones?' His breath was shaky.

'I don't think so.'

'They said they would send out a text. Have you had a text?'

'Mom has, but it just says stay indoors like always.'

'Great,' he muttered. 'They'll regret taking down the air raid sirens. Look. Are you somewhere safe?'

'We're in a caravan.'

I could hear his baffled dismay. 'Well, get somewhere safer than that. You don't have long. The military have spotted something on the ground. It. Well. The Army are saying it's almost military. Like when the D-Day troops hid underground in London. They're coming out of hiding, empty car dealerships, barns, warehouses.'

'What are? Animals?'

'What used to be animals. I've seen the aerial surveillance. It looks more like that tsunami in Japan.'

'Can we drive out of Oxford?'

'No time.'

'We're on a roof.'

'Good. Stay there. Text or phone other people, tell them get to safety.'

'There is no safety,' I said.

He didn't answer. 'Call me later,' he said.

We never heard from Dr Szenas again.

It was Faith's name I shouted. Both she and Mom stuck their heads over the edge of the roof. I told them both what Ivan had said – something was coming.

Mom asked, 'What kind of attack?'

'I don't know, he said something like a wave?'

'Well he must have said something more than that!'

'Yeah, *get to safety* and *there's no time to drive*.'

Faith said, 'Theres tins and things laid out. Could you bring them up? There's a lad.'

I jumped off the ladder, nipped back into the kitchen, grabbed my rucksack and began throwing the tins and jars into it. I heard Mom's feet on the ladder. 'Teddy what is this?'

'I don't know!' I shouted back and began to gather up our charging phones.

My Mom stepped into the caravan. 'Well what did he say?'

'What I told you. Call him yourself. It was Ivan, he was more concerned with his image.'

Mom started to gather up saucepans.

'Mom? Why saucepans? There's no power up there, we're not going to cook anything.'

'Store things. Put lids on them.'

'We could use them for water I suppose.' I grabbed the full rucksack, ran out and clunked up the ladder. I wasn't even all the way up when Faith said, 'Ammo.'

Ammo, right. I tossed the ruck onto the roof and turned right around.

Mom had come out carrying a big saucepan full of packets of pasta.

Why were the adults so slow? I wanted to throw the pasta over the back fence, but just shook my head and rotated around her, back into the caravan.

At first I couldn't see the ammo; it was in a neat cardboard box but I was blind to it. It was on the kitchen table where Faith always kept it to hand. I found an Aldi bag, put in the box (so clumsily that it opened and spilled the cartridges) and then started filling the bag with things to keep Evie amused, her colouring books and pens, *Frozen* and a bag of Haribo. Then I remembered we had nuts, sunflower seeds, and dried fruit in upper shelves, so I crammed those in too. And our one secret tin of dog food.

Back up top.

'Ammo's in the bag,' I told Faith. Without asking Mom, I took the packets out of the saucepan and started carrying the saucepans back down to the kitchen.

'What are you doing?' Mom demanded.

'Filling them with water,' I shouted.

I used the caravan's kitchen tap, but the water dribbled in as always, too slow.

'Mains taps,' Faith shouted from upstairs. 'Use bottles.'

Mom was suddenly standing at my elbow, pinch-faced. 'I'll do that, you fish through the recycling.'

We had a pile of uncollected recycling out front, so I took the bottles from there. The Close had taps for hoses with useful water pressure on the street corners. Standing out in the open as the bottles filled, I got scared, looking around me the whole time for animals. Faith stood on the roof with the gun ready.

I staggered back with two 1.5 litre bottles and one of Dani's huge oil jars filled with water. On the roof Mom had lined up brimming saucepans. Sitting in the middle of the roof was her big leather case of our documents. Dani reached down from the roof and took the bottles from me, so I nipped back in for one last check.

Our broadband was still working, a solid blue line of light across its front – it sent a strong signal up to the roof. I picked up a pen and Mom's big black hardbound notebook. Medical supplies! I scooped up bandaids, disinfectant, an aspirin, a box of face masks and toilet rolls. That made me think about passports and papers – Mom's residency card. She kept all that stuff in a belt bag. Sure enough the beltbag had been left hidden inside a shoe.

On my way out I remembered that Mr Keppel had bought a car charging battery from Olly the AA man. It was under the sink, all charged up but stowed in its box. My fingers shook as I tried to work out how to lock it to the input. There was key, a slot, you had to turn it twice – those batteries were too damn valuable to leave unsecured.

'Teddy? Can you hurry up?' Mom leaning over from the roof was looking anxious. The key turned twice, I gave the battery a tug and it was solid. I didn't know what else to do with the battery key, so I put it in Mom's beltbag.

'Look at what you forgot,' I said as I pushed the bag at Mom. She wilted. I'd been mean again.

'We all hide things in our shoes,' I said. My way of saying sorry.

'Ready as we'll ever be,' said Faith.

Text and call people, Ivan had said. I did want to warn people but there was no one to warn. We didn't know anybody in Oxford, and all the Oldies in Oldminster seemed to have disappeared. Crazily, I tried to text Dorothy, as if she could rise from the dead. I began to realize how devouring the disaster had already been.

We all sat down, crowded among tubs and jars, and finally at about four pm we ate something. Mom had a packet of fruit and nuts. Evie and I tabbed open our tin of dog food – *Chicken Supreme* it called itself. Evie and I ate it with our fingers right in front of Dani and Mom. Dani just stared; Mom sat hunched over with her back towards me.

Was I imagining it, or was that minty smell getting worse? Like we'd all been smothered in Vicks Vapo-Rub. Was there a buzzing in the air, as if from power cables?

We had a good view from the top of the trailer. I saw Mustapha the nurse slip out of the NHS trailer. He saw me and waved, 'Hello neighbour.' He was in jeans and white T-shirt, holding out a bag of garbage. Everyone was having to pile it up outside in the roadway.

'Get inside. Get safe!' I shouted.

'Don't worry, we have knives.'

'No. They're saying we're going to be attacked or something.'

'Thank you.'

'They're swarming or something.'

He broadcast his beautiful smile and waved again. 'We will be careful. We will be careful Little Man.' I think he'd heard Faith call me, but he'd heard my nickname wrong. Mustapha went inside the space he shared with four colleagues. I could hear his radio, gently pulsing Greatest Hits Radio. David Gray's 'White Ladder'. Joan Armatrading's 'Fast Car'. Songs from my world that you have never heard.

Through everything that followed, Mustapha's radio kept on playing. When the station was abandoned, an hour of music was left on repeat, over and over. 'Lady Marmalade' was a famous song about a prostitute, but I can't remember who sang it, and have no way of finding out now. 'We Are Family' by Sister Sledge. 'Happy' by Pharell somebody. 'We Are the Champions' by Queen. Meaningless, played over and over.

The buzzing sound got louder. I thought it was insects. Insects didn't seem to be getting sick; we needed insects; I thought that maybe buzzing was good. The sound was coming from the north, where trees screened the ring road. I stood up to see. Moving through the trees was something like a cloud, a swirling blackness filtering towards us.

'Mom,' I said. 'Something's coming.'

Mom jumped up. 'Looks like a plague of locusts,' she said. I was reminded of starlings in a flock, flowing into different shapes, swelling and contracting, then dive-bombing in a stream.

Then it was on us.

A gnawing, snarling grinder of a sound filled our ears, dimmed our eyes.

Something darted all about us, slammed into us. The stench was as sharp as onions, eye-watering, sinus-drenching. Mom coughed. I coughed, and then choked. My throat was full of crawling bits. I knew at once that they could choke your breath, stuff your stomach. Already, at once, we could not talk, communicate, unite. I chewed mouthfuls of something sticky like a toffee someone else had already chewed, stinking of decay and death. I dared not swallow.

I'd thrown a box of facemasks into the Aldi bag and I tried to find them. I had to keep blinking, my eyes stinging as these things burst apart under my eyelids. I glimpsed, like in shadow, the blue box. I tore it open pulled out the facemasks, put one on me – enclosing the horror already in my mouth and nostrils. I kept chewing them, though it made me retch – while I pulled a face mask over Mom's nostrils and mouth. She nodded vigorously up and down, *yes, yes, great*! She grabbed a mask from me and went to help Dani. I knelt and put one on Evie. Her face was clenched and strained. She looked so tiny, and her chest was pumping, trying to breathe.

Not able to breathe.

I stuck a finger into her mouth, and cleared dark matter that seethed and shifted. I reached deeper and pulled, and something seemed to have already grown roots into her, was matted together. I hauled it free, like weeds from around my leek plants, a clogged mass of mucous and blood, Evie's blood. She began to cough, and more stuff came out in red and black clumps. Blood streamed from her nostrils.

The coughing doubled Evie over. Then it rocked her back upright. Evie began to work like a hinge, flung open and shut by the efforts of her body to get rid of the gunk. I was coughing as well, expelling what looked like flexing tar into the face mask. I pulled off my mask and stared at it. The stuff was a mass of tiny bits and pieces that climbed over and through itself. I flung the mask away and put on a fresh one.

Evie calmed, and jabbed my leg and pointed.

Faith was on the ground thrashing, kicking. She still had the shotgun and in that fleshy twilight there was a flash from the mouth of the weapon – the sound of the blast nearly lost in the general roar.

I ducked. Jesus Christ, the gun was going off.

Out of nowhere Mom jumped forward, the gun pointing at her belly but she grabbed the barrel anyway. Fighting as she was, Faith was conscious enough to let go of the gun. I had lost the box of facemasks; I scrabbled for it, then felt it rather than saw it in that dark blizzard. I tore at a plastic envelope, but the bloody stuff just wouldn't give. Dani was next to me with her immaculate fingernails and she slit the packaging. She crawled towards Faith and pulled the mask on over her chin and ears.

Faith rolled to her knees, face down, and pulled down the mask. Dani tried to stop her *no no no* but Faith held up an intelligent hand then stuck four fingers down her own throat. Her whole body seemed to ripple, and black stuff gushed out of her. She cleared her own throat, then she blocked one nostril at a time and blew. Panting, weakened, she gave a thumbs up, and pulled the mask back on.

The storm seemed to clear around us and we looked out over over Marston.

Like a blizzard, only dark, that shitstorm reduced everything to dim silhouettes, a burning sun haloed by a grey ring, as if seen through a dragonfly's wing.

In that swirling shadow, we could only make out some of the other trailers, their white panelling gleaming.

Mustapha's radio was singing 'All Night Long,' by Lionel Ritchie. It was a song about dancing, having fun.

Mustapha staggered against that white panelling. He was just a silhouette himself now, seething with shapes that blanketed his arms, his face.

The ground was dark, bubbling like a tarpit. Light caught lumps, flotsam and jetsam; but I still had stuff in my eyes. The ground had been inundated with something.

Mustapha was covered by what looked like flies and mice. He held up an imploring arm, and its outline rippled and scurried. I think I saw a whole mouse clinging to the tip of a finger. There was a sound of serration. More like a sawing than anything else, a very gentle almost snoring sound. His torso was silently heaving, trying to breathe, but by then I think his throat and lungs were full of them. He collapsed onto his knees, then fell forward. Then he was still.

Bits of life were crawling all over my arms and legs. I picked one of them off to have a look. Individually, it looked like shredded beef, a little twist of fluttering hamburger squeezed into a vaguely aerodynamic shape, a twist with wings. Mom, Faith and Dani stood still, both hands clamped over their faces. I brushed things off my mask, then shielded it.

Then, as if on a signal, the cloud lifted like a curtain. It had a lower edge. It raised itself up, gathered like fist, and then punched itself east, towards the hospital. The swarm twisted and turned in the sky, stretched, contracted and caught the light in different ways. Other streams of life poured up from all over Marston to join it. The buzzing sound retreated towards the hill, to perhaps more populated ground. Heading towards all the helpless people in their hospital beds.

Below us, a flood moved in separate chunks.

Larger entities waded through it, some of them four-limbed and one-headed, but most of them now were small, scurrying and portmanteau. All of it stank, all of it was makeshift and hanging in threads. A warning sounded in my head: *wrong wrong wrong.*

Different kinds of impulses fired across my brain. I wanted to jump, flap, fly, run, charge or bite. I tried to open claws, I tried to bare fangs, and I could control none of it.

I couldn't talk. I passed the Bijou to Faith. She snatched it up. Mom still held the shotgun. Her eyes flicked to the chainsaw's battery light. I'd already used some of the charge that day on the Killer Chihuahuas. With her free arm, Mom helped me to sit, settling me gently onto the roof. I lay on my side and looked down at the road.

Mice, rats, moles, voles, squirrels, some of them still in separate selves, tumbled over each other. The depth of the inundation kept growing, coming in waves.

Pieces of dog helped each other limp, like old couples with walking sticks on a Sunday stroll. There was a hide, black and white so probably that of a Holstein cow, walking on stumps, with a fox's head, (well most of a head) sticking out of the prow. An amalgamation of at least three cats (judging from the colours of the fur) rolled past like tumble weed. I think I did a Plaintive Meow, but those cats were now silent. That was a most unsettling thing. These animals now no longer spoke.

Then finally there was a sound – a sound like motorboat roaring across a lake.

I was not entirely sane. For a second, I thought it was Ken on his speedboat on Lake Windermere.

Thrashing through the swamp-like tangle, accelerating through it came something huge and corrugated like a black rubber tire. It was making the sound, an urgent roaring, and I thought for a moment it was mechanical, or half mechanical.

It shot into our forecourt, rocking the Kia as it barged past it. My humans wailed and shouted but I couldn't understand what they said. *Fear Fear Fear* is all I heard in their voices

The thing flexed. Through its torn surface I could see its ribs, but its long narrow snout was whole and I knew what it was. It was a crocodile one of the creatures Dad had taken me to see in Crocodile Planet, by our river.

The thing was mostly crocodile--it seemed to have a white dove embedded in its back. The thing launched itself up the steps of the caravan as if onto a riverbank, then slammed through the door. My humans screamed and clutched each other and held onto the roof.

The crocodile thrashed its head inside the caravan; things splintered, clattered, crashed, glass and table legs. We could feel a thrill shake through the thin fabric of the house. We could hear its aluminium beams groan.

Then I heard another sound. A car horn. What kind of creature made that sound?

A Volkswagen Golf.

A car came round our road from the left, circling the loop in the wrong direction. It was beeping its horn, flashing its lights. Already claws of bone clung to the door handles. In its headlights, flakes of flesh danced like insects. The car drove through a puddle of silent creatures. They coated its tyres; seepages were flung up onto the windscreen, jamming the wipers.

The crocodile must have heard it. It tried to thrash its way backwards out of our caravan. Its head was caught at an angle in our doorway. The whole trailer leaned to one side and some of our food slid off the roof.

The croc flopped backwards into the tide of flesh, turned and surged after the Golf. The reptile accelerated faster than the car and slammed into its rear door. The humans inside screamed.

Then in a pincher movement, two of the larger amalgamations (mostly cow and horse I think) closed on the front and rear of the car. The one at the rear walked backwards like a reversed film. The one in front either collapsed or deliberately knelt in front. The car drove up onto its soft back. The front wheels sank then spun helplessly as if mired in mud.

Then the car managed to reverse, into the mass behind. A wave of flesh poured in like reinforcements, rising up like a tide all around the car.

The crocodile scrambled up the bonnet and flung itself through the windscreen. The head punched into the front and pulled out most of the driver by his head. The rest was held by a seat belt. Someone tried to open the back car door, but it was blocked by flesh. With the door half-open, tiny things swarmed in. The croc tossed its head from side to side, and some of what it held was flung into the swamp. Bits of life sizzled like boiling fat, up and over it, devouring.

Little creatures poured into the car through the broken windscreen; the thing nosed them aside, and tore something from the passenger seat. I glimpsed an arm, still in a long-sleeved shirt. The crocodile seemed to feed it to the thing under the front wheels. Then it slid back into the mass, and dove under the car as if into water. It clenched, swelling under the car and turned it over onto its side.

A wave of mice, squirrels, tendrils, thrashing guts, knitted twists of flesh, bones walking in structures that looked like marquees – all of it rose up and covered the Golf.

Then, as if it had discovered that cars contained delicious people, the wave surged forward, bubbled up under our Kia, and lifted it up.

The crocodile shot forward again, broke through our windscreen, shook its head through the interior, make a ripping sound, came out with part of a car seat, then flung it away. It turned, lumbered away and eased back into the mass. It swam along Albion Close.

I lost all motor control. I jabbered like someone tuning through radio stations. I was on my back in a pool of mess. I was aware something was bubbling up out of my throat. Things inside me were trying to dig their way into my brain so they could steal it. Maybe they already had. I could feel my vocal cords strain and give. I hissed. I groaned.

But for some reason I could still understand the songs on Mustapha's radio. They played a football crowd roaring out a song and those words made sense to me – music goes deeper for both dogs and humans.

When you walk through storm hold your head up high.
And you'll never walk alone.

But we were.
We were all alone.

Sixteen

'Shake Rattle and Roll', blared on the radio, an old, old song; and the trailer still shook like it had a fever, groaning and listing further to one side.

Faith, Dani and Evie had pushed what was left of our food to the centre of the roof and hugged it and each other into place. Mom was punching keys on the phone screen and talking, but I couldn't understand what she was saying.

Evie crawled towards me, knelt, stroked my head and whimpered. *Sad.* Then a solid abrupt little bark. *Work.*

Then her face hardened like setting concrete. She suddenly, piercingly shrieked.

Die!

I was an encumbrance to the pack, useless. I was to die and let myself be eaten.

And like Mr Keppel, my head cleared. Evie gave a hard, tight little smile and turned away. She would have let me die if she had to.

Mom was talking forcefully to Faith. 'They're saying evacuate, get to Kassam Stadium. Everyone. They say the military is there. They want everyone to leave. How? How are we supposed to get to Kassam Stadium?'

Faith nodded in my direction. 'He's back with us.'

Mom glanced at me misgiving and searched my face. 'Teddy?' she asked. She was firmly planted on her haunches and looked unwilling to move.

'Hi, Mom,' I said.

The whole caravan shook, and Mom shouted, and shot out an arm to hold herself in place. I looked over the edge. All of our windows were now under the black stuff. The Kia was buried.

The slope looked like the Battle of the Somme (World War One, look it up, or something, find an Oldie and ask them before we all die). Things on crutches of bone swung themselves up the banks. Loose sets of fangs like dentures chattered up the gathering slope.

I said, 'I can feel them inside, gnawing on me.'

'Right,' said Faith. 'I have a little something for that, as it happens. In emergencies.' She actually grinned, something I'd never seen her do. She crawled towards me on her knees, holding a small flat bottle of Famous Grouse. 'They hate it.'

She passed me the bottle. 'Don't swallow it, you're under age.' She grinned back at Mom. 'Corrupting the young.' Then back to me. 'Work it around like mouthwash.'

I took a swig and she was right, I could feel the little mites in sinuses shudder, bite, cling, shiver and let go. I frothed it up and around the lip of my sinuses. Some of the whisky went town the wrong way into my lungs, giving my tubes an internal sunburn, but that worked too, singeing the things out of me. I began to hack out a cough and the fluid spluttered out of me, now blood red with things crawling in it. Faith crushed them with her elbow. Evie came forward and wine-pressed them with her knees. They used a Tupperware lid to sweep the mess over the edge.

Mom said in a small voice, reading the screen. 'They're going to clear the area. What does that mean?'

Faith turned to her with a pirate's grin. 'Napalm,' she said, mugging a grin. She *had* been swallowing the whisky.

Mom stared watery with despair.

'Tell someone we're here,' I said. I stopped myself saying *Duh*.

Mom looked annoyed: *smart Alec*.

I said, 'If that's a text, text them back.'

Mom just passed me the phone. I texted *5 Albion Close OXZ 559 trapped on roof.* I scrolled through the previous messages and sure enough there was one with a blue link. So I tapped on that and there was an emergency form. I pasted in the same message and submitted it.

Then all we could do was wait. I looked over the edge. The tide was high. Something that looked more like an octopus than anything else waved thick tentacles at me like clubs.

Above us, I heard neeping.

Without meaning to, I growled. Evie sat next to me and growled as well.

'Something's coming,' I translated. 'Something else.'

And I was smelling smoke. I learned later that they were setting the fields around us on fire.

Bats were sociable creatures.

Miners killed them by coating just a few in arsenic paste. All the other bats wanted to help, so they licked the sticky stuff off their pack-mates, and died.

Bats lived on aerial insects and slept away from other animals. They became ill later than others, but then ill all at once.

Something was flying overhead and the stench came from overhead too. Black and pulsating against that deep starless blue.

I started to howl at them, my whole voice straining.

Evie and I both started to howl and leap and snap at them. I felt something flutter just over my head.

My head.

Suddenly claws clung to my hair, and I felt little snuffling nips. I slapped them, struck them, grabbed them and tore them away.

They were in an earlier phase of the illness and still had whole bodies. 'Tin opener,' one of the bats neeped in thin little voice.

They wanted a tin opener for my cranium.

'Where is my handbag?' a little voice neeped, with an Australian accent. Did I imagine, hard, swollen stomachs?

I clutched them, tore at them, felt my own hair tear free in their claws. I still have bald patches in streaks forty years later.

They clustered around Mom. Tiny fox faces with wings and teeth, and they were nibbling her hairline. Suddenly many of them closed like a shower cap over the top of her head. I saw a line of blood run down my mother's arm. I was shouting dog rage at them. I pulled them off with my hands, burrowed my face into the mass of them, and bit and chewed. They were dead and tasted of death, and I crunched then up and spat them out. I jumped up into the air and seized them with my jaws and leaned on them with my elbow, and tore them in half and kicked them from the roof. I saw Evie, with a corner of batwing in her mouth.

Bad Food Bad Food I howled.

Dani shrieked, beating her hair, fighting with her eyes closed, her cheeks puffed out. Faith was targeting individuals as they flew, slicing at them with the Bijou. One was burrowing in at the back of her neck. She had a stiff back, and would never be able to reach it, so I jumped. Something in my groin gave way from the strain, but I was able to tear the bat off Faith. Dani jumped in to help as well, but the Bijou grazed her forearm, flailing skin. Something large pulled me back. It was Mom. Faith lifted the Bijou high over her head and kept sawing at the bats, keeping the teeth away from us. Mom started tearing her shirt to staunch the flow of blood from Dani's arm.

I raged.

Ours ours ours

Evie: *Strong strong strong*

The neeping of the bats changed tone, went shrill, like a warning. They flapped wings uselessly as we held them in our mouths and snapped them. We were dogs but with thumbs who grabbed hold and tore off their wings and flung their amputated torsos into the night.

And while we fought the wall of scuttling dark had finally climbed up over the edge of our trailer roof.

It looked a bit like sticks and twigs caught up in a flood; bits of bones and teeth. The mess rolled itself up onto our roof.

I howled a warning, grabbing Tupperware lids, and started to push the stuff back. A tiny bare rat skull bit into my arm. I tore it free.

Dani was losing a lot of blood and was sitting up dazed in black leggings, staring at her thick soled boots. Bats were lapping at the wound in her arm.

A half-squirrel thing, limbless, snaked towards her. I kicked it away. I was standing one legged when the weight of the whole mess tilted the trailer and with a jolt, one side dropped. I was jerked off my feet. Like a maw of uneven rotten teeth, the mass of things hauled themselves towards us.

It started to rain rotten blood.

Flesh fell from the sky. Some of it still tried to walk. We were doused in it, stained with it, we stank of guts and death and marsupia. The sky itself made a sound like drum 'n' bass. Overhead, caught in a new flickering red light, there was a carousel of flesh, spun in arcs then flung aside. The neeping of bats started to fade.

A voice from the sky said, 'Do not bring any pets.'

Then voice then blared. 'Only two people in the basket at any one time.'

The thumping noise became a fist of air that slammed into us repeatedly.

I felt a sharp bite through my shoe. I was standing in a porridge of animal parts that surged like the sea. It didn't need to breathe, and was needled with teeth.

The last of the bats were shredded. Some few escaped – I could hear some of them retreat into the night.

Something large with a huge cow's smile was pulling itself up onto the roof. Two mismatched forelegs bent backwards.

And the voice of Zeus resolved itself into a helicopter, and a mesh basket being lowered. Mom and Faith had already hoisted Dani to her feet and kept her standing. Mom had one had on Evie's back. Evie carried her *Frozen* book under her arm.

The basket shuddered its way lower. Front and back were big orange tanks, for floating. This was meant for rescuing people from floods.

'Let's get Mum in first,' ordered the voice of Zeus. 'Then the little girl. Hold her in. We're about to hoist up.'

The shotgun went off right next to my ear.

The cow's head exploded. I had the Bijou. Deafened, I ran towards the thing and buzzed off its two limbs. Something dog-like sunk its jaws into my thigh. Another thunderbolt from Faith. Damn, she was a good shot. She missed my thigh, and hit the thing.

Mom had a little tin, yellow and black, containing lighter fluid. She'd been keeping it back. She squirted itat the tide around me, then pulled me back. She flicked a match. Flame danced on the surface of the stuff. It did not retreat, but it paused.

We backed into the centre.

Overhead, in the cradle, Dani was hauled skywards, her head resting out of love and exhaustion on Evie's shoulder.

The stuff heaved, regrouped. Scabs of burn were pulled in. Fresh faces assembled like a list of this year's upcoming new stars. They too all grinned, wearing other animals' skins.

'Holy Mary Mother of God,' said Faith.

I turned off the Bijou and let it droop. Save power for when it's needed.

Overhead, in the sky, Dani was being helped out of the basket into a maw that seemed to have opened in the sky itself. For some reason the helicopter was hard to see. My advice is to paint your rescue helicopters bright orange.

The basket descended again. Mom set alight the mass of stuff again. Beneath us, the aluminium frame of the trailer creaked and groaned. The helicopter's basket wobbled into reach.

'Only two,' the voice of God warned from overhead.

Faith gave us a push. 'Go!' She had the shogun. My hands made a foothold for my Mom. She stepped onto it. I staggered with her weight. She flipped herself in, turned around, seized my wrists and hoisted me in with the Bijou. The basket tipped, then righted itself and began to rise. Mom clicked a seatbelt around me, then one around herself.

Bam. Faith's shotgun. I looked back to see her calmly reload. A wall of stuff raised itself up in front of her. The whole porridge smiled. In the place of teeth were skulls, each skull full of teeth had inside it another mouth full of teeth, and another inside that. Concentric circles, fractals, a lamprey of heads and teeth.

It swept towards Faith. She slung the shotgun over her shoulder and jumped.

She caught hold of an orange tank.

The cable groaned, straining with the extra weight. We tipped dangerously; I reached for Faith to hold her as we even more slowly climbed.

From the mass below, an arm reached up after us. It looked like seaweed topped with a horse's nearly naked skull. Its jaws closed on Faith's ankle and held. We stopped rising.

I snapped on the Bijou. Over the noise of the chopper, I felt rather than heard it buzz and reached out with it, but the blade was nowhere near the thing. The horse-skull-thing jerked us, trying to dislodge Faith. I snapped open my seatbelt to reach forward, just as the thing jerked again. The Bijou swung and glanced off part of the cradle. Paint chips – well that's what they felt like – flew in my face.

'Turn it off!' shouted Mom.

A light blazed over us from above. 'Lean back,' ordered the voice of Zeus. 'Back,' Mom shouted, pulled me further into the cradle and encircled me with both arms.

Was I hearing thunder? I felt rather than heard bullets, a vibration though flesh, bone, metal and cloth. The buzz left a dazed numbness on my cheeks like someone had slapped me.

They must have shot the base of the thing. Suddenly the cradle soared skyward, released. My stomach dropped. We then swung in a wide circle, still tipped steeply. Faith shouted something like, 'It's still got me.' She kicked and jerked both her arms further over the orange floater and shouted, 'Don't pull me in.'

We rose up slowly, a kind of grinding tension in the wires that held us. Something below was thrashing. The maw of the helicopter suddenly seemed to open up around us – for a moment like it was trying to eat us.

The Army people – I think they were Army – shouted at us to keep down. They snatched hold of Mom and then me, and swung us in. I passed the Bijou to them. Faith was still howling and kicking. A mini-sun of light from the helicopter glared onto Faith's rictus smile. A length of sinew still held her ankle.

One of the soldiers knelt, aimed and blasted his gun at it. Like a snake, the thing coiled itself up and lunged, knocking the man aside and out of the helicopter. He gave a shout and somersaulted out of the light. The thing was naked now, all vertebrae. It roiled up into and into the cradle, hauling Faith by the ankle. The cradle pitched, righting itself, and the thing let go of Faith and reared up.

It was an amalgam of spinal cords seven, maybe ten feet long, healed into a chain and held by a lattice of string-cheese ligaments. A long skull seemed to survey us, smiling, looking smug. Its horse's mane was still in place, a jet-black mohican. Was it jewellery wound into that hair? Or just bits of metal flack or bone catching the light? The thing reared up over Faith's head and opened its jaws.

Then the horse's head exploded with gunfire, scattering into chips, the long neck breaking apart, parts dropping away into the night.

Faith wailed, held up her hands, and began to make panicked, disgusted noises. 'Hah. Hah. Hah!' She flung, then kicked bits out of the cradle. The Army reached out for her. Shaking, almost dancing, she shambled her way out of the basket. The personnel grabbed her arms, guided her inside and laid her next to us. 'Nothing the like,' she gasped.

'Poor Faith,' Mom said and hugged her. I had never seen Faith shaking, sobbing with terror. I'd hardly seen it at all in anyone and I couldn't imagine that it would not break her. I couldn't imagine that a person could be so turned upside down and not stay that way.

A radio voice blared. The sound inside the chopper was deafening.

'We're taking you to a facility,' a woman shouted at us.

'Where?' Mom bellowed.

'Kassam,' said the woman. She gave a thumbs up. Mom gave her a thumbs up back.

Another radio voice crackled. The woman passed Mom a canteen.

Below us on the ground, tongues of fire were being shot at the allotments – flamethowers? All along the main road, the evergreens danced, like they'd been hit by a nuclear bomb. Across the bypass, the half-built new housing estate with its empty basements, its sheds, its naked frames also burned, like skeletons in a bone-fire.

'Neighbours,' Mom shouted, and pointed down at the twenty-two other trailers.

The woman shook her head. 'Only ones left.'

I kept looking back at Faith. She looked fragile, like a leaf in autumn, brown, crinkled, and unsteady.

Amid the sea of fire, the burning hedges and the ashy remains of harvested barley, something huge and black moved, some of it still on fire. It looked like lava oozing from a volcano. Billows of black smoke rolled skywards towards us. We flew through it.

'You're just spreading it,' I said. The woman touched her ear.

It loved heat, it loved fire.

'It will fall as ash,' I told her. She nodded and smiled.

The ash would still be alive.

PART FIVE
Mountain of Ash

Seventeen

I didn't even know Kassam Stadium existed.

It looked like we were landing on the moon – a huge grey space with blinding lights in our eyes and dun-coloured dust blasting up from the pitch.

Three other helicopters were on the grass, and we could see a line of vehicles parked shoulder to shoulder all along the western side of the Stadium.

Dani looked awful, grey with deep creases down the middle of her cheeks and loose pouches of flesh either side of them, lightly blue with veins. The bandages on her arm had done little to staunch the bleeding. Evie kept circling her and whimpering, though the personnel tried to make her sit and wear a seat belt.

As we landed, one of the female officers held up a hand to keep us in place. She mimed how to leave the craft, crouching low, and warned us to keep our eyes shut. 'There's a lot of ash. We'll be taking off right away.' She rotated a finger. 'Blades keep spinning.'

Two personnel in masks, gloves and shoe coverings hoisted themselves up into the craft. They unfolded a hammock contraption and replaced the basket with it. They said something to Dani, counted aloud and smartly loaded her onto it. She howled 'Ow! Oh, wow!' She was swept away from us in some kind of hoist.

It was a bone jolting jump down onto the ground.

Everything smelled like there had been a fire, and nobody could have kept their eyes open in that blast of dust. I stumbled and let myself be pulled along. Getting away from the blast of air from the rotors was like stepping through layers of curtains.

Suddenly we could look up. The bleachers rose up on three sides of the pitch and they were already full of people. As bright as day, lights lit the ground and the seating. Even from below we could make out people slumped among their suitcases.

There was no stand along one side, but that was blockaded by vehicles – ambulances, one huge garbage truck and some military transport. One trailer had a large gun mounted on something rotary. Everything stank of petrol; blue clouds of unburnt fumes chugged out from generators, which added to the general noise level. For some reason in front of one of the tents, people in orange robes danced and played music. Hare Krishna?

Dani was being carried in a different direction, towards a large camouflaged tent. Mom jumped towards the medics, and sounding panicky asked how we would find each other later. Someone with a tablet asked Mom's name, and keyed it in, reassured Mom that we would all be seated together. Could we now register at the registration desk? An arm was held up inviting to one of the many tents, none of them with signs.

As our group split up, Evie walked calmly with her mum, hugging her book. She eyed me up from a distance and gave me an odd yip I couldn't translate into words. It immediately calmed me down. It was some kind of instinctive signal that the pack was not really splitting up.

Faith sniffed, looking around the Stadium. 'Don't think much of this.' She still had the shotgun slung across her shoulders. 'This place is a bugger to get out of at the best times.' I realized that I'd kept hold of the Bijou. The only thing Mom had was her belt bag with the passports. We'd lost everything else including the charger for the chainsaw.

'I feel safer here than in that trailer park.' Mom's voice was also raised over the din.

'It's like a henhouse. Draws the foxes.'

Faith looked firm, unflustered. She was still Faith. I sprang on her and hugged her hard, arms around her waist. Her breath reversed loudly, then she patted my shoulder and walked on after the officer. 'By the way,' she told me. 'You stink.'

We were deposited in a registration line, and the officer with us turned and jogged back to the helicopter. Arranged like the Last Supper along fold-out tables, sat more people in PPE with laptops.

'I'm sorry,' one of them said, a thin young man with a beard muffled by both a screen and a face mask. Volunteer, I reckoned. 'I'm afraid we're going to have to ask you for those weapons for safekeeping.' He waved for our gun and the saw. These were labelled with our names and carried away. We each got a cellophane pack of blankets, wipes, tin plates and cups, tin spoons, toiletries and a blanket. I found out later that Kassam Stadium had long been designated a disaster evacuation site – for London, in case of a chemical or nuclear attack. They'd been rehearsing this for ten years.

The strangle-voiced young man asked a series of questions about what animal life we had seen, what animals had attacked. 'They're merging,' I told him. 'The dead animals merge.' He had no category for that and didn't key anything in. Then he started to assign us seats. Mom said, 'We will be joined by a woman in a stretcher, very badly injured. She's in triage now.'

'Family member?' the young man asked.

Mom hesitated and then said yes. 'So we'll need seating that isn't too high up.' He gave us a seating assignment, 'This is so we can find you later if we need to contact you.'

Even now I can remember those seat numbers: EB 4, 11 to 15

'How are we supposed to remember that?' Mom asked.

Faith was a football fan and she'd been to the Stadium many times. 'Easy-peasy. East Bleachers Row 4.'

'Do you have a change of clothes?' the man asked. We didn't.

'In that case you'll need to shower. We have replacement clothes or you can shower in your clothes to remove most of the hazard.' He used his arms to flag-wave instructions to a row of blue cabins that looked like portaloos.

'Hot night. We can cool off,' said Faith.

The cabins had yellow radiation hazard signs. PPE-clad people told us what to expect – lower head so it's cleaned first, raise arms, turn, take off shoes and make sure the soles were cleansed. For some reason there was no queue. The whole floor was a drain. Jets of water pummelled me, smelling of disinfectant. Foul brown goop swirled down the drain. I opened up my mouth to rinse out the taste of death and washed and washed my hair. I stepped back out dripping wet – clean and cool for the first time in months.

Faith stood outside, waiting for us. 'We'll have go inside and then back around. There's no direct way to the bleachers from the pitch.' She started to lead us to the main entrance and a canopied walkway.

We passed the Hare Krishna tent and it steamed with beany curry smells. 'Oh food!' exclaimed Mom and made us all stop. She said to a young man with a white streak on his forehead, 'I'm sorry I don't have a credit card.'

A woman in sari stood behind him. 'It's all free,' she grinned.

Next to them was a grill selling German sausages and the usual range of burgers and kebabs. 'Ew. Meat,' said a woman in passing, wrinkling her nose.

The owners, a red-faced husband and wife tutted. 'Nobody wants anything,' said the wife, stunned.

Our tin plates were filled with steaming brown mush. It was lukewarm and the onions were undercooked, but even Faith did not turn her nose up at it. We ate standing up. Mom keyed something into her phone – sending the seat numbers to Dani, I supposed.

As we watched one of the ambulances pulled away, lights flashing but with siren silent. One military vehicle drove in front of it, another escorted behind.

There were no stars, no moon. I think I saw the mountainous outline of something like a thundercloud.

'I hope those hamburgers don't go for a walk,' said Faith.

Our seats were already occupied.

A man and his wife were nursing about seven large suitcases of stuff. 'Oh God no,' said the woman as we approached, her tan fake, her hair in streaks.

'These are our seats,' said Mom.

The husband was pale, pudgy with very black hair and stubble. 'Can't you sit somewhere else?'

'No,' said Mom. 'We have someone with us who is wounded, and we need seats lower down for her.'

The wife began to haul a case under her feet. 'I told you to leave them in the car.'

'Jesus,' muttered the man, and simply rolled one of the cases over the back of the seats into the row above.

'So what happens when the people for those seats show up?' Mom asked.

'Do you want to sit here or not?' The man said, and in a sweaty rage, tumbled another suitcase up and over. 'Years we worked for this.'

The bag clinked and rattled. 'Careful,' said the wife. 'There's valuable things in that bag.'

We sat down, me right next to the Mrs.

Sure enough about an hour later, a busload of evacuees from Waterperry squelched up the steps, each of them with a dripping rucksack and a suitcase. 'I'm sorry, you can't sit there someone else is coming,' the stubbly man shouted. They looked about them, wondering where. 'Well, you can't all sit together!' the man shouted.

Being numerous somehow made the Waterperrys more feeble. Murmuring they deferred and started to disperse, picking their way towards other, less aggressive people who grimaced, weren't happy, but made room.

'Bloody nonsense,' said Mr Stubble. His wife gave his forearm an approving stroke. Mom shook her head.

It was summer and a couple of hours before the sun rose.

By six am, the sun hammered those bleachers.

Bronze light from a bronze sky. It was like a dirty sunset. I realized my mouth had grit in it, a stinging grit I didn't like. I wiped my tongue on my sleeve. There was a texture like the cells of mulberries that went pop and left a dead-gut taste in my mouth and smeared grey-brown.

The roof was useless – sunlight blazed under it into our faces. We sweated and ached, far from any toilet and we'd already drunk our one bottle of water. My phone was nearly out of charge so I couldn't read my books. We weren't about to make conversation with the Fake Tans, and I wasn't going to be able to sleep sitting up in those chairs.

Mom's phone rang. She'd been holding it ready in her hand. 'Yes, yes, Dani love how are you?' She listened in silence for quite a while. 'Okay, babe I'm out of battery nearly.' She stared at the phone.

'She's had her arm nearly sawn through by a chainsaw, and all they've done is bandage it. They're sending her here.'

Faith stood up. 'This Stadium holds sixteen thousand people. They won't have space in that tent.' She turned sideways, almost disappearing she was so thin. 'Call her. Tell her to stay there, I'll meet her.'

'You don't have to do that.'

'Won't find us otherwise.' Faith had already slipped past Mom and me, and was bounding down the steps, back hunched. I slid over into her seat and couldn't stop myself looking at Mrs Fake Tan and growling.

'You mental or something?' she said.

'Yes,' I answered.

'Teddy,' warned Mom. So I growled again.

Nearly an hour later, someone tapped me on the shoulder. It was Evie. She climbed over the back of the seats and sat next to me, saying nothing. She fixed on *Frozen* again, opening out each and every tab, door, little wheel or fold-out page slowly and carefully. Water, snow, ice, palaces, dances, snowmen. She stayed silent.

Faith and Dani emerged from the first entry tunnel,. Faith had Dani's arm and the two of them inched their way round onto the very first step then past the four rows to us. Her leg was bandaged too, so the chainsaw must have grazed that, though it wouldn't have been turning – those teeth could still bite.

It seemed to take her hours to climb those steps. Dani collapsed next to Mom. 'You have no idea,' Dani said. 'Hundreds of people, in a terrible state.'

'Aw Babe, did they give you anything to eat?'

'Just water. I need to sleep.' Dani put her head on Mom's shoulder, and Mom sat still with her arm around her.

For hours.

Someone still in PPE came up the steps and threw bottles of water. People couldn't catch them and they landed like clubs on other people's heads. Mrs Fake tried to snatch one from me when she dropped her own. Faith's grim face shook in disapproval.

Sometime later the woman started to mew. 'Oh no. Oh no.' The front of her fawn trousers went dark, and pee started to splash over her shoes and mine.

'For Chrissakes!' her husband shouted.

'I can't help it.'

'Well, mop it up!'

Palaver as they tried to open the suitcases only a little bit and find something. 'No not that, that's my Dolce y Gabbana.' Finally a towel was found.

By then Faith had fixed them with slate grey eyes and chuckled at them thin lipped.

'What do you know about it?' Mrs Tan shouted.

'Enough not to piss meself,' said Faith. 'All that stuff of yourn. It's going to burn.'

Later Faith said to Mom, 'We need to get out of here. It'll be shambles with all these people if something happens.'

'When Dani's a bit stronger,' said Mom.

About two pm, up through the ticket entry just below us, came Dad.

My heart jumped. I stood up and wolf-howled. I saw him clearly, short and black bearded. And then I didn't see him. It wasn't Dad, black bearded.

It was Ken.

Ken had grown a beard too. Maybe he'd converted as well, to be with Dad. As he got closer, slowly, he held out his hands as if to show he had no weapons. One arm had a Waitrose bag around it like a handbag, and I saw that pretty-boy smile. I bounced up and down and barked and snarled and growled *Not yours! Go! Not yours.*

Evie joined in. She howled too.

Mr Tan said, 'They've got that disease.'

'They should be locked up.'

Mom stilled both Evie and me with her hands. Dani woke up blinking, and winced at once with pain.

Out of her cargo pocket, Faith produced the last of her whisky and passed it to Dani. 'Best medicine,' Faith chuckled.

'Ken,' Mom said. If she'd been a dog, she would have growled as well. 'Sorry. They're just being kids.'

I managed somehow to talk and growl at the same time. 'Hello Ken. Where's Barbie? Or is she dead too? Did you eat her?'

His face froze and he stared.

'It's been hard,' said Mom, like she was walking on glass.

Ken stammered. 'I tried to phone you a couple of times.'

And Mom didn't answer, I wonder why. Mom stared at him stonily, making no excuses for not picking his calls.

Ken stammered on. 'There's a helpline to call if you're concerned about relatives. They said you were registered here, and safe.'

'It's been difficult to charge the phones,' Mom said.

'I left as soon as I could. Lockdown's over,' he said with an odd blurting laugh. He looked shy, self-deprecating. *See how much I wanted to make sure you were okay?*

He was pudgy, pale like a frog's belly. Even with a beard, he looked soft enough to punch. I was beyond hostility. Part of me wanted to tear

217

out his throat. He'd taken my Dad. He'd taken my Dad by letting him fuck him and that made my Dad disloyal and broke our family.

Ken kept trying to make it friendly. He focussed on Mom and talked to her. 'I'm, I'm so sorry. Everybody at Well Being was just gutted to hear.'

Exactly what they said on breakfast television whenever somebody died.

I imitated TV in a sing-song voice. 'He was always so friendly and helpful to everybody, was always thinking of others, couldn't do enough for you. I miss him every day.' My voice went treble with sarcasm. 'The trauma never goes away. We're living with a life sentence.'

Fuckers.

He ran a shaky hand over his forehead. *Yeah Ken, this is even worse than you thought it would be.*

Mom's face clenched. 'Teddy's going through a bad patch.'

He looked down at the ground. 'Not surprising.' He put down the Waitrose bag and reached inside. 'It hasn't been that bad in London so I was able to get some food. Somebody at WBI told me you'd run out of food.'

Dani looked up. She had dark circles under her eyes. 'So this is the one is it?' she asked, her lip curling.

Ken took boxes out of the bag. 'I bought uh some vegan dishes. Humous and babaganoush. Mike always said you liked that.'

Dani was implacable. 'You've got a bloody nerve. You can see there's no space for you, so you can hop it.'

Ken looked up, his face settling. 'Hello, I'm Ken.'

'I know who you are. I never met this Mike, but the pair of you. Toof! You disgust me. Do you hear? Disgust me. You steal her husband, you wreck their lives. And now you show up here all friendly?'

Faith looked at him, the smile steady and thin. Mom said Dani's name, to calm her, and took her hand.

'No! I'm not going to make it easy for him. I've been living with Teddy. I've seen what you put him through. Well, you can leave the food thank you very much and then you can scarper.'

Ken held up a hand. *All right, enough. I got it.*

So why would that make me cry? I didn't like Ken so why would him backing away make me cry?

'Maggie, I know. But.' Ken was pleading. 'Can we talk for just a little? Somewhere else? And then I'll get going.'

Mom sighed, then said excuse me, sorry to the people to our right, so she could get out. I went with her, my eyes and fists swollen. I was defending my Mom. I wanted an excuse to hit him.

Evie was right behind me, growling.

There was no privacy, anyway. We had an audience of bored people in seats all around us. Ken walked down the steps, until Mom stopped. 'This will do,' she announced.

'Maggie. Do we know what happened to Mike?'

Mom just shook her head. 'He just disappeared.' *Like we told you.*

'No other sign? I mean how did it happen?'

Mom stomped in place.

Ken's voice went thin. 'I'm sorry. But I haven't heard, I don't know anything. Anything would help.'

And Ken started to get weepy.

No, you don't get to cry over my Dad. You don't get to mourn for him. You're the reason he's gone.

Mom made a smacking noise with her lips. 'We all feel like that, Ken. We're all just hanging in mid-air. It's been hardest on Teddy. He's regressing, he's acting up.' She looked at Ken squarely. 'And he hates you.'

'That's understandable,' said Ken. 'I don't hate him.'

'There's no news Ken. Mike went out to phone you. So Teddy blames you. I try not to. He didn't come back. His car wasn't locked, but the doors were closed, keys in the ignition, phone on the front seat. And he was gone. There were animals attacking people, but Teddy and Faith still marched up and down the fields trying to find something, anything. I was back home, tearing my hair out. There is nothing, Ken. We have nothing for you.' Her voice went savage at the end. 'I'm sorry.'

'Okay,' Barely audible. 'I'll be on my way. If you find anything…'

'We will let you know…'

'If you need a place to stay in London…'

Mom wasn't looking at him. 'It's my place, Ken. I'm the joint owner.'

Ken's face hung blankly.

Mom sighed. 'You are welcome to stay. I don't mean to be unkind. But you should be asking us.'

'Can I stay?' he asked, glum-voiced, not looking at anyone.

'Yes,' said Mom.

'Thank you. Will you go back to Beehive Cottage?'

Mom sighed. 'Ken. Will you please stop asking questions?'

He looked at her in silence, like a cow.

The worst of it was I could see that – he didn't *love* us exactly – but he did care about us. That as was bad as Mom kissing you when she'd been crying when her face was all gloopy. He cared about Dad and that meant he cared about us, cared about me, just because I was Dad's. He probably thought we were some kind of family. Or wanted us to be. That Ken had loved Dad, or held him, or took him from me or wanted us all to be together was like something jammed into my chest. I couldn't breathe.

I really had thought he was Dad. I hadn't been surprised to see Dad. I really was still expecting Dad to come home at any second, like seeing him would be normal. Constantly thinking he was going to come back any second was as bad as being sick.

Dad was gone. Gone completely. Evaporated. I'd never get to talk to him again. I'd never get to tell him he was the best Dad ever. I'd been mean to him. And then he went away.

'You're upsetting Teddy,' Mom said. Ken nodded. He turned to go. I threw Mom's hand off my shoulder.

I couldn't go back to those bleachers. They still smelled of that woman's piss; it was all over my shoes, the only ones I had. I couldn't just sit there listening to the whole world sink into mud.

I wiped my face. 'I'm going to get some food,' I said. Even then, I knew it was a lie.

'I'll go with you?' Ken asked.

I howled at him and ran jumping down the steps.

'Let him go,' I heard Mom say.

She had no idea how far I was going. It was not quite a thought, certainly not yet a plan, but I was going back to find Dad.

Eighteen

Counting on my fingers now I realize that Ken was only twenty-five years old.

Younger when we met.

Covid lockdown finally ended, and Mom went to see her family in Kokomo, Indiana. She hadn't been home for about fifteen years. And maybe the marriage was going through a bad patch. Mom's conscience wouldn't let her fly, so she travelled on a merchant ship and then by bus halfway across the USA. She was gone for four months.

Dad told me that we were meeting a friend of his in the pub. In came this kid who looked more like my brother than a friend of my father. I sat eating a beanburger and chips while Dad and the kid exchanged jokes I didn't get, hands on each other's shoulders, eyes sparkling. I was nine years old, my brain unclouded by puberty. I wanted my Dad to have friends. I wanted him to laugh and tell jokes. So why didn't I like this?

Dad would suddenly remember I was there and shake my knee and ask me if I wanted more chips. Dad would never normally ask me if I wanted chips. More likely tap water or homemade unsweetened yogurt. He was drinking beer, which he never did. It made him woozy, not like my Dad at all.

Maybe this is how Dad had acted when he'd been a kid. Maybe he'd made fun of kids like me. Maybe I wouldn't have liked my Dad when he was young. Probably not.

Ken didn't know how to talk to me. He asked me what computer games I liked. I told him what he should have known – that I wasn't allowed to play computer games. It was like trying to talk to one of those kids at school. He was young. Young guys scared me.

And there was something queasy in Ken's smile. His mouth always seemed to be curling into a sneer. It would have looked good in lots of lipstick like an old movie star. He was plump and nervous and I had to admit that I didn't like him at all.

Ken started to come around in the evenings.

Dad and Ken started an animal rights blog together and worked on it every Saturday night. Mid-week, they ran a political discussion group on Zoom. Ken always came with a gift of wine or cheese or venison or smoked eel or something else he wanted, like he didn't believe we were actually vegan. Then he'd scoff the lot himself. He sometimes stayed the night, though always in the third bedroom, and always with his bedding disarrayed in the morning.

Ken had a family house in Cumbria, and Dad and I spent at least two weekends that summer with him there. Ken's family house was on a lake. I loved snorkelling there even though the water was cold. It was another world underwater. I could hang suspended and look down at my feet like I was flying. The rocks had a coating of moss. Fools-gold floated glinting in the water. Light-worms wriggled over the surface of things; twigs floated like fish. I never saw a fish, though minnows would cluster round my feet, nibbling.

Ken had a speedboat. He loved roaring around the lake, skimming on the surface. He wore a crash helmet that didn't fit. It was too narrow but was huge and round and sat on his head like a muffin. It made him look like an alien. He kept smiling like it was all a clever joke, like he was being super-ironical. He knew he was plump and geeky and that he looked out of place in a speedboat.

Right at the end, just before Mom was due back home, Dad and Ken took a four-day trip to Scotland. We stayed by a lake in a national forest. They went for a long hike together and didn't take me.

Dad told me that there was a secret place where the animals had never been hunted. So they had no fear of people. Children weren't allowed there. 'In case they scare the animals.' He bought me a fresh set of books including *Just So Stories* which I didn't like, and a DVD of *Jason and the Argonauts*, which I loved, all the more because I was never allowed videos.

'You'll be okay reading, son? There's pizza in the microwave.'

And I was left alone for the whole day, at first enthralled by giant living statues, Poseidon, the hydra and skeleton warriors. Then it started to get dark and quiet and I went from bored, to cranky, to slightly tearful.

Oh they came back and told me that deer had eaten out of their hands. They said it was beautiful. I wished I could have gone, and it didn't quite make sense to me. It was hunters they needed to keep out of the Magic Forest, not me. I wanted to feed deer as well.

It wasn't until Dad left us that I got it. With a sensation like a sudden sprain, I realized that it wasn't animals that had made the forest magic, but Ken and Dad together. Dad had lied to me, to get me out of the way.

I think I'd become more of a cat than a dog – I didn't need or want a pack.

I wanted to prowl alone.

I'd said I was going for food, so I did end up at the food stalls. Apparently the hamburgers had indeed gone for a walk – well they'd eaten a customer's tongue, even after being cooked. That tent was now empty with a big sign in marker pen on whiteboard NO MEAT SOLD HERE.

The Hare Krishna guy with a white loop on his forehead and a very friendly smile, leaned forward and whispered. 'Are you okay?'

I think I just stared at him.

'Where are your parents? Are your parents here?'

Why couldn't Dad have converted to Hare Krishna? This guy would have been a nice extra Dad. I'd have played the drums. Krishna Krishna Hare Hare

'How about an orangeade?' he asked.

I think I nodded yes. I'm pretty sure I also made the Plaintive Meow.

So I was suddenly holding a huge waxed cup as long as my forearm full of ice and a drink the colour of Cheesits. (Cheesits – we had all kinds of horrible artificial food that actually everyone loved made mostly of air and chemicals, like eating baked clouds of carcinogen. I wanted to float off on Cheesits. They were the colour of sunsets. Forbidden fruit.) I wandered away with my big heavy cup and then remembered I hadn't said thank you for the free drink. It was cold, wet, and sweet.

Come to think of it, the sky was the colour of Cheesits as well.

It was nearly three pm by then, and in one corner of the field, rows of Muslims were kneeling, as if worshiping the eastern stand. All their faces were ranged toward me, and I supposed Ken might be among them. I looked away.

I felt invisible and who knows, maybe I was. I wandered past the military vehicles with their barking radio voices. I wasn't hearing the English. I was hearing the snarly, threatening, angry-dog noises.

Then I was walking among rows of parked cars with people checking their boots, looking anxious.

And then I saw little platforms with shelters and glowing electric notices. Bus stops.

I remembered that Faith said she took the bus from Witney to get to Oxford United FC matches.

There it was – Bus O3 labelled CARTERTON with electric-dot destinations parading past. One of them was MARKET SQ WITNEY. I could walk home from there.

I checked my pockets. They jingled. I hadn't spent any money in weeks, but there in my pocket were two pound coins and some change. That would get me somewhere.

So I sat down on bench that was rounded the wrong way to stop sleepers. I waited in the sun for a while.

Hybrid cars were more silent than owls.

A car stopped and opened its blue eyes, and inside was Ken.

'You do know there won't be a bus, don't you Teddy?'

I looked away.

'I'm sorry, but you're not going to find him this way.'

My hands were jammed into my armpits and I looked away.

'I could drive you,' Ken said. 'It's twenty minutes from here.'

I corrected him. 'Thirty minutes.'

He smiled, still sad around the eyes. 'I'm going there anyway.'

I'd been saving up the orangeade to let the ice melt. I leaned in the passenger window and threw the contents all over him and his burgundy interior.

Ken sat there blinking but looked only mildly pissed off, like he was enduring something. He said, 'We could find him together. It would keep us safer.'

'We don't have any weapons.'

He bit his thumbnail. 'You were going anyway. Or trying to.'

Ken had always been pasty faced – his black moustache had looked painted on like Groucho Marx's. But now he had a smooth sheen of sweat all across his dome of a forehead. Fever. We all had fevers; we'd stopped seeing the symptoms. Ken was so sweaty that he looked security-wrapped in plastic. He was quite ill, 25 years old and young for his age even physically. Age was the key factor in gene transfer into humans by the marsupia.

Ken let the orangeade drip, like he was considering something.

And then he made a dog noise.

The noise a pack leader makes, irresistible.

Hunt

Pack

Hunt

Now.

Ken knew exactly what he was doing. He dog-triggered me into going with him. The human part of me didn't even know I'd climbed into the car. Basically it was a legal kind of kidnapping.

Dogs are not wolves. We have been bred to be dangerously loving. Humans who also lack the equivalent chromosome sequences are trusting and sociable, freakishly sweet natured. It's a recognized genetic disorder called Williams-Beuren syndrome. People with Williams-Beuren have an elfin appearance – cute and wide-eyed – and so often end up duped, abused, raped, or loyal to tormentors.

What Ken did to me bound me to him. Made us part of the same pack, no matter what my human mind made of him. I was tame.

We headed out on roads I didn't know, driving around the south side of Oxford onto the bypass, and then onto the A34, another road with no traffic lights or crossroads.

I had time to think. I didn't want to be anywhere with Ken. But I did want to get back to Oldminster and driving there in a car was the safest way, perhaps the only way, to do that. I didn't protest or try to jump out of the car. I just turned my whole body away from him and looked out of the window.

We got onto the Botley Road. At lights next to some kind of old mall, he pulled over and took out his phone. He called Mom.

'Hello Maggie. I'm with Teddy, we're going back to find Mike.' I could hear Mom's voice shouting. 'I know, I'm sorry. He's in the car with me. We're fine.' Long silence. 'All of that is true.' Silence. 'Teddy, do you want to talk to your mum?'

I shouted instead. 'We're okay, Mom.' I knew what she was going to say. I didn't want to go back to that stadium. I wanted, needed to find Dad. We'd be okay in a car, so long as we kept moving. We'd drive to the house. Even more leaves and things would have died in the heat, so the ground would be more open. We'd find Dad in the broken grass; I'd see him; we'd bury him.

'Drink lots of water,' Ken told Mom, and pulled away from the lights.

We went under the ring road and headed out into fields. It was like a checkerboard – some were sun-blasted white, some were burnt black, still smouldering, with little dervishes of ash whirling across them.

I've tried now to reconstruct our route with old maps.

I think we must have taken the road to Farmoor where the water reservoir was. I saw what looked like a lake in the distance. What we know now is that the ash was blowing into the drinking water.

Ahead of us, car brakelights flashed red, slowed and then edged into the opposing lane. We crawled forward. On my side of the car, something had pulled itself over a dry-stone wall and slopped over onto the soft shoulder. It looked a bit like a porridge made of ash, only the surface of it seethed, covered with what looked like shreds of burnt onions and the odd flap of charred hide. Inside it were needles of blackened bone, and these worked like oars to pull the thing forward. It smelled like burnt tires and as always that chemical smell.

Ken swore, trickling sweat, and swerved the car away from it. He blinked and jammed a box at me. 'Wear a face mask.'

I remembered the goo in my nose and took one. Ken patted my leg. He thought we were friends.

Once past the ooze, cars accelerated and fled. As we pulled away. I looked behind us. Soon the ash would block that road. It was like a railroad barrier going down – we'd only just made it across.

We might not be able to get back. But I needed to get home.

The road narrowed onto a tiny stone bridge – a toll bridge designed to make traffic stop and pay a ten pence fee. Its high stone walls did not let us see the beautiful river. A bus was inching its way across and our caravan of cars had to stop to let it crowd past.

Ken looked at me with great misgiving, sweat dripping like tears. 'You're a great kid, Teddy,' he said. He searched my face. 'You look just like him. He was short too. Look at how big and strong he grew up to be.'

We waited, He looked back at the road ahead. 'Do you remember our drive north?'

His voice was faraway and he didn't blink. Cars horns beeped ahead of us.. In the wake of the bus, other cars bullied their way across the bridge. Ken kept talking.

'We stopped for lunch in Newcastle and walked across the bridge. And went to that big silver building that looked like a whale? Remember?'

'No,' I said. I did, but what I remembered most was feeling frozen out, Dad and Ken seemed so entangled in each other.

'You don't?' He sounded regretful. 'Remember your Dad talked about South Shields? His mum had lived there when she was little? So we drove along the river? They had these street lamps that were black metal ladies all lined up. The river was so wide, it was like the sea. His family had built boats there. We drove to Marston Rock.'

The beach there was all stones that hurt my feet, and I went off by myself to avoid Dad and Ken. I'd hugged my knees in the cold wind.

'And where we stayed the first night? We drove late? It got dark. It was in Scotland, near a place called Hoik... Only they spelled in Hawick. And we kept asking people where *Hawick* was. And people told us there was no such place.' He was smiling into another world. 'We built a fire. In the BnB, remember? There were owls, hooting. Your dad got so excited. He stood outside for hours hoping to see them.'

I had not remembered that, and then suddenly I did. I remembered it all, though a moment before I'd had no trace of it. That's one reason you need other people to stay alive for you. They give you back parts of your life.

We got across the bridge, and roundabouted away from Eynsham, onto the A40.

Then we stopped dead. On the A40, this was no surprise. Just beyond Eynsham there was a set of lights that always caused a queue. One car ahead of us did a U turn, but people often lost patience there.

Then a lorry also turned, unblocking our view, and we saw what the trouble was. It was like a lava flow, dark and glistening, another mound of black goo. Only much taller and bigger than the first one. This had strands of yellow in it like an infection. It had swallowed most of a car, just its white boot showing.

Ken slammed into reverse, then roared forward in a U-turn. He accelerated back the way we had come, wobbling. Ken was not actually a very skilled driver. We got back to the Eynsham roundabout. The car ahead of us took the first left and we swept along behind it. Then the car ahead screeched to a halt just in front of us. Another jam of cars. The dark mass had oozed across the fields from the A40 and over this road as well. Ken swore, grinding the steering wheel round, and eased us slowly back onto the roundabout.

He was a Witney boy, Ken. He knew the local roads. He drove east to a tiny left turn I'd never seen before with no-entry signs posted. We entered anyway, down an unpaved lane. Mud tire-tracks and grass extended into a village, Cassington. Beeping his horn, Ken wrong-wayed at high speed, hawthorn branches and grass slapping the car.

We bounced out of it into a circle of modern houses. The windows of one had been boarded up. I thought we'd have to turn left into the village – but that would just take us back to the A40. Instead, Ken turned right, heading as far as I could tell back to Oxford. Then in the middle of nowhere, Ken forked left, heading where I had no idea.

'It's like they're deliberately blocking the roads,' said Ken.

'They are,' I said. My body was buzzing again, another wave of fever.

Ken blinked and scowled.

So I said. 'That's why they always go for the head. It's how they learn.'

'Did Ivan tell you that?' Ken asked.

'Go ask him.'

Ken looked grim. 'Ivan won't talk to me.' He waited. 'I guess you won't either.'

Nope.

We had the windows closed and we baked in the heat. Ken's clothes were soaked, but he still smelled of some kind of scent. His eyes were fixed ahead, but he had to keep wiping sweat out of his eyes. Both of us dreaded seeing one of those things again.

But the Army had not got this far out – these fields had not been torched.

To my surprise we ended up in Hanborough, where the train station was, and from there it was the dear old B4095.

We came out near the almshouses in Witney. There was not a single other car, not a person walking. The only thing that seemed alive were the birds in the trees. They screeched loudly as if sensing they were the only ones left. Birds, insects and fish would inherit the Earth.

We drove out via West End, past farms that were without sheep, past houses with cars still in the drive. It was getting late – shadows lengthening, the light slanted and orange. Neither Ken nor I wanted it to get dark.

And then up and over the slope from Windrush village. Stretching below us, my little valley – the field, the dog run, the ruins, the old church, and the line of trees that no longer hid Beehive Cottage. The limes, beeches and elders all looked like skeleton hands, bare fingers.

The road home. The recycling bin was still outside our gate, as if this were a world that had regular collections. We seemed to float down the hill, past the kissing gate to the ruins. Ken turned into our drive and the car creaked to a halt. Ken got out.

Nineteen

The garden looked stripped, as if the only thing it had ever grown were stinging nettles.

Dad's Golf was still in the drive. My heart rose up and my skin prickled because for just a moment I thought he'd driven the car and that meant he was home. Then I remembered. That was where Mr Keppel had parked it a month before.

I got out of the car. Every single bush and tree had dropped its leaves. The stench of animal decay was rammed into my nose as if into someone's infected wound.

But Ken sighed with satisfaction. He'd loved staying here.

When Dad had chain-sawed the hedge in front of the door, he'd pulled the tangle of branches to one side. The front door stood broken and open, the interior wall streaked as if by rain or mildew. The air hung still like it was exhausted by the heat.

I began the Plaintive Mew.

Some part of me was calling for Little One, if anything was left of her. I was expressing grief, loneliness, fear, abandonment, my yearning for Dad, for Mom.

For home. I was mewing for home.

I could feel all of that raw in my head. My brain felt like a patchwork quilt; I would jink up and over the stitching into a different way of being. There was a buzz in my head down into my body, a bit like a chill. The marsupia still had me.

Round the corner of our house came two dogs.

From the size, one of them might once have been Big Boy. He hopped on three legs. He was covered with crawling insects, every part of him except for his head. I couldn't focus on it. It was snow white and elongated. For a second I thought he'd grown some kind of mushroom on his neck.

The other dog I think had once been Schizo. He was smaller and moved in fits and starts, not quite so covered in beetles, but his skull had been picked clean. Both Ken and I began to jump and howl and snarl, part of the same pack. *Our place. Ours.*

The dogs did not bark. Big Boy coughed out a swarm of flies. The white thing on his neck had ring of what looked like chewing gum and those lips mouthed, 'Hello, Teddy,' The voice was small and whispering.

His head was a duck that had healed into place. The lips were scars where the beak had been. A tiny black eye was turned towards me, reflecting light.

'Dead head,' said Schizo, in a voice remarkably like Bounce's. 'Must dead head the roses.' His eyes looked like red, bunched fists but somehow they could see.

Ken walked backwards while talking. 'Get into the car.' I couldn't quite understand him. I couldn't quite move. I was growling.

The dogs began to laugh. 'Lovely to see you,' rasped what was left of Big Boy.

'How are your courgettes doing?' Schizo asked.

Ken started to jog backwards. Both dogs lunged into him and he fell over. Schizo tore out his throat. Big Boy had no fangs, but spun round behind Ken and began to claw at his head as if digging up a bone. Ken's face was turned towards me. He looked wistful, as if regretting this life. *Why?* his eyes seemed to say.

Pollyfilla. I was stuffed full of disease and too much horror. I couldn't move.

'They want you,' I managed to say.

Ken rolled over onto his knees, holding his throat and then tried to stand. Big Boy jumped onto his back. Schizo's naked jaws found a flap of scalp and peeled it back. Big Boy turned on Schizo, hopped towards him three legged and tried to knock him away from the head. But Schizo had working jaws and fangs, and was now the stronger dog. Snarling, mouth open, he tore the top of Big Boy's leg.

Big Boy lurched back and then staggered towards me. He tried to snarl, but only a kind of hiss came out. I still didn't move. I started to whimper to comfort him, as dogs do for each other: *You hurt.*

There was a crunching snap. Schizo had broken through bone and his snout was now buried in Ken's cranium. Ken seemed to stare up at the sky.

Big Boy tried to whimper, but couldn't.

Old weak dog. I screeched at him to die. *Old dog. You die.*

Die now.

Big Boy turned and his newly torn leg prized itself from the socket. It jitterbugged free and started to writhe its own way across the brown grass. Big Boy fell sideways, one leg in front, one leg behind and started to pull himself forward. As he crawled, he broke apart like a wave subsiding into the pebbles at Marston. Bones came free, hide flaked, the rib cage twisted. The neck wrenched, and the spine crumbled, shedding vertebrae. The duck remains were freed and it ran, wingless, towards the field. Big Boy settled into a trail of dried skin and bits of bones. These still seethed on the ground like mince in pan. Exposed was a large round ball full of meat, covered in a membrane, filaments running from it.

Schizo was standing grinning in front of me, his snout all red.

I knew I should try to run for the car. I wondered vaguely if it were locked. I still could not move.

'I've brought you some eggs,' said Schizo. I held up my hands without claws, as if I still had the Bijou. All I felt was a bestilled sadness.

A furious grey blur shot across the garden and thumped into Schizo's ribcage.

There was a sound like twigs snapping, and Schizo danced sideways and fell, with the blur tearing furiously at what was left of dog-hide, sending up waves of flies and wasps.

The blur looked like a coral necklace, winding almost snake-like around Schizo. Twists of ligament held the necklace together, patches of black fur still clung to it. It was cat-sized, cat shaped.

Little One.

She rode Schizo's head, ripping out his eyes, then looping underneath to bite the boney throat and snap off the head. The ripple of tiny bones, articulated and sinuous, was beautiful to watch.

Little One dragged the skull-head away, even though it was still trying to bite. Then she burrowed her way into the dog's torso. Inside there was something swollen and hard, which she pulled out. It was yellowish-grey and filmed over like an unskinned heart, and she pricked it open.

Out spilled something like a cauliflower, rumpled and complex in different-coloured sections, instantly familiar. It was a brain or parts of them including probably Ken's – the stomached brain stored in the torso. The cat-thing began to devour it. The dog still kicked. I watched as if in a dream until the cat finished eating.

Then what was left of Little One plucked its way towards me and sat on its haunches as if expecting a fish head. It still had a tongue, so licked stuff off its snout. Its empty eye sockets looked at me with some kind of cobweb; and it said in voice more like the wind, 'Son.'

I couldn't move, I couldn't speak; I'd been stretched too far and I'd snapped.

It picked its way towards me and said, in a voice so faint I might have imagined it, 'Ted-dy'.

I was calm and detached, detached from myself, from everything. I remember thinking: *it's seeing without eyes, speaking without a thorax*. I peered and saw what looked like a fine cobweb of tissues, the ghost of a throat, healing itself into existence and pushing out whispering air.

Little One skirted its way towards Ken. It leaned over his face, what was left of it, and it hissed out in a gossamer voice, 'Ken'. It sniffed him and then reached out an assemblage of knuckles and pulled shut his eyes. 'Goodbye.'

I had no word for what it was, but I knew who it was, at least in part. There's a technical name for them now: animations. They were animated.

The animation came back to sit at my feet and wait.

'Are you going to eat me?' I asked it.

'No,' it whispered sounding dismayed. 'You're my boy.' Decades later, I'm still not sure which one was speaking, the cat or my father.

'Where's Dad?' I asked.

'Here,' it said. Again, I still don't know if that meant this place or what was talking to me.

'I want to bury him.' The words shivered out of me.

'Dish and brush,' said the animation, which I didn't understand at the time. Then it trotted past me and up our drive. It stopped at the lane and turned, waiting for me. It mimed licking its paws clean with a little hard, dry rose hip of a tongue.

I was weary. I clumped up the drive. The animation slipped up the opposite bank and waited again. The bank was steep but baked hard, and I trudged up it. I grabbed hold of a sycamore sapling to pull myself up.

We walked across the barley field towards the leylandii. Ahead of us were the sheds where Dorothy had kept her beagles. I stopped dead and began to growl.

A whisper of a meow told me: *safe*.

Underfoot, the brittle stems of barley broke. They'd been bleached white, lined up like someone had been planting memorial candles. The leylandii had dropped their needles. I could see the sharp outline of Dorothy's house through them.

Next to the dog sheds was a compost heap, a black and tangled mess neatly contained between sheets of corrugated iron.

'Here,' said the animation.

I stood and stared. What, Dad was buried there? Would I have to dig him up? I was dripping sweat and swaying where I stood. I saw a pitchfork leaning against the wall and I picked it up. I jammed it into the heap to shift it.

The mound squealed like a pig, shivered, then stirred itself. It slumped forward pulling itself off the heap. It was a mangle of beagle hide and bones, looking like branches caught in a flood. They bunched and extended, dragging clumps of what was now mostly soil with them, hauling themselves away from me.

They had nothing like a mouth or a head; they had no means to devour or to claw. They called out with a single voice, 'Help, help, please.' It was Dorothy's voice and accent, strong and loud. 'Somebody help me!' They kept crying out that over and over, the same words, notes and rhythm like a sampled dance record. I think they must have swallowed Dorothy's larynx and it healed in place.

'Dotty Dotty,' said the cat.

The beagles shrugged their way away from us, still shouting.

'She called,' said the animation. 'I ran.'

Dad had heard what he thought was Dorothy in trouble and taken off across the field to help, slamming the car door behind him. And the beagles attacked still calling with Dorothy's voice.

The mound moved away from us, still calling for help, crackling though barley as brittle as glass.

The compost heap underneath was a mass of plant skeleton, dried weeds that were intact and dusty. Nothing had rotted down – composting no longer worked when it was so dry. Nettles mixed with teasel mixed with rose prunings and brown mown lawn that looked like hair on the floor of a barber shop. Not even any insects buzzed.

'I'm here,' said the cat.

I had the pitchfork. The compost was a prickly tangle full of stings and thorns and grey dust, but it lifted up all together like a lid. I hoisted it up and carried it away to the hedge.

'Dust,' said the animation.

Amid the crosshatching of grey twigs, bones were laid out. Like the animations, they were held together by hide – blue jeans, a red tartan shirt. There were Dad's boots, looking clean and dry.

I stared. I kept expecting to see some aspect of him in the skull, but it looked cheap and gothic like a trip to Castle Dracula. It might be that the forehead was broader or the brow heavier than many. I could see nothing of his thick neck, his short black hair, his beard, his smile. 'Dad,' I said, but nothing came. 'Dad?'

What had I thought would happen when I saw him? Did I think all the grief would stop? That I could say goodbye, tell him I loved him, tell him that I forgave him? That I was sorry for being so shitty to him for so long? What had I thought would change?

The shirt, the shoes, the bones couldn't answer. The animation did. 'Ted-dy.'

'Why did you have to go away?'

'I didn't.' Such a tiny voice like wind in grass, nothing like him. Thinking about it, Dad did always come back to visit, and when the troubles started, it was us he stayed with. He tried to stay with us.

'Where are you now?'

'Here. Then everywhere. Everything goes.'

'I don't want you to. Dad? I don't want you to go.'

'Remember the hive? Up the tree with the hive?'

Yes I nodded. *Yes, I remember.*

'Remember we went to the town? The brown arches. Where Harry Potter?' Poor cat, it couldn't be expected to hold all of it, all my Dad's life, all of his language.

Once I had a photograph of him and me, (I can still see it) faces pressed together, in the Bodleian library where they had shot part of the film Harry Potter.

'Spain,' the animation said.

I remembered that too. 'We saw the Egyptian temple,' I said. 'Right there in the town. Where that overhead car stopped?' I couldn't remember the name of the city. 'Dad. How much of you is in Little One?'

Silence, then. 'Bits. Parts.'

Maybe it knew things Dad did about animals. I asked, 'How can you talk?'

'I don't know. I woke up and spoke.' Then. 'I remember being me.'

There was no connection between those bones, those old clothes and that voice. It was like talking to a tape recorder, or maybe Alexa. So why was I fooled? Why did it help? Why did I feel like I'd had one more chance to talk to my Dad?

'Miss you, Dad.'

'Miss you, son.'

The thin half-cat voice sounded like regret. Like Dad must miss having hands, trimming trees, building his hives. Like he must miss his research, the walk to work, the flat near the uni with Ken, going hiking, fishing, dangling halfway up trees. You're not there when you die to miss those things. But this new thing was here. It could miss life.

I found what I'd wanted to say, and it was unexpected. 'You never said sorry for leaving us.'

The animation didn't answer. The heat and silence hung.

So I said, 'Where do you want to be buried?'

'Our garden.'

I had a fever. It could be that I was insane with grief and pathogens, and was hallucinating. But even that doesn't matter, if I was. You get what you need.

'Ash,' said the cat.

I didn't know what to do with the remains. I didn't want to drop part of him or for the bones to clatter when I gathered them up. I wished I could lay him out on a bier in his jeans and shirt, but I was all alone except for Little One. So I took off my t shirt, and kind of rolled him up into it and hugged what was there close, and I carried him, them, it – a bit like I was holding a puppet – back down into shadow, across the field, to our house.

The cacophony of beagle was still shrugging away from us as if in fear. Then it suddenly collapsed, with a belching haze. The voice kept shouting for help.

'Hurry,' said the cat.

A shovel still lay on the ground by the gate. The lawn had been baked into a scab; the earth was hard. I picked up the shovel and clambered up the mountain of ash, our little magic circle of trees with the white plastic chair. The only leaves around us now were shrivelling ivy. The ash was light and crumbly.

I lay my father down and went back out into the skin-shrivelling sunshine to get the shovel.

I started to dig up the still loose coal ash from Mrs Tulp's Raeburn.

'Ash,' said the animation. 'In the ground. Over and over. A season. It comes.'

Layers of ash.

In the geological record there are thin layers of ash, mass extinctions when nearly everything dies so that life can start over anew. We had thought it was meteorites. But it's an earthly cycle, over and over.

The marsupia had done this before, over and over. Jurassic, Cretaceous, Tertiary. And now the Anthropocene, the time of humankind.

I dug deep into our mound, though soon there would be no animals to dig up the body. I stroked the smooth bald skull and put it in the ash so it could look up towards the sky. I tried to lay Dad out in some kind of order. I thought about burying him with his tools, or maybe one of his books, but nothing seemed right. I didn't believe in an afterlife, and I doubted that anyone would be around to wonder at the grave goods buried with him. Overhead, a pigeon cooed in a tree.

The animation said. 'Ash alive. Goes into sky. Rain. Plants. Flowers think. Trees whisper. Gods speak.'

Bastet had spoken.

Just about then, a cloud of devouring ash was settling over Kassam Stadium.

Every seat on the bleachers was occupied. No more helicopters were landing on the pitch because it was full of people on blankets. The Army were erecting more tents. There was a truck full of single metal beds being unloaded. The Stadium was giving refuge to more than twenty thousand people.

The ash was still alive, and it settled in a stinging cloud. Facemasks slowed it, but eventually breathing pulled it in over the gaps around the nose. It ate its way in, under fingernails or eyelids or worked its way into ears.

Like a line of acid it gnawed its way deeper and deeper through the ear drum or the septum and sinuses and then through the base of the skull. People began to scream and cover their ears, or beat the air. It felt like fire had been jammed into their ears; or their eyes stung and suddenly ruptured, blinding them. For some the pain subsided for a time. The ash was flaking apart the base of their cranium. The ash was driven to seek the contents of the head.

There was security cam footage and people's phone videos.

The lucky ones suffocated and died early on; their agony was over. Some lost motor control and started to dance and jitter, others to gibber or sing nonsense. Some could feel their memories unravel, then the sense of self, and they shouted, 'I'm going, I'm going!'. Others lost everything except their rage, striking out at people around them. A few, seeing what was happening, flung themselves off the top row of the stadium – perhaps to escape, perhaps to die.

Every single one of those people we'd seen on the bleachers, Fake Tan, the people who'd ear-wigged on Ken and Mom, the refugees from Waterperry, the Hare Krishna man, all of them were killed.

The ash settled, the blood and vomit dried and rose up into the air again. There was no one to clean it up. Drones showed a mass of bodies; all of Oxford was an exclusion zone. The marsupia lived on. It dried into dust and was blown on the wind. It settled into the ground, was pulled in by fungus mycelia and fed from there into the roots of herbaceous borders.

Eventually the authorities blasted the stadium with phosphorus. It blazed. The marsupia danced in the flames, rose up with the sparks, billowed as clouds. The stadium was burnt black. Plastic and bodies merged together. But the fire did not cleanse.

Unaware of the attack, I stood over the body of my father and tried to find words to say.

The Kia rounded our drive, horn beeping.

Mom jumped out, shouting my name, then cried aloud when she saw Ken; I called back from within the trees, and she fell on me with relief. She saw Dad laid out in the ash, and stood next to me, arm around my shoulder.

'That's his shirt,' she said. 'Those are his boots.'

Evie whimpered with dog sociability. *You hurt.*

Faith said, 'You did well to lay him here in the ash. Only place to dig,'

The coral necklace slunk out of the ivy. Mom cried aloud and tried to kick it.

'No, no,' I said. 'It's both of them.'

'Mag-gie,' the animation croaked.

Mom stood back. I went weak, and slumped down onto the white chair. The cat gathered itself for a spring, and Little One jumped on my lap. 'Lit lit lit…' I began, but there seemed no point.

She gave a Plaintive Mew and sighed apart on my lap. The chain of rumpled pearls broke and settled into separate pieces. I sat looking at them for a while.

Then because I couldn't think of anything else to do, I laid them next to Dad. They were entangled anyway. The hard round stomach-brain was still intact, stuffed full of neural networks that held my father's memories. Mingled with Ken's memories now too. That would survive in the ash for a time, mute.

Part of me, only part, now wonders and perhaps regrets, that I didn't eat that thing myself. Perhaps I would have grown a stomach-brain too? Might I still have Dad's memories, if I had??

In the beltbag, alongside the passports, Mom had been keeping three hundred pounds of emergency money.

She'd tried to use it to get a taxi from the Stadium to Oldminster to find me, but none of them would risk going that far. So she paid one of the Waterperrys to drive to our trailer. At the registration desk, Faith had demanded our chainsaw and gun back.

The Waterperrys dropped them off and roared away. They wanted, they said, to get back to the safety of the Stadium.

The animals had retreated from the Close. Our little Kia still stood outside the trailer, minus a windscreen and a front seat; but the portable charger was still clamped to it and there was juice in the battery and Mom found the keys in her belt bag. Faith had stood guard with the shotgun while what was left of our food, the ammo, and some clothes were loaded into the car. Including Mom's big brown case of birth certificates and photos.

My family had been on the A40 coming to find me when the Stadium was attacked.

Faith helped me bury Ken.

I told Mom that no, he was not going to be buried next to Dad. She said we should call the police; there would have to be an investigation; the death recorded. I told her, truthfully, that there would be no more police, no records, no one to come. I never afterwards lost my ability to shock my mother.

We dug a trench for Ken in the dog run. Without him, none of us would have been in Oldminster. We'd all be dead, though we didn't know that then. Ken and I never would have been friends, but we did owe him something, and I wouldn't have minded a few more memories of Scotland or of Dad.

I walked back to my vegetable garden. Though the bamboo framework leaned sideways and the beans had been blasted by drought, there was one late, red bean flower, and out of it flew one of Dad's wild bees. It hovered away towards the hive that Dad had hung in the lime tree. His bees were still with us.

I went to Mr Keppel's house, and I found the Syrian tablecloth. It was beautiful, all red and blue and flesh-toned stripes with gold thread and tassels, protected under a clear plastic sheet. A thing of beauty, a small summation of good things, some good things, about people. And a people.

There was a photograph of Mr Keppel in his twenties young and tanned and bearded, looking like a prophet; and another one of him as a handsome older man with an arm around Mr Ali (I suppose) in the courtyard of that Aleppo hotel. Wars descend into dust as well. I took all those things and laid them out in my house.

Marsupia have gnawed at us for decades.

The Delay killed Mom five years after Oxford, pushing her into dementia. I buried her in the garden and I can hear her living ash whisper to me from the soil and the leaves: *Teddy*. She wants me to be happy.

Dad guards his bees, and they are still here, still with us, pollinating our food. And they know it. Dad whispers when the leaves shiver in the wind and when I'm alone, scared, and feeling old I try to talk to him.

Otherwise the silence is as deep as the Mariana trench. No lowing of cattle, no sheep or dogs. The animals are gone and they will take us with them in the end. You who are young, you should record Evie and me when we howl or whimper or bark. We are what you have left of animals.

Sometimes at dusk I go out to fields and I howl. I can't stop myself. I need my pack. *Yee yee yee.*

Pack broken.

I Plaintive-Meow, to call up the dead, the legions of beautiful things that are gone.

In dreams sometimes, often, I howl out to the dead, and they stand up out of the ground. Big Boy and Petra and Jenny and Schizo and Charity and Donna Duck. Little One jumps into my lap and I am still somehow in the white chair. We are animals too. And they are people.

The birds remain, at least those that were not raptors. Owls, kites, eagles, those are gone. Nothing to eat. The swallows migrate, immune to marsupia, carrying them in their guts. While the ocean currents circulate, plankton and salmon carry them too.

It's everywhere.

Finches, woodpeckers, blue tits, rooks – they swarm ecstatic in the trees, chattering. Time moves through them. In far futures, they will grow huge and predatory; they will swim in the seas like whales. One day their wings might grow thumbs and perhaps they will record the death of the sun. Deep in the earth will be a layer of ash and one or two strange rocks covered with something that might be signs if only birds could read them.

I hear stirrings in the grass, in the leaves in the ground. I pray to the local gods of my garden to defend my plantings, keep my olives and tomatoes and prickly pear free from blight. I can almost hear the marsupia answer. But then I have always been an imaginative child.

On that day when we escaped the ash, Mom said in the dusk. 'Come on Teddy, time to go home.'

'This is home,' I said.

Standing by us both, Faith grunted. 'Home is where the ghosts are.'

About the Author

Geoff Ryman's work has received many awards including the Arthur C Clarke Award twice, a World Fantasy Award, a Nebula for best novelette, a Philip K Dick Award, a first place John W Campbell Award, the then Tiptree Award and BSFA Awards for short story, novel, and non-fiction.

He set up the UK government's first web design team in the 1990s; his team worked on the first official websites for 10 Downing Street and the British Monarchy. In 2011 he taught creative writing at Benue State University, Makurdi, and Taraba State University, Jalingo, both in Nigeria. He received a Levershulme Grant to study African SFF and published a series of interviews, "100 African Writers of SFF", with *Strange Horizons*. He helped set up the African Speculative Fiction society and administered their Nommo Awards from 2016 to 2022. His novel *WAS*, about the Wizard of Oz through history, was turned first into a play and then a musical. He worked briefly on the Australian archaeological site at Angkor Wat and wrote a series of stories around the history of Cambodia including the novelette "Pol Pot's Beautiful Daughter" and the novel *The King's Last Song*.

ALSO FROM NEWCON PRESS

Human Resources – Fiona Moore
Fiona Moore's work has been shortlisted for BSFA Awards and a World Fantasy Award. Her stories have appeared in *Clarkesworld*, *Asimov's*, *Interzone* and elsewhere, and have been selected for six editions of *Best of British SF*. "A collection of intelligent, thoughtful, disturbing but ultimately optimistic speculative stories" *– Oghenechovwe Donald Ekpeki*

The Hamlet – Joanna Corrance
The Hamlet is a new novella from Scottish author Joanna Corrance; a fabulous tale that dances between horror and science fiction with an added dash of weird. *The Hamlet* provides a mosaic tale of the inhabitants of a very peculiar rural community as they negotiate the time when 'things got strange' and face the consequences of where that leads.

Rowany de Vere and a Fair Degree of Frost – Chaz Brenchley
A graduate of the Crater School and of Oxford, Rowany has taken up service on Mars. As a spy. Her first mission is to escort a prominent defector, to see him safely across the hostile surface of Mars pursued by Russian agents. Success will require every ounce of her wits and her training, but, as it says on her card, she is Rowany de Vere. Of the Colonial Office.

Birdwatching at the End of the World – G.W. Dexter
When the world ends, the pupils of Near School for Girls are forced to fend for themselves on an isolated Scottish island with limited resources, no adults, and no prospect of rescue.
As the only boy present, Stephen Ballantyne has to be particularly wary of shifting politics and allegiances as the girls find a way to survive in this new and brutal world.

Different Times and Other Places – Juliet E. McKenna
Juliet E McKenna's novel *The Green Man's Gift* won the BSFA Award in 2023. This, her first collection in a decade, features a rich variety of stories; alternative histories, magical nursemaids, tree nymphs, and science fiction sit alongside traditional fantasies as the author leads us to… different times and other places.

www.ingramcontent.com/pod-product-compliance
Lightning Source LLC
Chambersburg PA
CBHW020638260626
47157CB00008B/2804